# SILENT GIRL

## M.L. ROSE

Storm
PUBLISHING

Ebook ISBN: 978-1-80508-270-5
Paperback ISBN: 978-1-80508-272-9

Cover design by: Lisa Horton
Cover images by: Trevillion, Shutterstock

Published by Storm Publishing.
For further information, visit:
www.stormpublishing.co

# ALSO BY M.L. ROSE

## Detective Nikki Gill Series

*Stolen Souls*

*Silent Girl*

# ONE

Charlotte was drowsy for a number of reasons. The alcohol and numerous chemicals in her bloodstream had created a numbness, a kind of dreamy comfort. She could be like this forever, stepping on a cloud, gliding away.

The tall summer grass, yellowing in the heat, was brushing her thighs. She could hear the buzzing of insects. The darkening dome of the sky seemed to blot out the land at the horizon, where it met the sparkling waters of the lake. She heard another sound: the faint cry of a voice. Someone was calling her name. Or was it the wind?

She half turned and almost fell over. She giggled, then straightened herself, brushing away bits of earth and grass. The sun had slipped under the horizon, the blue velvet spreading across the sky mesmerising her senses. She heard the voice again and squinted. Then she saw him. He was running over, coat tails flapping. She wondered why he had his coat on. He came closer, till he loomed above her, blotting out the sun. His face was ruddy, forehead pouring with sweat.

'I wondered where you went. I thought we were going together.'

Her tongue said something that didn't make sense. She giggled again, and he smiled. He grabbed her hand, and she leaned against him.

'Are you enjoying yourself?' he asked.

'Um hmm.' Enjoying wasn't quite the right word. She didn't even know if it was legal to host parties like this, but *they* obviously could. It was the last party of the summer, and boy were they going out with a bang.

He put his arm around her, and she could hear his heartbeat. The tinkling of bass beats came from the distance as the wind changed direction. She felt him stiffen and turn to the sound behind them.

'Come on, let's go this way.'

He practically carried her, and she let him. It felt warmer cocooned against his broad chest. They sank down in the grass, and his lips found hers. They kissed slowly, and his mouth moved to her ears.

'My mother would love to meet you,' he whispered.

He said it again, and the words finally made sense. It was a strange thing to say, and it penetrated the woolly fog in her brain. She opened her eyes and stared at him. His face seemed large, covering the sun. The brightness made his face darker. He was staring at her with wide eyes. She smiled, and so did he, but it seemed a distant smile that didn't touch the rest of his face.

'She really would,' he said.

Charlotte didn't know what to say. She pulled on his neck to lower his face to hers. The neck muscles were rigid, like the rest of his body. His hand moved up from her chest to her neck, then rested on her throat. She tried to move, but he pressed gently on her flesh, stopping her.

'Don't move,' he said softly. His hand circled her neck, slowly getting tighter.

Charlotte frowned, not liking this at all. Her dulled senses were struggling to keep up, but she knew something was wrong.

'Get off me,' she said, raising her voice. Her words alien to her, like someone else was saying them.

He increased the pressure on her neck, pushing h into the ground. Panic blossomed in Charlotte's gu kicked with her legs, but they were feeble. He draped ( over hers, holding her down.

'Just imagine if she could see you.' His face was now c the skin mottled.

With both hands he squeezed her throat. Charlotte f and bucked against him, trying to throw him off, but he wa strong. She couldn't breathe any more. She screamed, but o i croak came from her open mouth. As the light faded from eyes, she only saw his sweat-streaked face turning the sk black.

# TWO

DI Nikki Gill looked at her sixteen-year-old daughter, Rita. 'What do you mean, you can't stay?'

'I've got things to do. Like, stuff.'

With time, Nikki had learned to watch what she said to her teenager. She couldn't say the first thing that sprang to mind. No way. Often, silence was the best course of action, especially if Rita was in a bad mood. Which, thankfully, was less now that her exams were over. Rita didn't do exam stress very well. Her dad couldn't handle her, and she had stayed with Nikki throughout May.

Nikki had spent a lovely week with her mother, Clarissa, and Rita, in Bibury, a village in the heart of the Cotswolds. She had needed that time with them, to lay her brother Tommy's soul to rest and to heal together. It had been heart-warming to see how well Clarissa got on with Rita. Nikki had also opened up to Rita about Tommy. They had cried together, Rita wondering what life would be like if she had an uncle.

'Bibury was nice, right? What if we go to another place like that next year?' Nikki ventured gently.

4

Rita shrugged. 'Maybe.' She thought about something. 'When will I see Grandma again?'

Nikki hid her smile. Ever since she met Rita earlier this year Clarissa had shown signs of change. The bottles of alcohol that littered her house had vanished. She had stopped drinking, and was even smoking less. The change was slow but noticeable after their week together. The new bond between Clarissa and Rita, to Nikki's mind, was the biggest validation of her decision to return to Oxford.

'Tell you what. You know our plan to go to Stratford-Upon-Avon?'

'Yes?' Rita replied cautiously. 'I might not have time for it, like I said.'

'Well, why don't we go with Grandma?'

Rita pressed her lips together. 'We'll have to walk around a lot. Will she be OK?'

'I think so. Tougher than she looks, your nan is. She walked around all right in Bibury.'

'But not on the hills.' Rita shook her head, looking wiser than her teenage years. It made Nikki smile.

'I just don't know if I have enough time,' Rita said, turning down her lips in an expression designed for sympathy.

Nikki knew not to give in, even if the next step might be a little argument. 'But we have a plan! You wanted to see Stratford-Upon-Avon.' Shakespeare's birthplace wasn't far from Oxford, and Rita wanted to study English. She wanted to apply to Oxford as well, and she was clever enough to get in, Nikki thought with a surge of pride.

'Yeah, I know.' Rita wouldn't meet her mother's eyes.

Nikki stared at the tall teenager's long hair, recently washed. It was jet-black and shone in the sun. Rita was getting close to her shoulder height, which was scary. An iPhone was open on Rita's lap.

'So what's changed?' Nikki took a sip of cappuccino. They

were sitting outdoors, in a café in Kidlington, and the sun was warm on her neck.

'Just stuff, Mum. I got a life, you know. Need to get back.'

'Yes, I get that. But will anything change if you wait till Sunday?' It was Friday afternoon now.

Rita gave a shrug, her eyes still downcast. Nikki knew she was flicking through her phone.

'Stop that.'

Rita looked up at her. Then she sighed, did the teenage eye-roll thing, and put her phone in her pocket.

'Has anything happened? Bestie being *emo*?' Nikki smiled, then wiggled her eyebrows. Rita grinned.

'Stop it,' the teenager said, punching her mum playfully on the arm.

'Right then. If there's no problem, then you can stay, right? I'll put you on the train on Sunday.'

'You don't get it, Mum,' Rita whined. 'I'm busy with stuff.'

Nikki's pager beeped, and she cursed in silence. She was SIO till the end of shift, and it had been quiet so far this week. One robbery, a couple of burglaries, nothing to interest the Major Crimes Unit. She lifted up her pager and groaned. It was Detective Superintendent Dean Patmore, her boss. She had to call him back urgently. Another message arrived before she could answer; this time from Detective Sergeant Thomas Armstrong, Tom. It was more informative.

> Young IC1 female found in Turnham Green.
> Homicide suspected.

Nikki sighed. Officially, she was due to be off from 6 p.m., so the weekend was still on, if she could convince Rita to stay.

'Duty calls, huh?' Rita asked.

Nikki blew her cheeks out. 'I just need to make a call. Back in a moment.' She rose, pulling her work phone out.

'Famous last words,' Rita called out behind her.

Nikki shook her head and waved back. She called Patmore first. He coughed once, then drawled in his guttural, twenty-a-day voice, 'Got the news?'

'Yes, sir. Anything you know?'

'No, but the girl was wearing a nice dress and shoes. Looks like a college girl. You know what that means.'

She did indeed. Any crime in an Oxford college was treated with kid gloves. It was kept from the press for as long as possible. In many cases, the perpetrator was never caught. The colleges liked to do things their own way, which meant hampering an investigation because, frankly, they were bumbling, old-fashioned idiots who didn't have a clue about modern policing. Nikki knew there was another, more sinister aim – to ensure no blame was cast upon one of the college members.

'I guess you've told the units to keep it quiet, sir.'

'Yes, and keep it that way until we have a positive ID. I got a bad feeling about this one.'

That wasn't a sentiment DS Patmore often shared, and it gave Nikki pause. 'I'll get on it now, sir.'

She called her sergeant.

'Guv,' came Tom's flat, business-like voice.

'Sitrep, please, Tom.'

'A jogger found the body, guv. It's deep in the woods, near the Waterperry turn-off on the A40. Uniforms have cordoned off the woods.'

'Have you put roadblocks in place?'

Tom hesitated, and she had her answer. She also knew what his objection would be. 'Block the exit and entry to the A40. I don't care about the traffic, Tom. Do it now.'

'But, guv, it's going to be peak time soon...'

Nikki glanced at her watch. It was 3 p.m. 'We still have an hour, maybe two. Besides, it's summer. Traffic will be less. Has Scene of Crime arrived?'

'On their way,' Tom said in a subdued voice. He liked to sulk when he didn't get his way.

'Dr Raman?' Sheila Raman was the veteran and formidable pathologist for Thames Valley Police.

'Not called her yet.'

'Don't worry, I will. See you there, okay?'

She hung up and made her way back to the table. Rita was on her phone. She looked up at Nikki, eyes glinting.

'Dead body? Or drug dealer?'

Nikki frowned and put a finger to her lips. 'Shh.' She sat down, gulped her coffee and glanced at her phone. Rita was watching her closely.

'You need to go, right?'

Nikki hated this. But she had no choice. 'Yes, darling,' she sighed.

'Can I come with you?'

'No.' Nikki's tone was hard as steel.

'Oh please. You never take me. I want to see a real crime scene. I won't take any photos. I promise.'

'Answer is still no.' Her eyebrows twitched. 'Why are you interested in this anyway?'

Rita twirled a strand of hair near her shoulder. 'Because it's like, no one's ever done it, and it's like—'

'It's like not going to happen,' Nikki interrupted. She eyed Rita's phone. 'And don't you go snapchatting or TikToking any of your friends about this either.'

Rita's mouth fell open with a look of hurt. 'As if. What do you take me for?' She rolled her eyes again. '*Momcop.*'

They had watched *Kindergarten Cop* one night, because Nikki wanted to show Rita a film she liked from when she was younger. Rita came up with the name *Momcop*, which they both found funny.

She grinned at her teenager. 'You better believe it. Come

on, I'll drop you off at home. Hopefully, we'll still go out for dinner.' She took the keys out of her bag and stood.

'I'm still going home tomorrow,' Rita declared, strapping herself into the seatbelt.

Nikki didn't say anything as she reversed the car and started driving. An argument was brewing, and she was crestfallen that she wouldn't get the weekend with Rita. This new case would be more than a distraction, though, and she wouldn't rest till she had solved it.

# THREE

Nikki drove fast, indicating to leave the A40, and then zoomed up the empty road to Waterperry. On either side, verdant green fields undulated, dotted with white sheep. Within minutes she was pulling up next to the two squad cars parked near the roadside at the woodlands.

Broadbent, the new uniformed sergeant, was standing to one side of the cordoned-off path that led up the hill, thumbs hooked on his chest rig.

Nikki got out of the car, inhaling the smell of damp heather and earth. She had tied her hair back into a tight bun, and she lifted her eyes briefly to the sunny sky.

She smiled at Broadbent in a reassuring manner. The poor bloke was two months off basic training.

'Thanks for setting up the perimeter, Neil.'

The young man's pale face took on a relieved expression. He tipped his cap. 'No problem, ma'am.'

Nikki stopped short. 'Don't call me ma'am. Got that? Guv is fine.'

She wasn't some old fuddy-duddy who had arse-kissed her way to the top. School of hard knocks had been her tuition, coaching and graduation. Hell, she even managed top marks in her detective-level graduation class. Ma'am made her sound old.

Neil swallowed as the harsh rebuke hit him. 'Sorry, ma— I mean guv.'

Nikki squeezed her eyes shut and sighed. 'Don't worry. Where is it?'

Neil pointed up the slope. 'There, guv. Right at the top.'

'SOCO here?'

'Not yet, guv. Sarge Armstrong is up there.'

As Nikki climbed, small rocks scattering and twigs breaking underfoot, sweat broke out on her forehead. She stopped and took off her light coat. The victim must've been terrified to clamber her way up here.

Nikki tried to keep herself fit with running and yoga, but the last four weeks with Rita home she had done neither. This jaunt reminded her she needed to get back into shape.

As she climbed, she examined the ground. Tangled spines of twigs, branches, small rocks. But she didn't miss the splash of dark crimson when she saw it on the grass. It was about five centimetres wide and already getting oxidised to its black colour. Blood, no doubt about it. She found another splash not far away, and they became smaller, harder to see without the untrained eye.

But they were present. Small, dry puddles of blood, aligned up the hill like the footprints of a cat on snow.

Her lungs were burning by the time she spotted the blue and white tape flapping in the wind. The short, slim figure of Tom Armstrong was visible, a grey outline against the corn-flower blue sky.

Two Uniform constables were keeping watch at the perimeter of the tape. Tom turned as he heard her approach. His lips were pursed, a deep frown covering his face, and it only let up fractionally when he tilted his head towards her.

Nikki nodded back. Then she looked at the ground and

realised why the veteran sergeant looked so troubled.

# FOUR

A young woman, fully dressed, lay on the ground. Her black dress was knee length, but it had rolled upwards. Blonde hair plastered the dark-brown ground, forming a halo around her head. It looked artificial, like a carefully arranged feature. The eyes were open, the blue of the pupils just about visible. Pallor had seized the sunken cheeks. The mouth was slightly open, and with the eyes, the face had a ghastly, stunned look, like she couldn't believe this had happened to her.

The dress looked expensive. So did the black-heeled shoes. Nikki shook her head. No way had she climbed up that slope on those heels. They weren't huge, definitely walkable, but certainly not for hill climbing. She noted the lack of mud on the heels as she stepped closer and looked for signs of injury.

The victim's hair was matted near the left of her forehead, probably from a cut. That wasn't the cause of death, though. The skin on the neck was smudged, and the windpipe was twisted to one side. A dislocated windpipe only meant one thing: death by strangulation. Some of her red-painted fingernails had come off. She had struggled with her attacker. Dr Raman could probably get some DNA off those fingernails.

At the base of the neck, on the left, she could see a tattoo. It was three black hearts, in different sizes, each larger than the one on top. Nikki looked carefully elsewhere but didn't see any other marks on her exposed skin, but it was something that would be checked for at the PM.

The dress wasn't torn anywhere. There was no congealed blood behind her scalp to suggest a head injury. No signs of laceration on the limbs. There was a necklace, and it had slid down the V-neck and caught on the dress. It looked like the pendant had been torn off and the necklace snapped in two. The chains were made of gold, and it didn't look fake.

Nikki felt movement beside her, and she rose to her feet, her knees popping. DS Armstrong nodded at her.

'Guv.'

Nikki returned the greeting. They had worked together for a few months. Switching over from the Met hadn't been easy. A baptism of fire, not made any easier by Tom's rule-driven personality. But they had managed to set up a working relationship.

'Have you questioned the jogger who found her?'

'Yes, guv. He's squeaky clean. Banker in London, commutes from here, five days a week. Took his prints, nothing to see on IDENT 1.'

'Let's get a proper statement off him. He's not off the hook. No prints means sweet Fanny Adams at this stage.'

Nikki knew most violent killers were unknown to the law. And many of them took a sick pride in playing with the police.

'Of course, guv. Goes without saying.'

She looked at Tom, and he swallowed, then looked away. 'Bring him in,' Nikki said shortly. 'Any ID?'

Tom shook his head. 'Uniforms have searched around, down to the road. No purses or phones.'

'So we have no idea who she is.'

'Sorry, guv.'

'Nothing on her? Did she have a coat?'

'Not that has been found.'

'Keep looking. Anything is important now, even a box of matches, or a piece of tissue.'

She looked around the body. It was placed under the shade of a tree. How did the girl get up here? The ground was hard, and she hadn't seen any obvious footprints. She had run, presumably. She was trying to escape her assailant, but he caught up with her. She was bleeding from the cut on the forehead already... Nikki stopped her ruminations. That laceration on the forehead wouldn't cause the blotches of blood she had seen on the slopes, would they? Dried, blackened blood that had been there for a few hours at least.

Her old boss, DCI Arla Baker, of the Met, had taught her how to look at blood splatter and tell the age of the spilled blood by its colour. Any more than three hours and blood gave up its oxygen, and it turned black. Arla had also mentioned it had to be venous blood to begin with, which had low oxygen for starters. Nikki missed Arla sometimes. She had been a good boss, and Nikki wished they could have continued working together. But Nikki was glad she'd come to Oxford.

She shook her head and dragged her errant mind back to the present. Her jaws hardened.

'Here they are, guv,' Tom said. She followed his gaze. At the bottom of the hill, two more cars had pulled up. One was a blue and white Ford estate, which had 'TVP Forensics' written in black letters on the side. The other was an electric car whose brand she couldn't tell. The small, sprightly figure of Dr Sheila Raman came out of the electric car, while Hetty Barfield, the podgy, bustling SOC chief locked the forensics van, and they walked up the slope together. Hetty almost slipped, and Dr Raman had to hold out a steadying hand. That made Nikki smile. In all the rushing around, she wondered how many times Hetty lost her balance.

While she waited, she walked over to the other side of the body. Her back rustled against the blue and white tape as she crouched on the roots of the large oak tree and looked at the head and neck. Again, apart from the marks on the neck, no obvious injuries.

Was she strangled up here? Or was she killed elsewhere, then the body placed on this spot? The careful way the body was positioned made her think it was the latter. On her back, arms by her side, in perfect repose.

Those blood drops... perhaps they could have dripped from her forehead as she was carried up the slope.

The sound of strenuous huffing and puffing caught her attention. Tom and one of the uniformed constables gave Hetty a hand as she made it over the hill. Dr Raman did it easily, almost swinging her little black leather bag. And she had twenty years on Hetty, Nikki thought with a grin.

Nikki gave them some time to compose themselves. She walked to the other side of the tree. There was a flat clearing, and then the slope moved downwards again, ending in a small valley. In the distance she could see the black river of the A40, cars moving on it like small speedboats on the River Cherwell. This spot was isolated enough for the body not to be spotted for a few days; it was placed up here, under a tree, like a macabre offering to a bloodthirsty god. Nikki shivered. She couldn't rule out a ritual killing.

Hetty set up her tripod and, once she nodded that she had finished taking photos, Dr Raman crouched by the body's feet. She had her mask and gloves on and wore a blue disposable apron round the front. She moved the woman's feet and looked under the heels. Then she raised the legs, and Nikki moved forward to help.

'Thanks,' Dr Raman grunted. Blue and black bruises were forming on the underside of the calf muscles. The pathologist pointed to the back of the knees.

'Important artery passes through the padding there. Popliteal artery. No cuts there which is good.'

They examined the other leg as well, then put both legs down. Dr Raman zipped open her bag and took out the long rectal thermometer. Nikki looked away. It was best to give the doctor privacy. As expected, Dr Raman inserted the probe into the vagina. That would give her the core temperature she wanted.

Dr Raman took the probe out and held the digital thermometer up to the light. 'Fourteen degrees. It's about twenty-three here, now. Nine degrees difference.' She pursed her lips and looked around.

'It's a slim body so will lose heat quickly. And the ground isn't wet, nor is there any water nearby,' Nikki said as she walked around the body.

Dr Raman looked up at her. Her silvery hair glistened in the sun, and her chocolate-brown eyes, the same colour as her skin, danced.

'Good observations, DI Gill.'

Niki shrugged. 'I picked up a few things over the years. Dissipation of heat from the body would've been at the normal rate. Correct?'

'For her body size, yes. You're right, she lost heat quickly because there's not much fat padding to stop the heat. And because it's hot outside, that drags heat out from the body. Funny, isn't it? In the cold, bodies lose heat more slowly, as there's less of a temperature gradient.'

'Time of death?'

'I would say close to twenty-four hours. It's past 4 p.m. now. It may not have been a whole day, or the rigor mortis would be a lot more advanced, and the skin would be changing colour.'

Nikki raised her eyebrows, and Dr Raman nodded. 'Okay, okay. I would say perhaps around 8 to 10 p.m. last night. But I will have a more exact time when I put all the numbers into the software.'

"Ok."Tom nudged closer. 'Guv, there's traffic building up. Shall we send Hetty out there to see if she finds anything on the exit road?'

That made sense. 'Yes,' Nikki said. 'Please send two Uniforms with her.'

'I'll go as well. We'll start at the bottom of the hill, where it joins the road. Then walk up to the junction with the A40. That should do?'

Nikki looked around the woodland. As far as she could see, a green and pleasant land unfurled in rolling hills and clumps of trees. It was only to her right that the A40 thundered away, Oxford's main artery to the outside world.

'For now, yes. But we need to scour all around here. Two-mile radius, minimum. Get three more teams from St Aldate's. While Hetty's here, we might as well make the most of it.'

'Roger that, guv.'

# FIVE

Tom and Nikki returned to the Kidlington South HQ. Dr Raman had promised to treat the autopsy as a priority. Hetty and her team were still there and would be until nightfall. The reinforcements from St Aldate's, Oxford's central police station, had turned up.

'What do you think, guv?' Tom asked as he drove. Nikki was busy responding to a text from Rita. She promised to be back by seven in the evening. They were going to the Duke of Marlborough, a gastro pub in Iffley, which wasn't far from Kidlington. She put her phone down and sighed.

'I think it's a shame she's so young.'

Tom didn't say anything. Despite being seasoned police folk, it was never easy uncovering the destruction of a young life.

'She was no more than twenty-five. With that dress on, she must've been at a party. It's not like she was wearing a jacket. Yes, her killer took it, obviously. If she had one on in the first place.'

'The boss thinks she was a student. Do you agree?'

'Yes.' Nikki closed her eyes. She massaged her temples for a while. 'We need to ask around the colleges if anyone's missing. Also if there was a big party last night. Summer balls are happening now, right?'

Tom nodded. 'A few of them. Most are finished by end of June, and the students go off in the first week of July.'

Nikki had grown up in Oxford. She didn't study at the university, though; she couldn't wait to get as far away as possible after she finished her A levels. Oxford held nightmares for her that she didn't wish to relive. And yet, relive them she did, almost every other day.

'From what I remember, there's a lot of summer balls. Not to mention the balls organised by the secret drinking societies. Not so secret, I mean.'

Tom said, 'Yes, not so secret. Did you see the photos of the Piers Gaveston ball?'

'Nope. I thought those balls were secret. How did the press get hold of the photos?'

'The students queued up at a bus station in the middle of the day. Stupid really.'

'Oh, I believe.' Nikki exhaled. Everyone in Oxford knew the utter bacchanalia the drinking societies got up to. In 1986, a girl even died after taking an overdose of heroin at her graduation party. That shocking event didn't stop the parties from happening.

Nikki knew her victim could have been at any of the summer balls. Her traditional dress meant one of the more 'boring' events was more likely, like the annual Students' Union or university ball. But she could be wrong.

They arrived at the Kidlington South station, and Tom drove past her car and parked at the rear. They took the stairs up to the fourth floor, both panting slightly by the time they reached the office. Kristy Young, one of the detective constables, came out of the office as Nikki stepped inside the large open-plan space. Scores of desks were laid out, with both detectives and uniformed officers busy at work on their laptops. Fax machines and printers whirred quietly in the corners. The air conditioning was on, a faint drone in the background. Nikki had her own office to the side, next to DS Patmore's.

'Hello, guv,' Kristy said. She was in her early twenties. Her friendly face was attractive, framed with brown hair that she had tied up. She wasn't just a pretty face, however. It was her fifth year in the force, the first three spent in uniform. She had taken to detective work like a duck to water.

'I heard. Just got back from the crime scene?'

'Yes,' Nikki said. 'Where were you and Nish?' Nish Bhatt was the other detective constable in the team.

Kristy glanced at Tom, standing behind Nikki. 'Skipper told us to stay put and look for missing persons.'

'I see.' Nikki sighed. It wouldn't have been her preference. She wanted the inexperienced ones to get as much experience as possible of crime scenes. Police work was about getting one's hands dirty and looking people in the eyes to uncover what lay in their dark minds.

'Well, did you find anything?'

'Nothing that fits our victim. Over the last few weeks, two people in their fifties have been reported missing. One from Headington, the other from Botley.'

'No one else missing from their households?' Nikki asked.

Kristy shook her head. 'Do you want coffee, guv?'

'Yes. See you back in the office.'

Tom walked ahead of Nikki, but she stopped short. A familiar figure rose from one of the desks opposite. Detective Inspector Monty Sen looked like the side of a cliff, a tall, sinewy man with an intense, focused expression on his face. He had a three-day stubble on his light-brown cheeks that ended in square, firm jaws. He put his light summer jacket on and spoke to a younger man who was probably a DC, stopping mid-sentence as he caught sight of Nikki. He smiled, an easy, attractive smile that Nikki liked. He spoke rapidly to the younger man, who wrote something down. Monty walked over to Nikki. She folded her arms across her chest.

'What're you doing here?' she asked.

Monty was one of the CID inspectors in Kidlington North. The Thames Valley Police covered a large area, most of the Cotswolds up to Cheltenham. The North office dealt with cases outside Oxford.

Monty's eyes had that sparkle and a hint of a smile on his full lips. 'Keeping an eye on you. Still my job, you see.'

They had started off as sworn enemies when Nikki landed her first case here. She had left the Met in a state. The relentless grind of work had worn her out, and, too, the harrowing child's death case which sent her down a vortex of remorse, stress, and finally breakdown. TVP had been her refuge, but she'd had to accept a supervisor. That man had been Monty.

It was only six months ago but seemed longer. They had become friends since then and even been out on a couple of dates. Not much had happened. But Nikki knew there was a potential something might. She had to watch herself. Monty was her colleague, and she didn't want to jeopardise their working relationship.

'Done for the day?'

'Hardly. Just getting started. No rest for the wicked, you see.'

They smiled, and Nikki shook her head. Monty was a handsome devil. Her insides did a little somersault when he smiled, and she wasn't sure if she wanted that.

'Why're you here?' she demanded.

'Been transferred. Myself and Dom.' He pointed to the DC he was speaking to. 'More manpower needed here, apparently.' The smile vanished from his lips. 'Heard about the dead girl. How old?'

'Early to mid-twenties, no more.'

'Shame that. You were duty SIO for the week, right?'

She eyed him suspiciously. 'Were you checking up on me?'

'Always,' he said with mock seriousness. 'No, Patmore told me. Let me know if you need any help. I'm the duty SIO from Saturday.'

Nikki blinked in surprise. 'Really? From here?'

'No, the moon. Yes, of course from here. I told you, I've been transferred.'

She didn't know whether to be pleased or alarmed at that. She was still finding her way around TVP, and Oxford in general, although she knew the place like the back of her hand. Too well, in fact. She wished she could forget her past, but now she was right bang in the middle of where her horrible life had been. And she was here to get away from what happened in London. One bloody vicious circle. Funny how life was like that sometimes.

'I better go,' Monty said. He went to say something more, hesitated, then thought better of it.

She gulped and nodded. 'Okay. Later.'

It was rather awkward in the end. Nikki put it behind her and stepped into her office. Nish, the young DC who was about the same age as Kristy, looked up from his laptop.

'Hello, guv.' He smiled. Nikki liked Nish. He was bright-eyed and bushy-tailed, like Kristy. A far cry from the morose Tom, who was the only team member who didn't understand what a team really meant.

Nikki greeted him, and Nish pointed at this laptop. 'I'm going through the university pastoral website to see if there's anything.'

'Pastoral website?' Nikki asked, pulling up a chair.

'Yes. It's where students and teachers can post any concerns they have for a student's welfare, anonymously. I got a visitor login from the university chaplain after I explained what it was for.'

Nikki switched on her laptop and looked at the depressingly full in-tray. It had been empty this morning. She went through it quickly. Mostly reports of the sighting of the dead body and memos for the same from various offices. She breathed a sigh of relief when there wasn't anything else.

'That's good,' she told Nish, putting the stack of papers back in the tray. 'Nice way to look after students' welfare.'

'Absolutely. They didn't have this stuff even in my day. Not that I went to Oxford.' Nish smiled sheepishly.

'Did you find anything interesting?' Nikki asked, opening her emails.

'Nope. A couple of students with mental health issues, but nothing else. No one's been reported missing.'

'Cast the net wide. That girl could be from anywhere. For all we know she's still doing her A levels.' The thought filled Nikki with sadness. With it, came the first blossom of anger. What sort of animal stoops that low? She knew the answer well enough.

Kristy and Tom came back in, Tom holding the door open. Kristy put the tray of biscuits and three coffees on the table. Nish didn't want one.

Nikki went up to the whiteboard, and used the cloth to erase it clean. 'Okay, guys. We need to have a plan of action. You know how critical the first forty-eight hours are. And given Dr Raman said the time of death was about 8 p.m. last night, the clock is ticking loudly.'

She wrote number one. 'We need a positive ID. I doubt we will find anything on fingerprints, but worth a try. Hetty will look at dental records as well, I'm sure.'

She wrote number two. 'I'm puzzled by how she got there. She didn't walk out into the woods with those shoes on. Dressed like that.'

Kristy said, 'She arrived by car. Maybe to meet someone.'

Nikki pointed at her. 'Good. We need to check CCTV for

all cars taking that exit off the A40 yesterday evening. I would say from 6 p.m. till midnight, and the rest of this morning.'

'I'll call Traffic now and set it up,' Nish said, reaching for the phone.

Tom cleared his throat loud enough for everyone to look at him. He had a stony look on his face, Nikki thought, like a child who wasn't getting enough attention. He was a married man with two children. She wondered how happy the marriage was.

'Yes, Tom?'

He shuffled in his chair. 'I think we need to look outside Oxford. Maybe the whole of the Cotswolds. If her body was dumped here, she could be from anywhere. It makes sense the killer would go as far as possible.'

Nikki thought about it. 'True,' she said. 'But then again, think about the way the body was laid out. Legs together, arms by her sides. Like she was put there for a reason. Some killers like a ritual. That would indicate he knows the area.'

Nish said, 'That spot might mean something to the killer. Maybe he did something there before. Not necessarily another murder, or even anything bad. But it holds a place in his memory. Perhaps, in his mind, this is where he wanted to put the girl to rest.'

Tom smirked. 'Psychologist now, are you? Let's not get ahead of ourselves.'

Nikki raised a hand. 'Yes, let's not, but I also see the point. These sick people tend to stay local. They follow a pattern. I'm not saying we have a serial killer on our hands. But we do have a violent, dangerous person.' She pointed to her head. 'You know what the research shows. They can't control themselves. They don't understand normal feelings.'

Kristy spoke up. 'And they substitute a pattern instead of standard emotions.'

'Exactly.' Nikki smiled at her. 'It's our job to find that pattern. So, while we will spread the word everywhere, I think this person is local. By that I mean in Oxford, or within a five-mile radius. And he knows this place well. Like Nish said, that spot means something to him.'

Tom's face looked stormy, and he stared at the door in silence.

Nikki wrote number three. 'Motive. No murder happens without one. I guess this will emerge as we find out more about the girl.'

There was a knock on the door and Hetty Barfield's cherubic face, framed by black locks, pushed in. Nikki waved her inside. Hetty sat down and promptly picked up a chocolate biscuit.

'God, that feels good,' she moaned. 'Abi's gone to get some coffee. I told her to come back here if that's okay.'

The small office was getting tight for space, but it could hold six at a stretch. 'I guess we won't be long,' Nikki said. 'Anything of interest?'

'I sent photos to the blood splatter expert. He thinks the drops on the slope are venous blood, and a slow drip from a small laceration.'

'Which could be the cut on her forehead,' Nikki said. 'These are blood drops on the slope, going up to the crime scene?'

'Yes. Abi and I looked around, but there was nothing else. The extra Uniforms team joined us, and when I left, they hadn't found anything else. Nothing to make a positive ID, I'm afraid. Fingerprints on IDENT 1 showed nothing.'

'Did you find anything near the road?' Nikki asked.

Hetty looked thoughtful. 'Lots of boot prints. Given that it's summer, and the ground is hard, difficult to get any meaningful prints for the gait analyst. And all of us have trampled over the grass as well. So...'

Nikki nodded. She suspected as much. Hetty seemed to read what was on her mind.

'I looked for a man's print. She was killed by strangulation, correct? That points to a man.'

'As far as we know,' Nikki said. 'She could've been poisoned, or assaulted by other means before she was strangled. In any case, did you find anything?'

'Nothing that wouldn't count for one of ours, unfortunately. But I did find car tyre marks on the grass, a few hundred yards below ours. They dented the ground under the grass, so the car was heavy. Maybe a four-by-four.'

'Any other marks nearby?'

'None that I could see. And these marks were fresh. No more than a day old.'

Nikki's eyes brightened as she felt a jolt of excitement. 'Then that could be the car we're looking for.'

She glanced at Nish, who had already reached for the phone. He spoke to someone in the traffic department. They would get busy downloading films from the relevant cameras.

Tom raised his voice. 'The necklace she was wearing. Looked like the pendant was torn off. Any sign of it?'

Hetty shook her head. 'Not so far, no. But the Uniform teams will keep looking till dark tonight, and then first light tomorrow.'

Nikki felt conflicted. She wanted to be there early tomorrow morning, but she had her weekend planned with Rita.

'Thank you,' was all she could say for the time being. 'I want a full report please, even though I'm not working.'

'I'll be there, guv,' Kristy said, and Nish agreed.

Tom remained silent. Nikki looked at him, and he averted his gaze. She wondered what was eating him. He was a lot more grumpy than usual.

'I can't expect you guys to be there if I can't be,' she said softly, almost to herself.

'Nonsense,' Hetty remarked. 'If not now, when are they going to join the fray?' She grinned at Kristy and Nish.

'Exactly, guv.' Kristy looked at Nikki hopefully. Nikki nodded.

'Okay. Keep me updated.'

# SIX

'White tent is up on the site and Uniforms are keeping guard overnight,' Hetty said. 'The roadblocks have been removed. I'll be there tomorrow morning, but not at the break of dawn. I need my lie-in.'

Hetty left, and the meeting broke up. Tom was going out, and Nikki left her bag and followed him out swiftly.

'Tom, can I have a word, please?' she called from behind.

He came to a halt, then turned around slowly. She nodded, then walked down the service stairwell through to the underground car park. Tom followed without a word.

'What's going on?' Nikki didn't waste time. Her eyes searched Tom's face. 'You're upset about something. I need your full attention on this case. You can't be distracted.'

Tom rubbed his jaw, then kicked an imaginary stone. 'Nothing, guv. I'm fine.'

'Don't give me that.' Nikki hardened her voice. 'If you've got a problem working for me, I need to know.'

Tom turned his head slowly to look at her. Then he averted his face. 'No problem, guv.'

She didn't believe him. Tom had been a sergeant for a

while. He wanted to make the inspector grade, but all of a sudden, she arrived from London. Nikki knew he didn't like it, and she suspected the fact that she was a woman made it worse.

'Look, Tom. You're a good detective. You've been doing this job a while. But I need to do my job as well. While I don't want to tread on your toes, you need to understand that I'm the leader of this team.'

Tom said nothing. He wouldn't look at Nikki. She said, 'You question my decisions at every turn. When things don't go your way, you sulk. It was the same with the last case. I'm wondering if you need some time off.'

His head jerked towards her, and his eyes hardened. 'You know what, guv? I think that's exactly what I need.' His voice rose a notch. 'Get out of your hair, and get out of this fucking shit hole.'

He turned back towards the building.

'Tom!' Nikki shouted and ran after him. But he wouldn't slow down.

'I'll leave my warrant card on the desk. Bye.'

Nikki swore and smacked her fist into her palm. Great. So much for her team management skills. Did she just make a bad situation worse?

Kristy was upstairs, waiting for her. 'What's up with skipper? He stormed in, told me to hand in his warrant card. Said he's going away.'

'Oh god.' Nikki closed her eyes.

'To be honest, guv, he's been acting strange for a while now.'

'Has he said anything to you or Nish?'

'Not that I know of. By the way, the boss wants to see you. Said it's urgent.'

An ominous cloud gathered in the corner of Nikki's mind. 'Did he say what it's about?'

'No, sorry.'

* * *

Nikki smoothed down her shirt and walked the few steps to DS Patmore's door. She knocked, but didn't hear a response. There was a muffled, slamming sound from inside, like a window being shut. Patmore must've smoked another of his cigarettes.

'Come in,' his gruff voice barked. The smell of cigarettes was faint but still present. How he got away with it, Nikki didn't know. Then again, he was the boss.

Dean Patmore had the appearance of a grizzled bear who had lost the bulk of his youth. His shoulders slumped, his back was bent. He wore a perpetually irritated look on his stubbled face, which looked like it had been dragged through bushes. He coughed onto his fist, then hacked up some phlegm, which he spat into a tissue. Nikki closed her eyes briefly.

'Any progress on the girl?' Patmore asked as he took his seat again, having dropped the tissue into a bin. Nikki was glad the window was wide open.

'Not yet, sir. Early days.'

'Have the media got hold of it yet?'

Nikki shook her head. 'Not that we know of. The jogger who reported it has been warned not to speak to the media.' She lifted her arm and let it flop. 'We live in the age of instant news, sir. It's only a matter of time.'

Patmore's jaws clamped tight, and the corners of his lips moved upwards in a grimace. He picked up a phone and scrolled through it.

'Matter of time, eh?' he grated, looking up at Nikki. 'Then what the hell do you call this?'

He pushed his phone across the desk. Nikki picked it up, her heart doing a crazy dance against her ribs. The TVP official Twitter account was open on a link from a well-known journalist's feed. The photo on the screen took Nikki's breath away. She tried to swallow, but a heavy weight blocked her throat.

It was the same body she had seen this morning, but the photos had been taken with a flashlight, and at night. The girl's figure was visible from several different angles, with close-ups of her face.

The phone almost fell from Nikki's hands. It clattered onto the desk. Her chest felt hollow, she could barely breathe.

'Sit down,' Patmore said.

She complied without a word. She stared down at her lap, fingers twisting. When she looked up, Patmore was glaring at her.

'Who leaked it?'

Nikki blinked several times, then frowned. 'What do you mean, sir?'

'You know bloody well what I mean! Who from your team leaked the news?'

Nikki recovered from the earlier shock quickly, her mood sharpening into anger.

'No one as far as I know. You're talking about experienced officers, sir.' For a second, her mind went back to Neil Broadbent, the new kid on the block. She dismissed the suspicion quickly. Neil was too scared to put his career on the line for a few pennies from a media vulture.

Nikki leaned over and stabbed a finger at the phone, frowning. 'If you took your time to think about it, you'd see these photos were taken at night, with a flashlight. Our team didn't get there till daylight.'

Patmore's jaw dropped, then his face turned purple. His nostrils flared, and muscles jumped at the side of his temples.

'How dare you speak to me like that,' he seethed.

Nikki wasn't having any of it. She was used to Patmore's moods, just as he was to hers. It didn't mean she would tolerate her team being slandered.

'Well, like I said, if you—'

'Enough!' Patmore bellowed, slapping a hand on the desk.

The phone jumped in the air, and a couple of pens skittered off the table, falling to the carpet.

Nikki held his eyes for a few seconds, then dropped her gaze. Patmore was her superior officer. He knew all about her and had helped her join the TVP at a difficult time of her life. She owed him some respect.

But she was only pointing out the truth. Patmore was upset that a media storm was coming to his department, but it wasn't his department alone. Nikki was a part of this too.

'I'm sorry, sir,' she said. 'But I hope you can see the logic of what I said. This offender is a freak. He wants the publicity. He took photos after the crime, and he posted them on Twitter.'

Even as she said the words, Nikki knew how ridiculous they sounded. A murderer on social media? Was this guy mad? The police could trace his account within minutes, get an IP address, and then a location.

She asked, 'Do you know which account the photos came from?'

Snorting, Patmore picked up his phone. He scrolled through it, then handed it back to Nikki.

'There you go.'

The account was registered to 'Night Crawler', with the animated picture of a black owl on a white background. Nikki checked the account details. One sentence of description – *As you sow, so you reap*. She frowned. What did that mean?

There was no link to a website, and the only media on the account were the four photos taken last night. A journalist, who worked for a tabloid paper, had retweeted the images to TVP, as he had been instructed to do by Night Crawler.

'I'll get on to Cyber Crime, ASAP, sir.'

Patmore bunched his fists on the table and looked away. 'Okay. But I don't want anyone knowing that stuff was sent to this journalist. Or to TVP. God knows where else this idiot has sent the photos to. It's ridiculous.'

'No problem, sir.' She stood. 'I understand perfectly.' She didn't explain that TVP tweets were public.

'I didn't want this thing to blow up, and now it has. Just wait till the bloody colleges talk to their rich alumni, and they start to breathe down our necks.'

That, Nikki realised, was always a possibility in Oxford. The colleges would do anything to preserve their reputation.

'He hasn't identified the woman, sir, and we don't know if she's a college student. Let's wait and see.'

'I hope you're right,' Patmore said, calming somewhat.

Nikki hesitated. Now didn't seem the right time, but she didn't have an option. 'Sir, about DS Thomas Armstrong.'

Patmore looked up at her. 'What about him?'

'He's got some problems. Not sure what they are. But I think he's not happy working under me. Nish and Kristy are,' she added quickly.

Patmore exhaled and stood up. He went to the open window through which warm sunlight streaked in.

'He took it badly when Rutland left. They were close.' James Rutland had been Nikki's predecessor. Nikki arrived as his replacement.

'I'm sorry about that, sir. But I've been here for six months now.'

'I know.' Patmore turned around, and the look on his face changed. 'I see Monty's fortnightly reports have stopped. You did well. Transferring from London isn't always easy.'

Nikki smiled. 'It's quieter, that's for sure. But there's more than enough to keep me occupied.'

Patmore wagged a finger at her. 'Don't be fooled by the empty roads outside Oxford. There's a lot of money in the Cotswolds. Rich people like living here. I mean big money. Money draws in crime.' He coughed, then his scarred face moved in what was a close approximation to a smile. 'Not to mention what the rich people get up to themselves.'

34

'Thanks, sir.' She wondered if Patmore was changing the subject. 'What about DS Armstrong, sir? He seems to have a problem with me.'

Patmore leaned against the window and crossed his muscled forearms across his chest. 'Give him some more time. He will settle down. It's just that...' The words died on his lips, but Nikki knew exactly what he wanted to say.

'He's never worked for a female boss,' Nikki said, raising her eyebrows.

'Right. Maybe. Look, he's a quiet one. Always has been.'

'With all due respect, sir, he's worked several major cases with me. I hope he settles down soon, or I might need a new DS.'

Patmore's eyebrows lowered. So did his voice. 'Be careful now, Nikki. That sort of talk can be dangerous. We have to make the best of what we have.'

'I need to be able to trust him fully, sir. Will you please have a word?'

Patmore looked skyward as if there was an answer there. 'Okay. I will.'

# SEVEN

Kristy jerked her head up as she spotted her coming. Nikki beckoned her over, and they walked round to the new Cyber Crime Lab, where three full-time technicians lived, surrounded by servers, wires and screens.

Will, the oldest technician, looked up as they entered. He was in his thirties, but with his paunch, balding head, and nicotine-stained teeth, looked at least a decade older. His skin was a pasty colour, and every time Nikki saw him, she noted with revulsion his nose-picking habit. Gross wasn't even the word. Thankfully, his hands were on a keyboard this time.

She opened up the TVP Twitter feed on her phone, showing him the recent tweets. Will blew out his cheeks.

'Jay-sus.'

'Yes. Can we trace whose account this is?'

'Night Crawler?' Will's nails scratched the back of his neck, then his jaw, and Nikki watched with relief as they returned to his side.

'What do you mean by tracing the account?'

'I mean his IP address. From that you can get a location, right?'

Will shrugged. 'Yes, but that location can change. If they're in Starbucks and using their WiFi, we get the IP of that server. If they're at home, on a different server, we get that address.'

'Yes, I know,' Nikki said. 'It can change. But if we monitor it, we can see a routine. Maybe he uses the same three servers every day. Or stays in the same place. Can you do it?'

'I can try.'

'How will you do it, though?' Kristy asked.

Will's eyes lit up like he was a kid in a candy store. 'I can insert a webpage as a clickable link on his account. Every time he clicks on it, I get his IP address.'

'But won't he see it?'

Will rubbed his hands gleefully, getting more childlike by the minute. Nikki tried her best not to laugh. She looked down at her shoes, sucking her cheeks in.

'That's the cool part. These webpages are like cookies. You can't see them, but they can be inserted anywhere.'

'If you can't see them, then how can they be inserted? I mean, won't the user see them?' Nikki was confused. Will appeared to be as well, then he understood.

'No, I mean the IP address of the pages will be concealed. So they click on the link, it takes them to this page, but the location of the page is a fake one. If they try to trace it, then they will realise, but most people don't know how to trace an IP address.'

'You never know with this guy. He could be quite tech savvy.'

Will shrugged. 'Worth a try, I guess.'

'Okay, let's do it. Will you please report back to me in two to three days?'

'Yes,' Will nodded, staring at Nikki for longer than necessary. She moved quickly, picking the phone up from the table.

* * *

'Looks like you have a fan,' Kristy said as they walked down the corridor.

Nikki raised an eyebrow at her, and Kristy grinned back.

'If this doesn't work,' Kristy jerked a thumb back, 'then we can always issue a warrant with Twitter's HQ.'

'Which will take days and weeks to process.' Nikki sighed wearily. 'This is quicker. If we don't get anywhere, then the warrant is a fallback. But to be honest, I don't know if Twitter even has an office around here. Even if they did, it's going to be a nightmare asking them to reveal their user's data.'

Kristy nodded, looking downcast. 'It's a shame we don't have access to them. However, this could be a fake account.'

'I think so. He would be stupid to use his own WiFi and laptop or phone to post those photos.'

'He wants to play a sick game. Sending the photos to the TVP account is just ridiculous.' She thought of the serial killers she had caught in the past. By definition, unless three murders were committed with the same MO, a killer wasn't given that term. She just hoped this wasn't a new kid on that unwanted block, starting his twisted game. The thought made her shiver.

Nish was coming out of the office, and he saw them. He walked over. 'Traffic called, guv. They've pulled in the images from CCTV and have sent me the files.'

'Anything interesting?'

'Not seen them yet. I came to find you. Where's skipper?'

Nikki sighed. 'Let's get inside and I'll tell you.' She waited till the door was shut and the two DCs were sitting down.

'He's been a bit weird all day, and I asked him what's going on. He got angry and stormed off.' She looked from Nish to Kristy. 'Do either of you know what's bugging him? You worked with him under James Rutland, right?'

Both DCs were quiet for a while. Nish spoke first. Nikki knew Tom was closer to him.

'He took the guv's leaving badly. They used to be family

friends. And he also thought he might make the grade to become inspector. Patmore was meant to back him for it, but it didn't happen.'

'Why not?' Nikki asked, but she already suspected the answer. Nish wouldn't look her in the eyes.

'Well, you came along. Patmore told the skipper there was no need for him to get promoted just yet.'

Nikki sat down at her desk. No wonder Tom was funny with her. She knew how department politics worked. Paying for a new inspector's salary made no sense when an old one could be shipped over. She knew Patmore had done her a favour by agreeing to her transfer. She needed a break from the Met, and her mother was here. But maybe her being here wasn't just Patmore being nice. He was also looking to save money.

'He doesn't blame you, guv,' Nish said softly. 'He's just getting used to you, that's all.'

'I hope so. I need him back at work. Anyway, let's have a look at the CCTV.'

Nish opened up his laptop as they gathered around him. His fingers clicked on the keyboard and four boxes filled up the screen. The exit for Waterperry had a steady stream of traffic. On the top right-hand corner of each box the time was displayed. Nish stopped the film at thirty minutes past seven, and he pointed at the black and white image of a black Range Rover that indicated and turned left into the exit. It went around the bend and vanished from sight. Nish clicked again and the cameras picked up the Range Rover, coming out of the exit and joining the A40 traffic. The time was eight thirty. Nish zoomed into the car, but the driver's image wasn't easily visible.

'Let's check the plates with DVLA,' Nikki said. Nish did as asked, and came up with an insurance and MOT certificate. Using his clearance, he was able to download the vehicle owner's certificate, which had the address.

'Bingo,' Nish whispered, his eyes shining.

Nikki said, 'Who is that car registered to?'

Nish went through the vehicle owner's licence. 'A Mr Barry Henshaw, in Cheltenham.'

# EIGHT

The wind was howling outside, its icy blast roaring through the cracks of the windows. Ten-year-old Danny shivered in the cold, and hugged his little sister Molly closer. Their mother, Janet, was on the phone and pacing up and down the room. Janet's hair was straggly and loose, and sweat poured down her forehead. Her skin was a sickly pale colour. Her nose was running continuously, and she wiped it on her dirty sleeve. Her thin fingers clenched and unclenched, her reed-thin arms moving continuously. She spoke in a high-pitched voice.

'What do you mean you can't come? You've got to come, please. I don't have enough left.'

Danny knew who Janet was speaking to. He didn't know the man's name, but he came round frequently. The man and Janet went upstairs to the bedroom, and stayed there, sometimes for hours. Sometimes, the man was nice to him and Molly. He once bought them burgers from McDonald's, which was a real treat. Normally, Janet didn't have enough money to do their weekly food shopping. Danny stole bread and eggs from the

41

corner shop, and sometimes, when things got really bad, he rooted around in the neighbours' rubbish bins desperate to find something he and his sister could eat.

In some ways, Danny wished the man would come back. He wouldn't mind if they could leave this godforsaken house. If the man took them away, then with their mother, maybe they could start a new life. Danny promised himself the next time he saw the bloke, he would ask him his name.

Janet hung up the phone and chucked it on the sofa. She sat down and swore loudly, then dug the heels of her hands into her eyes and dropped to the floor. Molly went up to her.

'Mummy, I'm hungry.'

Janet stared at her daughter like she was seeing her for the first time. Then she got up and started pacing the room again. She screamed at Molly.

'Just leave me alone. Leave me alone, please.' She started to cry, and then left the room. Molly was crying too, and Danny went up to her and gave her a hug.

'Come on, let's go and get some food.'

They put their coats on, and holding each other's hands they walked to the local off-licence. There was a crowd at the counter, a few drunk teenagers buying cans of beer. That occupied the shopkeeper, and Danny swiftly put a few tins of baked beans and a sliced loaf inside his jacket. They slipped out of the shop before anyone could notice.

They got back into the house, and Danny fed Molly. He put the TV on and left Molly snug in a blanket. He checked the radiators: the heating wasn't on. The boiler was broken, and he had asked Janet to fix it. She had brushed him off as usual, and then gone up to her room. When he checked, she had that needle sticking out of her arm, and she was fast asleep.

He had no doubt he would see his mother in the same condition again. He crept up the stairs and listened by the bedroom door. He could hear movements inside, and then his mother cursed. He pushed open the door: she hadn't locked it. Janet was on the floor, on her knees. She was searching for something, and she looked up as Danny entered. She carried on, desperately looking all over the carpet.

'What have you lost? Money?' Danny asked.

Janet didn't answer. She started muttering to herself in a low whisper that rose steadily higher.

'I can't find it. I can't find it.' Then it became a scream, and the words wailed out of her lungs. 'I can't find it, dammit all, I can't find it.'

Danny looked round the floor. He had to be careful: a couple of needles lay on the carpet and he didn't want to step on them. There was some broken glass and a spoon, its underside blackened and some dried material on the top. He didn't know what these things were. But he had seen his mother inject herself with a needle and syringe. There was that heavy, sweet smell in the room, a cloying, deep aroma that reached inside him. He would never forget that smell for the rest of his life. Danny could sense his mother's desperation. He lifted the bed sheets and found a couple of rubber tourniquets on the stained sheets. He looked under the pillow and found a small brown rubber ball, the shape and size of a large P. He picked it up between thumb and forefinger, and he held it up so Janet could see it.

'What's this, Mummy?'

Janet's eyebrows shot up, and she jumped up from the floor. Her eyes were red, nose running. She sniffed and climbed over the bed, then grabbed the small ball from Danny's hand. She set to work, and Danny looked on, fascinated. Normally, Janet locked the door when she did this, but she didn't know that Danny watched through the keyhole. Just like now, he had seen his mother empty the brown powder into the spoon, and heat it up by lighting a flame from underneath. He saw her pick up a needle and draw some of the fluid into it.

Janet seemed to be in a world of her own, now; she seemed to have forgotten that Danny was standing just a few feet away. He looked at her face, at the streaks of sadness, the lines etched deep into her forehead. His mother was always sad, always in pain. She only felt better when she took the medicine.

He watched as Janet put the syringe on the bedside table. She tied the rubber tourniquet above her left elbow, then picked up the syringe with her right hand and injected herself. She released the tourniquet from the left arm and slid down on the bed. Her eyes closed, and her breathing went from fast and ragged to slow and peaceful. Her lips opened as she breathed deeply.

Danny stepped forward. The needle was still half full with the brown liquid. It was still sticking into his mother's elbow. This was the medicine that made his mother happy. What would it be like if she never woke up? She would always be happy, wouldn't she?

The air in the room seemed to get sucked out, and even the breath in Danny's chest was still. He almost didn't know what he was doing. It was as if a voice inside him was telling him to grab the needle and do something. He reached forward and placed a hand on the plunger of the syringe. The needle was firmly inside the vein. The skin was white with marbling patterns of veins. Danny held the syringe and depressed the plunger. The brown liquid went inside Janet's veins, and it kept going till Danny depressed the plunger to the full.

44

# NINE

Rita left on Saturday morning, much to Nikki's disappointment. But Nikki understood. Rita had stayed with her for a whole month, and her father missed her. Rita also missed her friends in London.

After she left, the house seemed quiet. Nikki tried to keep herself busy. Ironically, the one weekend she wasn't working was when she wanted to. She went running and learned to make a new type of salad.

She knew Clarissa was feeling a little lonely after their holiday in the Cotswolds, so she called her, and, when she said she was at home, Nikki made her way over to the house in Jericho, where she'd grown up.

She sat down opposite Clarissa, who coughed and hacked up some phlegm into a tissue.

'This place is looking nice. Did you get a cleaner?'

Clarissa looked at her daughter. 'No. Can't afford it.'

Nikki knew that wasn't quite true. Clarissa had some savings, and she used to work as a teaching assistant. In any case, Nikki was glad she had done this off her own back.

'Rita rang this morning, to say goodbye. She's back in a couple of weeks.' Clarissa's face relaxed and her eyes became animated.

'Yes. I'm sure she'll come around when she's back,' Nikki said. 'Please keep that weekend free.'

Clarissa nodded. A shadow seemed to pass over her face, and then her jaws hardened. It seemed as if she was trying to decide on something. Nikki watched her mother with interest.

'Come and sit here.' Clarissa pointed to the cushion next to her on the sofa.

'What's going on?'

Clarissa patted the seat, then her right hand snaked behind the cushion she was resting on. As Nikki sat down next to her, she pulled out a green, worn-out photo album.

Nikki felt an odd sensation in her throat. She had a vague memory of this album, but she couldn't recall the last time she'd seen it. Clarissa opened the first page and stopped. Nikki's heart boomed slowly against her ribs, and the room seemed to darken. A baby boy's photos were on the page. Slowly, like she was turning the pages of a rare and ancient manuscript, Clarissa opened a new page, and then another.

They were photos of her half-brother, Tommy, when he was little. He was a baby in the photos, but there were also images of him as a toddler, aged perhaps three or four.

Clarissa stopped at a photo that showed Tommy in the arms of a man.

'You once asked me who Tommy's father was,' Clarissa's voice was like paper scratching on the floor. She cleared her throat, then coughed. 'This is him. His name was Steven.'

'Let me see,' Nikki said, extending her hand. It shook, and she swallowed the heavy weight in her throat. The photo was fading at the edges, but the man was clearly visible, grinning from ear to ear as he held Tommy. Nikki had never seen him before.

'I didn't really know what he was like. I was young. He got me into...' Clarissa's voice trailed off, down a dusty, forgotten path, mired in regret.

Nikki stared at the photo. Steven was a good-looking man, on the thin side, with sunken cheeks and prominent, lively dark eyes. This was the man who had introduced Clarissa to heroin, the drug that destroyed her life; and she'd had to give up Tommy.

Nikki had never seen Steven before, and she wondered if her mother had kept the photos hidden and only showed her what she wanted.

Clarissa sniffed, the tip of her nose red. She wiped her tears. 'I just wanted... to let it go. He meant nothing to me after a while, and he never got back in touch. But I'd never shown you this.'

Nikki put a hand on her mother's shoulder and felt it stiffen. Clarissa turned to look at her, and they held each other's eyes for a second. Nikki realised it had taken Clarissa a lot of courage to do this, to open up old wounds, in the hope of letting the old demons go. True, the guilt over Tommy's death would never leave her, but at least she could start the journey to come to terms with her tragic past.

'Thank you,' Nikki said.

'I don't know where he is, or what happened to him. He never stayed in touch. Then I was with your father, and you came along.'

Nikki thought for a while. 'Was he in trouble with the law? Drug addicts often are.'

Clarissa nodded. 'He was caught for shoplifting and also for drug dealing. Well, we were doing it all the time then, anyway.' Clarissa shook her head, then covered her head with her hands. 'Good job I never heard from him, to be honest.'

They sat in silence for a while, Nikki's hand now clasping her mother's.

'But I'll never stop missing my little boy,' Clarissa whispered. A sob ripped from her chest like ribs being pulled out.

Nikki pulled her into a hug, her own face crumpling with bitter sadness.

# TEN

Nikki phoned Monty when she was back home.

'How are you?' Monty's warm voice came down the line.

'Not too bad. Can I ask you something?' She had spoken to Kristy the night before. There was no progress report from the crime scene. Nikki couldn't stop thinking about it.

'Sure, go ahead.'

'About this dead girl. What do you think?'

There was a pause. Maybe Monty hadn't expected that. But he took it in his stride. 'He's a sick exhibitionist.'

'That's for sure. I feel we're missing something.'

'Have you looked through old cases to see if there was another case with the same MO? Or a cold case that looked similar.'

'Yes, we've started on that. But—'

'I was in Cyber Crimes, and Danny was working on those tweets. He hadn't got anything, in case you were wondering.'

Nikki sighed. 'We're nowhere. It's the waiting. Waiting for Hetty's report; waiting for the post-mortem; waiting for Cyber Crimes. I really need a positive ID at least. Maybe...' Nikki hesitated: a second pair of eyes would be useful. 'I thought about going to the scene today, take a fresh look. I know you're on shift, but would you have an hour or so to spare?'

The static of silence filled up the void between them, and she almost took the offer back.

She bit her lower lip, adding, 'If you do come to the crime scene, it would be only as a lay person. It doesn't give you any rights to the case.'

She heard him smile down the phone. 'I won't tread on your toes, don't worry.'

Monty knew the lie of the land, literally. His views might be useful. What did she have to lose? Him attending the crime scene meant nothing, after all. If he had been the SIO on Friday, then it would be his case, anyway.

'I'll see you there.'

* * *

Nikki parked her Volkswagen on the dirt track near the slope and waited. She could see the trees at the top of the small hill bent from the wind's rebuke. Close to them, she also saw the white forensics tent. A bank of clouds had scuttled across the sun, and the air suddenly chilled. Nikki pulled her coat collar up as Monty's dark, two-seater BMW pulled in behind her. She watched as his tall frame unfolded itself from the driver's seat. He stretched, then glanced at her and smiled. He rubbed his shoulders. She wondered how he fitted into that tiny car.

'A bit cramped, is it?' she asked as Monty leaned forward, touching his toes. He was dressed in casuals, jogging bottoms and a vest with a hooded top.

He grimaced as he stood and raised his arms upwards. 'Lovely car, but small for me.'

He was honest, and she liked that about him. 'That's what I was thinking. You must be well snug in that seat.'

'It's fun taking corners at a hundred miles an hour. But yes, rather snug.' He grinned at the shocked expression on her face.

She put her hands inside the pockets of her top as they walked up the slope. 'Didn't think you were a speed freak.'

He hooked an eyebrow at her. His dark eyes glinted. 'It's a natural high. But I'm not a freak. It's more like a sport.'

'Not my type of sport. I prefer going for a run.'

'Me too, when I get the chance.'

His long legs were making short work of the hill, but he slowed down for her. Walking up the path was so much easier with trainers on. The blue and white tape was fluttering in the breeze. The sun broke through, shining over the white tent that looked so misplaced in the surrounding greenery. A uniformed squad was guarding the crime scene. One of the constables waved at Nikki, and she nodded back.

The car units would be doing their patrols every hour. If they had seen or heard anything, it would be reported. As it happened, Monty would be the first to know, as he was SIO for the weekend. Considering that, she was puzzled by his laid-back dress. She was used to seeing him suited up in his dark-blue blazer, she thought with a warm flush to her cheeks.

Monty took out two pairs of purple nitrile gloves and gave her a pair. He unzipped the tent and had a look at the empty ground inside.

'She was laid out on her back, palms up, feet together. Very prim and proper. But horrible, obviously. It would be better if she was in a heap, actually. I hate seeing them laid out like that.'

'Like they want to make a show of it.' Monty shook his head in disgust. He looked up at her, his large, soulful eyes suddenly holding her captive.

He straightened his lanky spine and went around the tent. She followed. They stood under the tree, looking at the rolling hills of the Cotswolds. The sun came out. The hills were a patchwork quilt of green and brown. Silver-bellied clouds browsed over their tops. Monty pointed to the left. A village was nestled in a valley. Two church spires were visible and a couple of large manor houses.

'That's Burton. It's your typical desirable village. Too expensive for our salaries.'

'Aren't they all?' Nikki replied. She looked around and saw a few more villages she had missed last time. They were a couple of miles away, she guessed.

'So. What do you think?'

'I think you might be right about the placement; it looks like she was left here for a reason. Did you notice that hiking trail?' He pointed to a dirt track going down the other side of the hill. 'That's a well-known running track. I've done it too, a couple of times. He knew she would be found; he didn't try to hide the body.'

'And he took photos, and sent them to TVP and the press, just to make sure we knew. Assuming it's a he, anyway. The MO points to it being a male.'

Monty nodded his agreement. 'He's also likely to be young, given his social media abilities. Although Twitter isn't exactly cutting-edge any more. There's so much these days.'

'I know what you mean. I can't imagine a sixty-year-old pervert doing this.'

'He'd also have found it hard to drag the body up this slope. Unless she came up herself, which I doubt, given the dress and shoes she was wearing.'

'She was brought here,' Nikki whispered, almost to herself. 'I know it.'

# ELEVEN

Jacob Winspear was used to getting his own way in life. Given the amount of wealth he was born into, and the life of privilege he enjoyed, it came naturally. When others didn't do his bidding, he knew how to make life difficult for them. But when that other happened to be his own daughter, Jacob had a problem. Lottie had always been a wild child. Too emotional, and too argumentative. But worst of all, as she had grown up, she'd got her own political beliefs.

Jacob sipped tea from the china cup as he looked out over the lawns that merged with the woods far beyond. There was a fountain in the middle, spouting water. Topiary hedges stood on either side. It was a lovely summer's day, but Jacob was too distracted to enjoy the idyllic view to its fullest.

His stupid old father had changed the family company structure when it came to inheritance. The first born got the land and house now, regardless of whether it was a boy or girl. His boy was fine. Rupert was still a teenager and docile. A bit simple, well, dumb frankly, a dumbness even his expensive boarding school education hadn't been able to change; but Jacob thought being an idiot wasn't a bad thing in a child born to the manor. Aristocratic families were full of idiots – and they were all stinking rich. All they had to do was listen to their father and make money off the land. How hard could that be? Farmers, developers, everyone wanted their land. It was the easiest money to be made in the world.

But Lottie, his daughter, well, she was a different kettle of fish. She was a socialist, who thought one person or family owning all of this was too much. Stupid girl. One day, she would rue her actions. Actions? Jacob had no intention of letting her act on her beliefs. He needed to do something before that. But Lottie was clever too. She had taken herself to Oxford, which Jacob admitted made him proud. After all, he was a graduate of Merton College himself.

If only Lottie would just marry a suitable boy and start a family. All this nonsense of getting girls educated just made life difficult. It upset the age-old balance of things. Like his dad had done. The old fool got married to a young actress who had no money but a lot of ideas above her station. Women had been mistreated since the beginning of time, that stupid bitch used to say. And his doddery old father fell for that crap. Now, Jacob had to deal with the fallout. If Lottie, with her radical beliefs, got hold of the family fortune... Jacob shuddered, a sudden fear squeezing his guts. He remembered one thing his grandfather often said:

*Never let an outsider in.*

Now, Jacob feared his own daughter might do exactly that.

And that was not the only worry he had. He stared at the piece of paper on his desk. It was the last thing he needed. Lease and rental income had fallen this quarter. This was a problem because Jacob was funding his Conservative Party membership battle. He was a councillor already. But to become a Member of Parliament was another matter. Competition was much stiffer. The Cotswolds and southeast England was the bastion of the Conservative Party voter base, and there was no dearth of super-rich Tories wanting more power for themselves. Every candidate was well connected, their lives were squeaky clean, and virtually everyone was an Oxbridge graduate. Well, their public lives were clean; what they got up to behind closed doors was no one's business. But Jacob's life wasn't clean. He was tarnished by association, and that too by his own daughter. The ugly photo on the front page of the tabloid newspaper said everything. Lottie, holding a placard over her head, shouting for the statue of the famous statesman in front of her college to be brought down. The statesman used to be a slave trader. So what? He had donated millions in today's money to that Oxford college. If his statue was taken down, should that money also be removed from the college? To Jacob, the whole thing was totally stupid. As far as he was concerned, it was old history, and everyone should let sleeping dogs lie.

Obviously, Lottie disagreed. Her name was written under the photo, which meant she had given it to a reporter; she must have said yes when those cretins wanted to take a photo of her. Bloody ridiculous, Jacob fumed, closing his eyes. No wonder the land rents were falling. And with it, his chances of becoming the next Witney MP. One of the previous Witney MPs was David Cameron, who had gone on to become the prime minister. It was a prestigious constituency. Several Cabinet members had emerged from it over the years.

Jacob had also held high hopes for himself – once. Until his daughter started to become a loony lefty.

The phone in his pocket started to vibrate. He looked at it and cursed. He thought about not answering, but the man had already called once this morning.

'Have you seen the papers?' Charles Topley asked in his low, smooth voice. Jacob had never heard the man say a word in anger or get emotional. He juggled a hundred men and women and never got stressed, no matter what they did. Nor did he suffer fools. An ideal man to handle an election campaign.

'Of course I've seen the bloody papers.'

'We don't have much time till the hustings at the Houses of Parliament. This doesn't look good.'

Jacob paced the room. 'You don't have to tell me that, Charles. I need a solution; I know what the damned problem is.'

Charles was as unruffled as ever. 'Lottie shouldn't give any more interviews to the press. Have you talked to her?'

'You think she listens to me? Or her mother? She thinks high taxes and income redistribution will solve all the world's problems.'

Charles was silent for a while. 'Is there a chance the college will remove the statue? Because if that happens, then they win. And given Lottie's involvement, that's a mortal blow for you.'

Jacob slumped into his red leather armchair. His initials were carved in black.

'I don't know. I know they're thinking about it. The college's governing body are meeting about it.'

'You need to influence that meeting. Make sure they don't vote to take the statue down.'

'Okay. I'll try.'

'Good. And, Jacob? Control your daughter, before she destroys you.'

# TWELVE

Jacob Winspear stared at the completely bald man sitting opposite. His scalp was shiny and tanned, but he had a large moustache that looked incongruous on his otherwise hairless face and scalp. He seemed like a man who would benefit from wearing a wig.

'I'm sorry,' said the bald man, whose name was Justin Dickens. He was the bursar of Merton College. 'The governing body have started the meeting already. I will let them know that you came.'

'I must insist that I speak to them.'

'If you pass the message onto me, I will make sure—'

'No, I have to give it to them myself. Please tell Professor Smith to speak to me. Now.'

'Mr Winspear, this is most irregular—'

'You're not listening.' Jacob leaned forward. He put his elbows on the table. 'I don't want to have a situation where I have to pull out the scholarship funds.' The Winspear family currently provided tuition, accommodation and meals to three masters's students in Economics. Jacob had studied PPE –

Philosophy, Politics and Economics was a popular liberal arts degree in Oxford – and Economics was his favourite subject. 'And I need to make a decision by the end of this week.'

The bursar frowned. 'What's bothering you?'

'All the noise around the statue of Basil Bones.' He dropped his voice an octave. There was a secretary typing outside when he came in. But the old harridan had stopped typing and Jacob knew she was listening. He leaned forward, almost whispering.

'I don't want my daughter's name in any publication.'

Mr Dickens understood. 'I can assure you, that won't happen. No publication from this college will bear your daughter's name. And Basil Bones's statue is staying, by the way.'

Jacob was relieved. But Mr Dickens had an apologetic look on his face. 'However, we cannot censor publications at the university, although we can speak to them and let them know of your concerns. And we certainly cannot control external media.'

Jacob's relief rapidly turned to consternation. 'You need to stop the papers. I don't care how you do it.'

'Perhaps you might want to have a chat with your daughter, first?' Mr Dickens said politely.

'Don't you think I've tried that, you idiot?' Jacob was past caring now. 'I need to ensure that for the next week, nothing about my daughter or my last name comes out in the papers connected to Oxford. Is that too much to ask for?'

'Like I said, we will try our best for publications within the university. And you don't have to worry about the college papers. We can control those.' A crafty gleam appeared in Mr Dickens's eyes. 'Apart from an embarrassment to the family, is there any other reason for this, Mr Winspear?'

Jacob stood. He wasn't a tall man, and he had always hated that. He wished he could tower above this cretin of a bursar. Leeches, all of them.

'No. Nothing at all.'

Jacob walked out of the college grounds and crossed the road. He got into his two-seater Bentley Continental, then took his burner phone out. He turned off his usual phone before he spoke into the burner. A man answered on the first ring.

'Are you alone?'

'I wouldn't be calling you if I wasn't. Meet me at the usual place in ten minutes.' He hung up.

Jacob started the car and drove out of Oxford. He made sure he wasn't being followed. As he drove, his phone rang. He answered, and Charles Topley's voice came through the speakers.

'Joan Birch, the Minister of Transport wants to speak to you. I think she wants assurance we have the situation under control prior to the election.'

'Have you not assured her already?' Jacob couldn't believe it. Who knew politics would be this stressful?

'I have, but she wants your word on this. She said if you're going to have the party's backing, the party needs to be sure you can control the situation.'

'Not only that, Charles, tell them I can turn it into an advantage.'

'She's coming down to Oxford tomorrow. Where do you want to meet her?'

Jacob groaned inwardly. Joan Birch was a dragon. A dragoness to be precise. Ironically, she also held the title of baroness. She was tight with the prime minister. Any fledgling Tory politician would be honoured to see her, but Jacob knew she was coming on business, and her ruthlessness was legendary.

'At home, I suppose. When is she coming?'

'Afternoon. We have to give her some good news.'

'Don't worry. I'm working on it.'

Jacob hung up. He went east from the centre, towards

Headington and the John Radcliffe Hospital. Behind the hospital buildings, and after some woodland, there was a BMW factory that had fallen into disrepair. The giant warehouse was rusting, its once-shiny production line now littered with graffiti and needles. Jacob parked his car, but stayed in the car for a while, ensuring he was alone. Then he got out and walked swiftly inside the main warehouse.

A bearded man was waiting for him. Ryan Siddle was the Labour Party MP for Donnington. He was dressed in a light-brown linen suit, but he was still sweating.

'Why do we have to meet here?' His dark eyes settled on Jacob. 'I can think of a hundred other places.'

'Because no one will expect us to be here. Was the protest rally a success?'

Ryan smiled. 'Yes, thank you. I made my office pull out all the stops, like you wanted. We got hundreds more volunteers, and from all accounts the university is spitting bullets. Some of the volunteers even sprayed graffiti and wrote rude words on some statues. I thought that was a nice touch.'

'Good.' Jacob felt a bit better. That should turn the tide against these fuckers. Now all he had to do was give an impassioned speech to protect Oxford from hooligans at Friday night's hustings. That should ensure everyone in Witney voted for him to become the next MP.

'What about my daughter?' Jacob asked.

Ryan frowned. 'The leaders said she wasn't there. That works out well for you though.'

'She wasn't there?' It was Jacob's turn to be both perplexed and elated. At the same time, he felt a tinge of concern. 'Are you sure? She's not answered my wife's calls, so I don't know where she was. Or is, for that matter.'

'And even if she was, she would be barred from giving interviews to the media.'

'Good. Thank you. The donation to your party will come from a shell company in the Cayman Islands.'

'All good,' Ryan said. Then he leaned forward. 'Our arrangement still stands, right? I don't want the new stadium, and you do. We kick up a fuss till the developer is forced to increase his price. Then I can sell it to my people.'

Jacob pointed a finger at him. 'And that will take a couple of years, at least, if we kick up the right type of fuss. That makes you look good. The valiant left-wing fighter, protecting the environment.'

'And you make more money on the deal than before.'

'I scratch your back, and you scratch mine.'

Ryan smiled. 'Precisely. You won't go back on your word?'

Jacob shook his head solemnly. 'You've done us a big favour with this one. Going ahead, we can be of use to each other.'

Ryan's lips flattened and a hard look came into his eyes. 'Don't tell your aides anything. If word of this ever gets out, it will be political suicide for both of us. And if you try to use any of this against me, then I will destroy you.'

'A war won't help any of us,' Jacob said, 'when we can benefit each other.' He stuck out his hand. The veteran left-winger pumped it enthusiastically.

'I hope you win hands down on Friday.'

'Thank you for the help.'

'No problem. Have you seen the headlines this morning?' Ryan laughed. 'Everyone hates the protestors now, after all the vandalising they did. Even the cops turned out. They arrested someone.'

Jacob frowned. 'That wasn't my daughter, was it?'

'No,' Ryan reassured him. 'It was a bloke. If I hear about your daughter, I will let you know. Try not to worry though. I'm sure she's fine. I'll ask some of the party members to hunt her down.'

Ryan looked at his watch. 'Are we all done?'

'For now, yes.'

When he got back to the car, Jacob took the burner phone out. He rang a number and waited for it to connect. It went to answerphone. He left a message.

'Benjamin, it's me. Where's Lottie? Wasn't she at the party with you? Call me back ASAP.'

# THIRTEEN

Twenty-five years ago

Danny woke up with a start. He felt Molly next to him, and he thought his sister had crawled into bed with him at night, like she sometimes did. Only this time they were on their mother's bed. Molly was still sleeping, and Danny sat up. His eyes fell on his mother. She looked different. Her eyes were open, and her face was puffy. Her skin was a strange greyish colour. He shook her shoulders once, but she didn't move. He noticed how still she was, how nothing in her body moved, not even her chest. Danny's heart raced. He didn't know what to do.

He got out of bed and went over to his mother's side. He pulled her arm, and it fell limp to one side, over the bed. He touched her cheek; it felt cold. For some reason, Danny couldn't help but be fascinated. Janet looked so calm, like she was in a dream world from where she had never returned. For once, she wasn't sweaty, agitated, or cursing. Gently, he brushed the blonde hair from her forehead. She was ice-cold to the touch. He realised his mother was dead. He lifted her thin arm and tucked it under the covers. Then he went over to Molly. She was still fast asleep, thumb stuck inside her mouth.

Danny let her sleep; he left the door wide open. He ran downstairs and thought about what he should do. He had to call the police, or ask the neighbours for help. He started to put his coat on, but then the door opened. The man who visited his mother entered.

'Hello, kid,' he said, flashing Danny a toothy smile. He held a packet of food and gave it to Danny. 'Some burgers and chips for you and your sister.'

Danny stared at the man. He wasn't hungry. He didn't take the packet. The man frowned, aware something was wrong.

'Where is your mother? And your sister?'

Danny didn't know what to say. He simply gaped at the man.

The man brushed past Danny; he looked around the tiny lounge, kitchen and bathroom. He shouted Janet's name, then went up the stairs. A few minutes later, Danny heard him come downstairs. His face was pale, his eyes wide. He seemed to be in shock.

'You need to call the police. Your mother...'

Danny spoke for the first time. 'She is dead.' He felt emotion as he said the words. In his own mind, he thought his mother being dead wasn't a bad thing. At least she was calm and in a happy place.

The man blinked a few times, staring at Danny. Then he pulled out a phone from his pocket and called 999, and an ambulance.

'Shit,' the man said, running a hand down his face. 'Hello, 999? Yeah... reporting a dead body found in 24 Ashmore Close, in Sutton. No... I don't know. There're children here. No... no.'

He hung up. His eyes were bulging, and he stared at Danny for a while. Then he blinked and squeezed his eyes shut, thumbs pressing on his forehead. Then he breathed out.

'Stay here, kid,' he said. 'Where's your sister?'

'Watching TV.'

'Help is coming. See ya.' The man opened the door, letting in cold air and rain. He paused at the threshold and gave Danny a look.

'Have a good life, kid,' he said, then left.

Danny watched him get into a silver two-seater BMW sports car. As the man drove away, he noted the registration number of the car, the letters and numbers etching deep into his mind.

# FOURTEEN

'Mr Henshaw?' Nikki said on the phone. It was Monday morning, and it hadn't taken long to get the phone number of the Range Rover's owner.

A male voice answered. 'Yes. Who's speaking?'

'Inspector Nikki Gill of Thames Valley Police.'

There was silence on the other end, as expected. Nikki didn't mind that. If people were worried after hearing her title, then they were more willing to share information.

'What... what is this about, Inspector?'

'Do you own a black Range Rover Sport HSE, reg number PO22 USV?'

'Yes, I do.' The voice became louder, with a hint of panic. 'Oh please, don't tell me. Has he been in an accident?'

'Who are you referring to?' Nikki asked calmly, but she could guess.

'My son, Ben. Benjamin. He's crashed the car, hasn't he? The stupid sod. Was he drunk?'

If only that was Benjamin's only worry, Nikki thought to herself grimly. Secretly, she was pleased she was getting somewhere.

'Do you know where Benjamin is now?'

'No, I... has he not been arrested? How did you get hold of the car?'

'Mr Henshaw, please calm down. I need to ask you a few questions. I will explain everything as we go along. Was Ben driving the car on Thursday?'

'I assume so. He normally has the car. It's in my name, but he drives it when he's at college.'

A light bulb clicked on in Nikki's mind. Her pen was poised over the notebook.

'Which college does your son attend?'

'Oriel College in Oxford.'

Nikki scribbled quickly on her notepad. 'Do you know if he has a girlfriend?'

'I think his mother mentioned something. I've never seen her. Why do you ask?'

'I will answer all questions soon, Mr Henshaw. Do you, or your wife, know what his girlfriend's name is?'

'I have to ask my wife.'

'Okay. When did you last see your son?'

Mr Henshaw hesitated a while. 'He hasn't come home from end of term as yet. I've not seen him for a few weeks.'

'Cheltenham is no more than a couple of hours' drive from Oxford. Can you remember the date when you saw him?'

More hesitation. 'Maybe in April, the last weekend. That was the Easter break. He's been studying for exams, hence he's not been back.' His voice was worried, and now Nikki detected frank panic. 'Inspector, is my son all right? What's happened to him?'

Nikki felt bad immediately. 'I'm sure your son is absolutely fine, Mr Henshaw. We want to find the person who was driving your car on Thursday, last week, between seven thirty and eight thirty. He or she took the A40 exit from Waterperry, and we have the car on CCTV. Is that person likely to be your son?'

There was more silence for a while. Nikki heard a woman's voice, and Mr Henshaw went offline, speaking in a hushed tone.

'Sorry, I had to speak to my wife. She hasn't seen Ben since Easter, either. He's been busy with his exams.'

'When did you or your wife last speak to him?'

Mr Henshaw spoke to his wife again. 'Glenda spoke to him last weekend. She's calling him again now.'

'Thank you. I'll hold.' Nikki wondered if there was a perfectly reasonable explanation for all of it. After all, the Range Rover being on that road meant nothing. He could just have been driving to somewhere else. However, it was interesting that Benjamin was a student at Oriel College.

Mr Henshaw came back on the line. 'It went to voicemail. We will keep trying.'

'Could you please tell me where your son lives in Oxford?'

'He rents a house with a couple of other students. It's 24 Rosemary Lane. I can send you the postcode.'

'Thank you. I'll see if I can contact your son. Could you please send me his phone number and email?' Nikki gave Mr Henshaw her contact details.

Nikki heard his wife's voice again, and this time they had a mini argument. Then the woman took the phone. 'What's going on? Is Ben all right?'

'Mrs Henshaw, is it? Please don't worry. I don't know where your son is, but I'm sure he's fine. We just want to know where he was on Thursday evening, and who was driving his car.'

'Why?'

Nikki sighed. Their son owed them an explanation, but she couldn't exactly share details so early in the investigation. 'It's a police matter, that's all I can say at the moment. I will be in touch, and please contact me if you hear from your son.'

The office door opened and Nish entered. He was surprised to see her, as it wasn't 9 a.m. yet, but Nikki liked starting early.

'I've got the address for Henshaw's son, where the Range

Rover's usually parked,' Nikki said, grabbing her warrant card and rising. 'Let's go.'

She left a note for Kristy and, hopefully, Tom, to call her when they arrived in the office. She was still bothered about the way Tom left on Friday. She didn't know what was going on with him, but if she had to guess it was trouble at home. Tom might have an issue with her being his boss, but it wasn't the only reason why he was disturbed. She made a point to visit him soon, if he didn't turn up to work by tomorrow.

* * *

Rosemary Lane turned out to be a pretty street with multicoloured terraced houses. It was a short distance from the main complex of the colleges, behind University Parks and Lady Margaret Hall. Nish drove up and down the street, and the surrounding area, but they didn't find the black Range Rover.

Nikki knocked on the door and waited. It was the end of term now, so the students should be at home. Unless they were back home already. The street looked deserted, but cars were parked at regular intervals. Resident permits were necessary for the cars, which meant some people still lived here. Most of the streets and the houses around Oxford were owned by the colleges. They loaned them to the university, who in turned offered them to student and staff for rent.

There was no answer, but the curtains were open in the front bay window. Nikki cupped a hand over the glass and looked inside. She could see three sofas around a TV. A couple of pizza boxes and some beer cans were littered on the floor. At the back, she could see the kitchen area. The place looked a mess: a typical student digs. Nish had moved to the opposite pavement, and he was looking at the upper floor. Nikki banged on the door again, louder. She was rewarded by the sound of someone coming down the stairs.

'Who is it?' a sleepy voice grumbled.

'It's the police. Open the door, now.'

There was silence, and Nikki put her ear to the door. She heard creaks, as if someone was going back up the staircase.

'Break it down,' she said to Nish. He was bigger than her.

Nish kicked the door twice and the lock broke. He surged inside, shouting. The ground floor was empty. Nish ran to the garden, and then came back as Nikki went up the stairs.

'No one there, guv,' he panted as they got to the landing. The house, like many terraced properties, was bigger than expected. Upstairs, three bedroom doors were shut and the bathroom door was open. Nikki ducked inside. The bathroom was empty. Swiftly, she noted one toothbrush in the holder by the sink. That would come in handy for DNA sampling later. From the bedroom furthest down the corridor, there was a crashing sound. Nikki ran towards it, Nish close behind.

The door was locked, and she pushed against it but it held. Nish's heavy boot came in handy again. Two solid kicks and the lock splintered, the door smashing open on its hinges. A wall of heat hit them, and there was a blaze of lights in the left corner. The room was in disarray. To the right lay a single bed that was piled high with clothes. On the left lay what looked like a science experiment. Rows of plants were laid out on growing trays that looked like fish aquariums without the fish. Strong lights hung over them, too bright to look at. A distinctive smell hung over the room, and Nikki knew what it was before Nish whispered it.

'Cannabis plants.'

It was a hydroponics growing system, and the lights were blinding, not to mention the heat they produced. But, more importantly, the window was open. Nikki gripped the ledge and looked out. There was a flat roof underneath: the ceiling of the kitchen downstairs. A hooded figure, dressed in black, was scaling the back garden fence. It led to another garden with clothes flapping on a line.

'You go after him, and I'll cut him off from the road opposite,' Nikki shouted, running down the stairs.

# FIFTEEN

Nish jumped out onto the flat roof as the figure made it to the other side of the fence. Nikki had the radio in her hand as she raced down the stairs. She called for more units and gave them the address. On the street, she had no idea which way to go, but knew she had to find her way around. She ran left, down another block of similar terraced houses, then skidded to a halt. She could only go left as the road went straight for miles, rows of terraces on either side.

She heard a muffled scream and stiffened. Seconds later, a door from one of the houses on the street to her left burst open, and the black hooded figure fell out on the road. He scrambled to his feet, looked around and his eyes met Nikki's; she was already charging towards him. He was tall and skinny. He turned to the other side and raced down the road, Nikki huffing and puffing after him as he disappeared into an alley. Nikki's radio chirped, and she took it out. They would have her location from the radio's GPS in any case.

'Suspect IC1 male still on foot wearing black hooded top. Heading away from the colleges.' That much she could tell. He was going out of the centre, into the green parks dotted around

Banbury Road. Probably had a car parked somewhere, on a street that was a dark spot on CCTV. Nikki heard footsteps pounding behind her, and soon Nish overtook her, followed by a uniformed PC. Nish had discarded his heavy stab vest. Nikki wasn't even wearing one. She had dealt with gangs in London's inner cities and thought she could do Oxford without a stab vest. She slowed down, panting. At the far end of the alley, she saw the hooded figure vanish and there was no police car to block his way. She heard the sirens in the distance, but they still hadn't arrived.

Nikki emerged out of the alley, into another terraced row of houses. Nish and the other PC were disappearing on the main street, down to the left. She ran after them, taking out her radio. It was Nish's voice that greeted her.

'All units,' Nish panted. 'He's going round, back to the centre. Repeat, he's heading back to the colleges.'

That was interesting, Nikki thought. She went in the opposite direction to where Nish had just gone, asking where he was on the radio.

'He's going into University Parks,' Nish shouted. 'He jumped over the railings.'

'Surround all exits to the Parks,' Nikki ordered on the radio, running faster now. 'There's a bridge over the Cherwell. He'll head for there.'

The University Parks was Oxford's common park, with rugby and cricket pitches. All the colleges had their individual parks and sporting grounds, and the University Parks, despite the name, was used mostly by Oxford's residents.

Lady Margaret Hall was next to University Parks. Nikki debated whether to go through but then decided against it. The grounds of any Oxford college could be confusing, with hidden exits. She skirted around it and came upon University Parks. She ran inside and saw Nish and two more uniformed officers, running in from her left.

'This way,' Nish roared, pointing to the northern exit which opened onto the main road into town.

'Parks Road,' Nikki panted on her radio. 'Close it down. I want roadblocks.'

Static crackled and then she heard a male voice. 'Inspector Stevens from Traffic. There's a gathering at the Radcliffe Camera. It's spilling out around the covered market and Trinity College. Sorry, can't block Parks Road.'

Nikki could see Nish and the others up ahead. They were running past the spacious playing fields. Cricketers looked up momentarily from their games to watch them pass. Nikki didn't have time to appreciate the view as one question turned over in her mind – could the man they were chasing down be Benjamin Henshaw? Whoever he was, his guilt was greater than growing some cannabis plants at home. In the past, Nikki had seen industrial-sized hydroponics operations taking up an entire floor. In comparison, this was nothing. The man clearly had more to hide.

She was getting tired now. The day had remained mild, sun behind clouds, but it was humid, and her shirt was sticking to her back like a second skin. She saw the men ahead run into Parks Road, and she shook her head in frustration. She had a feeling the man would escape that way. She came to the road and noticed the throngs walking down towards the colleges and the centre of the Bodleian and Radcliffe Camera. It was odd, she thought as she dodged past them. These roads were normally empty, even in the tourist season, which was just starting. The crowds grew thicker as she approached Oxford's de facto nerve centre of the Radcliffe Camera.

Placards were raised in the air, and the crowd chanted, 'Pull him down. Pull him down.'

In a flash, Nikki understood. The statue of Basil Bones, the former statesman, and infamous colonialist and imperialist, had become a focal point recently. Mr Bones, and his family, had made significant contributions to the university over the years, but there was no escaping the fact he had ruled like a dictator over parts of central Africa. International students felt offended by his prominent statue over the college entrance. The campaign to remove his statue had been going on for months, and it was reaching boiling point.

The area around the Radcliffe, normally a natural meeting point, was clogged with people shouting and waving placards. Nikki looked around helplessly. Her radio crackled to life. It was Nish.

'By All Souls, guv. I think I see him.'

'Coming,' Nikki said. She pushed her way through the crowd. She feared the man had taken his hooded top off, and now he would merge with the masses around her. She was blocked by a crowd of students holding up a banner and shouting. Others took up their chant and screamed loudly: 'No voice, no vote.'

Nikki tried to get through but there were too many people, all pressing forward. She wanted to take out her warrant card and shove it in their faces, but she knew it might have the opposite effect. She had been a uniformed officer once and done crowd control. She had no wish to get smacked around by a thousand angry students. Instead, she barged ahead, deciding to shout out a single word – *Emergency*. It seemed to have the desired effect. Some of the bodies moved, and she was able to slip past, but then the knot tightened again. Someone had a loudspeaker, and they were shouting out slogans, and the crowd started to chant as one and pressed forward.

Her radio crackled again, and there was a commotion up ahead. 'Got him,' Nish's voice came, out of breath, 'Suspect apprehended.'

'Roger that,' Nikki said.

'Hey, are you a copper?' a voice said.

Nikki ignored it and moved forward. She heard a few more

words, but ignored them. Someone pulled at her hair, but she didn't look back. Cursing, she turned down her radio to silent. She was hemmed in on all sides by the crowd. Panicking wouldn't help. She kept pushing through and, suddenly, to her relief there was a clearing. Some students had sat down on the cobbled stones and made a circle.

'Oi, watch it,' a man shouted as Nikki almost fell on top of him. She apologised and moved away. The crowd still pulsated behind her like a living organism. A man with a loudspeaker was whipping them up into a frenzy.

*'Pull him down. Pull him down.'*

In front of her, ahead of the clearing, Nikki could see the boundary wall of All Souls College. Four uniformed police officers stood there, and two more joined them. Nish was leaning over a man on the ground. He twisted his hands behind his back and handcuffed them. Worryingly, some people had strolled over to watch the fun. Nikki saw one of them ask an officer something, which he ignored.

She ran over and showed her warrant card to one of the uniformed constables. Nish heaved the man to his feet.

'I saw him slip off the hooded top.' Nish pointed with his feet at the garment on the ground. 'He tried to mingle into the crowd. Just glad I saw him when he took it off.'

The man was very young, early twenties if Nikki had to guess his age. There were bruises on his forehead and his left cheek.

'Are you Benjamin Henshaw?' Nikki asked. The man looked at her sullenly. Nish gave him a shake from behind, holding his collar.

'She asked you a question.'

'No,' the man replied. 'I want a lawyer.'

'I bet you do, sunshine,' Nikki said, stepping closer to him. 'You're going to jail for a long time. Growing cannabis with intent to supply, evading arrest and assaulting a police officer.'

The young man had paled visibly. His lips trembled as he looked around him. Nikki knew his type. He was a college student from a good family, but had gone astray. It often happened to rich students who had daddy's credit card, or a trust fund to bail them out. She had met boys like him in her younger days in Oxford.

'You need more than a lawyer.' She showed him her warrant card. 'I am Detective Inspector Nikki Gill of the Major Crimes Unit. You're now a suspect in a murder inquiry.'

The man's mouth hung open as his eyes bulged out. From behind, Nikki heard voices.

'What are you doing to him?'

'He has a right to protest. Let him go.'

'Is this now a police state?'

Nikki ignored the babble of voices, but looked at Nish, who understood. He yanked the man in front of him and started frogmarching him up the road, past the Bodleian Library, heading out of the main square. Three squad cars had arrived and also a riot van, all with blues flashing. The crowd was thinner out here, but still present, and students still marched out from the streets, joining the main group in front of the Radcliffe Camera.

Nish and a uniformed officer put the man in the back, and Nikki rode with them. She looked at the placard-waving throngs crowding the roads. Oxford was transformed from its quiet haven of learning into a cauldron of conflict. She almost didn't recognise the place.

# SIXTEEN

Monty was the first person Nikki saw when she stepped out of the car. His concerned eyes swept over her.

'I heard it's bad out there. Are you all right?'

Nikki exhaled. The adrenaline was still bubbling and she felt energised, oddly enough. Nish and the others took the suspect into custody, and she walked back in with Monty.

'The protest seems more like Trafalgar Square than Oxford,' she said. 'Where have that lot come from?'

Monty's jaws firmed. 'Mostly students. But political parties are making some capital out of it as well. Tensions are running high over this statue business. Neither side is giving way.'

They took the lift up to the third-floor canteen, and Monty got Nikki a coffee and doughnut. She looked at him in horror.

'I can't eat that and you know it.'

He shook his head and exchanged it for some biscuits. He wagged the packet in front of her face.

'You need some energy after that. Have the biscuits.'

Nikki's guilty secret was dunking chocolate biscuits into her tea and coffee. She had more or less given up on the chocolate ones now, but every other biscuit was fair game. Her current favourite were the jammy dodgers. She bit into one and sipped the coffee gratefully.

'The man you caught is a student?' Monty asked.

'Not sure. He looks like one. Have to interrogate him now.' She tried not to look at his mouth as he chewed on a biscuit. It was distracting in a nice way.

'Do you think he could be our killer?'

Monty's brows furrowed. 'I'm not sure. But stranger things have happened. He's guilty of something, or he wouldn't have run.'

'He was running a hydroponics factory in the bedroom.'

Monty's eyes widened in surprise. 'Mind you, the students get up to all sorts. A combination of too much money, youth and freedom can spell trouble.'

He continued. 'As I was in the building anyway, I was speaking to Kristy about the case. Do you mind?'

She eyed him warily. 'I guess not. This isn't your way of keeping an eye on me, is it?'

'I think we're past that stage.' He stared at her. 'Even Patmore knows you're well settled now. But if you don't want me to, it's fine. I had some time this morning, so I looked into it.' He shrugged. 'But you can tell me to bugger off.'

With Tom not around, she needed all the help she could get. And Monty's experience made him a good substitute. But she also had to be careful. She didn't want Tom to come back and find Monty effectively a part of the team.

'What did you find?' she asked, curious.

'Mr Henshaw is a colourful character. Used to be an antique car dealer. There's a lot of money in it, if you can get hold of the right cars. Somehow, he managed to build a big business out of it. He's had some skirmishes with the law as well. Some of his cars were brought from overseas, and no one seems to know how they crossed the Channel from France or Holland. He was also getting them at a knockdown price, which meant he was perhaps paying cash. That's illegal.'

'And now someone his son lives with is growing cannabis, and they're selling it as well for all we know,' Nikki said. She drained the rest of her coffee and stood. So did Monty.

'If you hear about the autopsy, call me. I'd like to come and see what Sheila has to say.' Monty smiled. 'She's a legend. No one messes with Sheila.'

Nikki said goodbye and walked back to the office. Nish was still downstairs, handing over to the custody team. Kristy was on the phone.

'His name's Brian Robinson,' Kristy said when she hung up.

'Right. Let's see if that's correct.'

'He's not saying anything else. Wants to wait for a lawyer,' Kristy said behind her as she went downstairs.

\* \* \*

Brian looked up as she entered. The holding cell was large enough, a remnant of the days when dozens of men were stacked into one cell. There was a loo without a lid in one corner, and a sink that was recessed into the wall. A microwave ready meal lay uneaten to one side, a white plastic cup next to it.

Nikki indicated the meal. 'Not hungry?'

Brian didn't answer. He was looking at the floor. Nikki leaned against the wall and folded her arms across her chest. Brian was tall, but he was little more than a boy. His thin shoulders sagged, and his posture slumped in defeat. He had messed up in a big way, and he knew it.

'The solicitor will call soon. There's no reason for you to talk to me.'

Brian said nothing. Nikki continued. 'If you were growing

less than ten plants, you won't be prosecuted. Less than ten can be counted as for personal use.'

Brian looked up slowly. His grey-blue eyes had a sudden sparkle of hope in them.

'How many plants were you growing?' Nikki kept her voice low.

'Nine. And one of them is dead anyway.'

She nodded. 'Which is your college?'

Brian looked away, then seemed to make his mind up. 'Somerville. Look, I'm sorry I ran. I panicked. I don't want to...'

'End up in jail?' Nikki asked.

Brian shook his head.

'Do you know Benjamin Henshaw?'

Brian looked up at Nikki again, his eyes widening slightly. Then he nodded. 'Yes. He lives with me. He's also at Somerville.'

'Do you know where he is?' Uniforms had told Nikki the house was empty.

Brian shook his head. 'He was busy...' His voice trailed off as he bit his lower lip.

Nikki came closer and sat down on her haunches, directly in front of Brian, and made him look at her. 'If you talk to me, it's going to be a lot easier than ending up in a courtroom.'

Brian sighed. 'I guess it's common knowledge. He's one of the organisers of the Piers Gaveston Society. They had their annual summer ball on Thursday evening.'

'When did you last see Benjamin?'

'A few days before the ball. He was busy with organising it.'

Nikki asked, 'Are you a member?'

He shook his head. 'I'm not a member, no. But Ben invited me to the ball. There's only sixteen members of the club. But each member can bring twenty-five guests, and their partners.'

'Did you go?'

'No. My girlfriend had invited me to the VOM summer ball.'

'VOM?'

'Veritable Orgy of Mayhem. It's another drinking club.'

'I see. And that was held on the same day as the Piers Gaveston ball?'

'Yes.' He shifted in his seat. 'Why are you asking so much about this?'

'Answer my questions, Brian, and trust me, your life will be a lot easier.' She looked at him with dead, cold eyes, and the boy dropped his gaze.

'I want you to think about this carefully. Does Ben have a girlfriend?'

Something changed in Brian's attitude. His cheeks lost some colour, and the sparkle in his eyes faded. Nikki held him with her gaze.

Eventually, he nodded. 'Yes. Her name is Charlotte Winspear.'

'Can you describe her to me?'

'Average height, five feet seven or eight, I think. Blonde hair. Bluish eyes.'

Nikki's breath came faster, and she made an effort to control herself. 'Slim or large?'

'Slim girl. Why do you ask?' There was now a guarded look in Brian's face.

'Did she have any distinguishing marks?'

Brian said, 'She had a tattoo of three hearts, each one larger than the other, on the base of her neck.' He narrowed his eyes, and he sat up straighter. He looked uneasy. 'What's going on? Why are you asking me about Charlotte?'

'When did you last see Charlotte?'

'I can't remember.'

'Was she with Ben? Think carefully, Brian, this is important.'

He did, lowering his head. 'I've not seen her recently. She used to come to the house. But she was busy with her campaign.'

'What campaign?'

'She's a socialist, and she does all sorts of stuff with the Socialist Club at the university. Recently, she was also involved with the campaign to take down the statue. Basil Bones.'

Light dawned at the back of Nikki's mind. 'The gathering you ran into today? You knew it was being held because you're friends with Charlotte.'

'Well, I am kind of. I only know her through Ben. But yes, I did know about the protest.'

Nikki opened her notebook and wrote down the names. 'Can you remember if Charlotte wore a necklace? It had gold chains, and maybe a pendant at the end.'

Brian frowned, then his eyes opened wide. 'Oh yeah. She wore it all the time in fact. Wait.' He frowned at Nikki, and a slow circle of shock appeared in his gaze. 'What's happened to her? Is she here?'

Nikki took a deep breath.

'No. She's dead, Brian.'

# SEVENTEEN

Benjamin Henshaw removed the phone slowly from his ear. His heart thudded loudly as panic unfurled slowly in his belly. What had he done? A horrible guilt got hold of him, squeezing his guts. He bent forward, head between his knees. He couldn't forget Charlotte's eyes. His Lottie. He used to lose himself in those blue depths. Her wide open, dreamy eyes. The touch of her fingers on his lips. Emotion clogged his throat. He had loved her with passion, but then things went wrong, that passion morphed into... into something dark and sinister he couldn't control. That had always been his problem. His feelings were always intense, and then suddenly, he would go blank. His old friends knew, and his parents had tried to help. His father's money had bailed him out.

Not this time. He squeezed his forehead with both hands. His brain seemed to be slowly coming apart, thoughts squeezing out into a dull haze. Lottie had been his last hope, he knew that. He couldn't do to her what he had done to the others. And yet... fate had a habit of repeating itself. Would he never get out of this cycle?

He stared at the damp wall opposite. He was renting a

bedsit, paid for with his last cash. Soon, he would be out of money, and he was already out of luck. He needed to dump his car, quickly. The cops would be out searching for it, and he couldn't let them find it. Automatic Number Plate Recognition, or ANPR, meant his car was now a liability. Every police car and camera on the street had ANPR installed. Jacob had told him his car's registration number would be installed on that system as a priority.

His phone rang again, and it was the same number. With trembling hands, he raised the phone to his ear.

It was Jacob. 'Where's Lottie?'

'I did what you wanted,' he whispered. 'Now leave me alone.'

There was silence on the line. Jacob's voice returned, harsher than usual. 'Listen, you idiot. Get a grip. You've got all these big plans, but you can't fall apart once you execute them.'

'Fall apart?' Ben couldn't believe his ears. 'She was your daughter, for heaven's sake.'

More silence. Ben said, 'Look, I need money. I need to get out of here. My parents—'

'Leave your parents to me,' Jacob said. 'I'll speak to them. Don't worry. You need to disappear for a while now. Where's the car?'

'I covered it up with tarpaulin, and also put black paint on the number plates like you suggested.'

'Good. Tell me where you are, and I'll get someone to come and take the car away. They'll come at night.'

Ben chewed his fingernails. He had no choice but to trust Jacob. His voice quavered, and he hated that. 'I didn't want it to end like this. I'm sorry.'

Jacob sighed. 'It's too late for that now. What's done is done. You need to control yourself. No stupid moves. Do you understand?'

'Okay. I'm in Headington, at the back of the high street.' Ben gave Jacob his address.

'Don't call me. I'll call you from this number. Are you using the burner phone?'

'Yes, I am.'

He hung up. He was sitting on the threadbare carpet, his back resting on the bed frame. He stood up, feeling restless. The cops would be on him soon. He felt unreal all of a sudden, sights and sounds merging into a kaleidoscope. He felt dizzy. What had happened to his perfect life? A week ago, he was organising the ball of the year at Oxford University. An unparalleled spectacle of drugs and debauchery. And it had all ended with a shocking event that had torn his life completely out of joint.

He needed to get to his house and remove the rest of his belongings. He had to speak to Brian. They had to get rid of the hydroponics plant, and Brian also had to get lost for a while. It was good that term was ending and they were going home. But home was one place that was now out of bounds. If Brian went home, the cops would catch up with him there. If they hadn't already. Panic curdled in his gut again, making him sick. He had to get out of this awful, damp bedsit.

He put on dark glasses, and a hooded top. He took the bus to Oxford town centre, then another bus to his house by Lady Margaret Hall. He stopped at the corner of the street and peeked in. Their house wasn't far from this end. His pulse skyrocketed, and his breath came in gasps.

There was a police car in front of the house, and a policeman was standing guard outside. He was looking around, and Ben jerked himself back, flattening against the wall as the policeman looked in his direction. He had to get out of here. He walked quickly and went to the bus station. He looked behind him, and with a sigh of relief, didn't see anyone following.

Now, he had no chance of getting his stuff. Police would get his DNA. The bus came and he got on it. In a daze, he got back to Headington. He walked around aimlessly till he found a park. He shook out a packet of cigarettes and lit one. His hands trembled.

Had the police found the body? They must have, otherwise why were they here? Thank god the Range Rover was hidden. The cops must've got CCTV views of him in that area... He covered his head with his hands again.

Did they have his DNA as well? He had been careful... but he knew how detailed and accurate modern forensic science could be. And he wasn't exactly in a rational state of mind when it happened.

He threw the cigarette away and pulled out his burner phone again and called Jacob.

'What is it?'

'The police know. They're outside my house.'

Jacob was silent for a while. 'My man will come tonight to take the car away. After he leaves, you have to as well. Got that?'

Ben thought for a while. He didn't trust Jacob fully. He had done Jacob's bidding, but what if the man now discarded him like a piece of trash? If he cared so little for his own daughter, what could he do to *him*?

Ben didn't trust this bloke who was coming to take the car away. He was dodgy obviously, probably a car thief. He didn't even want to think how a man like Jacob knew such common crooks.

'Tell your man I will leave the keys to the car in the exhaust pipe. I don't want to see him. But I want some cash. Can you leave some for me at the usual place?'

'Why don't you want to see my guy? Don't be stupid.'

Ben didn't answer. Jacob hissed urgently. 'Listen, you idiot. No one's going to hurt you. Don't be paranoid.'

'I've done what you told me to,' Ben said. 'But you don't

control me. You said the police would never find out – and now they're outside my house. Looking for me. I'm going to end up in jail for life.'

'That won't happen.'

'Fuck you.' Ben raised his voice. 'I want twenty thousand in cash at the usual place tonight. If it's not there, I'm going to the police myself.'

Jacob went quiet. When he spoke, his words were laced with menace. 'I know where you are. My men can pick you up anytime. And don't forget your parents. What will happen to them?'

Ben gasped. 'You wouldn't dare do anything to them.'

'Don't push me. This can end very badly for you, if you don't listen. Meet my man tonight and give him the keys.'

With a click, the line went dead.

# EIGHTEEN

'Dr Raman said the dental records of the victim match that of a Charlotte Winspear, twenty-one years old.' Kristy held up a piece of paper. Nikki, Nish and Monty faced her. Nikki had texted Monty to join them, once Brian confirmed the victim's ID.

Kristy continued. 'She went to Merton College. She shared a house with three students, according to council tax returns and the electoral roll. I've got their names and contact details here.'

'Get in touch with the parents,' Nikki said. Now they had a positive ID, it was a question of piecing together her last few days leading up to the murder.

Nish spoke. Father is Jacob Winspear, scion and heir of the Winspear family. They have breweries all over England. They make cider and beer. I've seen their bottles in supermarkets.'

'So have I,' Monty remarked.

'Mr Winspear is a Tory councillor, and is hoping to become the next Conservative MP for Witney. Polls on the Conservative Party website indicate he's got a good chance of victory.'

Nikki tapped a pen on the desk. 'Let me make the call. Do you have a number?'

A man's voice answered.

'The Winspear residence. May I know who's speaking?'

Nikki gave her name and status, and the voice changed immediately. 'What is this about?'

'Who are you?'

'I am Mr Winspear's secretary and the house coordinator.' In other words, a modern butler, Nikki thought.

'Can I speak to Mr or Mrs Winspear at once please? It is urgent.'

There was a pause, then a woman's voice came on the line. 'This is Beatrice Winspear.'

Nikki introduced herself. 'Mrs Winspear, I'm calling about your daughter, Charlotte Winspear.'

'What's happened?' The anxiety was apparent in the woman's voice, and Nikki felt heartbroken for her. It was the worst part of her job, and there was no other way to do it but be blunt. But there was a procedure for it.

'What's going on? What's happened to Lottie?' Mrs Winspear's voice kicked up a notch.

'I need to speak to you urgently, and it would be best if I came to see you. I will be with you in half an hour. Please wait there.'

Nikki hung up; she pointed to Nish and Kristy. 'I want Uniforms to secure Charlotte's student digs, and SOC to be there ASAP. I want to know who her friends are, her daily routine, her exam grades, everything. Please get cracking on that.'

She turned to Monty. He was leaning against the wall, his wide shoulder almost touching the door. His face was grave, eyes solemn.

'Will you please come with me,' Nikki said. It was a statement, not a question.

Monty detached his long frame from the wall. 'I'll drive,' he said quietly, then held the door open for Nikki.

* * *

The gates to the mansion house were open. Monty drove the black BMW through and down the long drive, where mature oak, birch and maple trees offered shade. In the distance, they could see the sprawling house to the left. On the right, green expanses opened up, and a fountain flashed into view.

'Wow. This is how the other half live,' Monty remarked.

'I doubt these people occupy a half. More like a sixteenth of the population.'

'A millionth,' Monty countered. 'You're right. I doubt they're even resident in England, or pay any taxes. They take a private plane to Jersey or Isle of Man five days a week.' Both locations were tax-free havens where England's super rich stored their money.

'No money will compensate for what they're about to hear,' Nikki said quietly as the car pulled up at the bottom of a flight of stairs which led up to the four sets of main doors. Only the middle double door was open, and a man wearing a suit came hurrying down out of them.

Nikki and Monty showed him their warrant cards. The man, who had spoken to Nikki earlier, ushered them upstairs. They were led across a giant reception room the size of two tennis courts stuck together, and through a set of double doors into a long lounge. The walls had tapestries and dark wallpaper, and Nikki felt she was in some baroque castle in the middle of Italy. Large oil paintings of old ancestors – all men, naturally – hung from the walls. A man and a woman were sitting on a sofa opposite a fireplace large enough to roast an entire cow in.

Both of them stood. The woman had a haggard, drawn look on her colourless face. Her eyes were red-rimmed. The man looked calmer, but the pensiveness in his eyes betrayed his anxiety. Nikki and Monty introduced themselves.

'Please sit,' Jacob said.

'I'm very sorry to be the bearer of bad news. A body we believe to be your daughter, Charlotte Winspear, was discovered on a hill near Waterperry last Thursday.'

They stared disbelievingly at Nikki.

Beatrice stammered. 'How can you be sure... how?'

'We won't know for certain until a family member has made a formal identification. Would that be possible?'

Beatrice dissolved into tears, and Jacob comforted her. Nikki gave them some time. Then she showed them a photo on her phone, taken when she first saw the body. Beatrice broke down while Jacob struggled to control his emotions.

'If you don't mind, we would like to collect a personal item like an article of clothing she wore recently, if you have it. We will need DNA samples, too, from both of you, and also anyone else in the house. By that I mean all of the staff here as well, not just those who came into contact with Charlotte.'

'Who could've done this?' Beatrice sniffed. She looked at her husband, whose stony face gave nothing away.

'We don't know as yet but we will not leave any stone unturned to find the truth,' Nikki said, and she meant it. 'But I will need your help as well. We believe she was killed on Thursday night between the hours of six p.m. and midnight.' She looked at both of them in turn. 'Do you know where Charlotte was on Thursday night?'

Jacob was silent, but Beatrice spoke. She took a tissue out and wiped her nose. 'Yes, she told me. She was going to this ball, some Gaveston Society dinner. It's meant to be a big thing to get invited to these things, I believe.' She looked at her husband. 'Jacob knows. He went to Oxford.'

Nikki turned her attention to him. 'Which college did you attend?'

'Merton. I don't think my time at Oxford has anything to do with my daughter, however.'

It was a strange thing to say, and Nikki watched him for a while. While the comment was unnecessary, she couldn't help thinking it sounded defensive. From the expression on Jacob's face, she also suspected he knew he'd made a wrong move.

'What do you mean?' she asked, pinning him with a stare. Jacob's cheeks flushed slightly.

'I mean things were different in my day. These drinking societies and clubs were all...' His words trailed off.

'Only for men,' Monty said. 'Like the rest of Oxford was in your day.'

All eyes turned to Monty, who stared at Jacob. The older man swallowed. 'Yes, I guess so. That's what I meant.'

There was an uncomfortable silence for a while, then Nikki continued by asking Beatrice, 'Did Charlotte send you any photos or videos from the party?'

'She told me photos were not allowed. They had to leave their phones at home.'

Nikki thought that was a shame. She could've tracked Charlotte's last location if she had her phone on her.

'Did she mention if any of her friends were travelling with her?'

'No.'

'What about her boyfriend?'

Jacob shifted in his seat. Beatrice pressed her lips together. 'She had a boyfriend. I didn't really approve of him, but Lottie seemed obsessed with him. Hung onto his every word.'

'Why didn't you like him?' Nikki asked, stealing a glance at Jacob who was staring at the floor.

'He was the flashy type. Drove around in a big Range Rover. A little too full of himself.'

Jacob still said nothing. Nikki noticed his wife glanced at him once, then went silent.

'Mr Winspear, what did you think of Benjamin Henshaw?'

At the mention of the name, both of them looked at Nikki with surprise.

'You know who he is?' Jacob asked.

'Yes. We picked up his black Range Rover on CCTV taking the exit for Waterperry on Thursday night.'

'I see,' Jacob nodded. 'Where is he? Have you got hold of him?'

'No,' Nikki said. 'Do you know where he is?'

Jacob shook his head slowly. 'Have you checked where he lived?'

'Yes,' Nikki said shortly. She didn't want to give too much away, and she was getting some strange vibes from Jacob.

Monty cleared his throat. 'As we understand, Benjamin invited Charlotte to this party. He is a member of the Piers Gaveston Society. Do you know if that is that correct?'

Both parents nodded. Monty said, 'Was Charlotte with Ben that evening? I know it makes sense, as they were both attending the party. But do you have any messages from Charlotte that mentions she was with him?'

Beatrice nodded, and Nikki's heart skipped a beat. This could be the proof they needed to mark Ben as a suspect.

'She sent me a text to say she was going with him.'

Nikki wrote this down, and asked Beatrice to send her a copy of the text. She exchanged phone numbers with her and noticed Jacob put a hand under his collar and tug at it. There was a film of sweat on his forehead, and his fingers drummed on his thigh.

Monty asked, 'When did you last see Charlotte?'

'About four weeks ago,' Beatrice said. 'She was busy with exams, and then busy letting her hair down after.' She smiled sadly and wiped the corner of her eyes. Nikki glanced at Jacob.

'How about you, Mr Winspear?'

He seemed startled by the question. He composed himself

quickly. 'I can't remember. Maybe the same time as what my wife just said.' He looked at Beatrice, but the woman didn't reciprocate the glance. There was something strange going on here, Nikki could feel it.

'Were both of you close to Charlotte?'

They stared at Nikki. Beatrice was the first to answer. 'Yes, Inspector, I was. I mean when children are older they have their own lives and so on. But we stayed in touch.'

'Me too,' Jacob said quickly. Too quickly, Nikki thought.

'Do you mind if we take DNA swabs from you?' Nikki asked. Monty took out the sterile packets and put gloves on. He took the cheek swabs and put the packets away.

'We would like to see Charlotte's room, if that's okay,' Nikki said.

'You can,' Beatrice said, 'but most of her stuff is with her at college. You will have more luck there.'

The butler showed Nikki and Monty into a marble-floored hallway that would look at home in Downton Abbey, and he took them up a winding staircase wide enough to fit an elephant. They went down a hallway, and the man opened a door. They stepped inside. Nikki saw a room that was rather tidy. Then she remembered what Beatrice had said.

The bed was neatly done, and it didn't look slept in. The desk was clear, with a monitor and desktop computer. Nikki put gloves on and opened the drawers of the desk. In the bottom drawer she found some exercise books and leaflets. The butler was standing at the doorway, watching them. Monty shut the door gently, in his face.

Nikki looked out the windows on either side of the bed. They faced the large garden on the side of the house. Monty showed her a book from the shelf.

'*Das Kapital*, Volume 1. Seems Charlotte was quite the communist if she was reading Karl Marx's definitive work.' He pulled down a few more books by Marx, Lenin and other

Russian leaders. His gloved fingers leafed through a slim volume. 'Even the communist party manifesto.'

He looked up, and his piercing eyes met with Nikki's. She averted her gaze quickly, her cheeks reddening.

Monty whispered, 'I didn't expect these books on her shelf. Surely the Winspear family didn't make all this money by practising communism.'

Nikki looked at them, and thought back to Jacob's strange reactions. 'Take a couple of the books; there's clearly some family tensions.' She took out her phone and called the station. 'We need someone over to take Charlotte Winspear's computer into evidence.'

She shook her head, and said to Monty, 'Like the crime scene, there's nothing here. I hope the team have more luck. We need a break soon on this case.'

# NINETEEN

Kristy and Nish knocked on the door and waited. It was a terraced house in Cowley, just over the bridge from Magdalen College. Cowley was a run-down area but that didn't deter the students; in fact, their influx had made parts of Cowley fashionable. Cocktail bars and restaurants had sprung up in places, along with the cheap student digs.

Kristy looked at the house as they waited. A rubbish bin had overturned in the front garden, but was thankfully empty. Graffiti was scribbled on the side wall. One of the windows was boarded up with plywood. She wondered what the daughter of a millionaire many times over was doing living like this. A sign hung from the top-floor window facing the street. Black words on a white cloth.

*Pull him down*

Kristy wondered if Charlotte's friends had been at the protest rally. The door opened a fraction, and a young woman in her early twenties poked her head out. She had brown hair with braids on the sides. She was wary, her eyes flicking from Nish to her.

'What do you want?'

'Are you a housemate of Charlotte Winspear?' Nish asked.

'Why?'

'We need to come in to ask you some questions.' Nish stepped forward and put his foot on the doorway. The woman couldn't shut the door.

She frowned. 'What is this about?'

'If you let us in we can tell you.'

Reluctantly the woman opened the door wider. The hallway had seen better days. It badly needed a paint job and new carpets. There was a smell of cigarette smoke, cannabis, and perfumes that sought to neutralise the odour but failed. They followed the woman down a short corridor into a living room. Another woman sat on the sofa, dressed in shorts, holding a cup of tea. She jumped up when she saw them.

'What the hell?' She eyed the other woman. 'Taby, what's going on?'

Taby shrugged. 'They want to talk about Lottie.'

Kristy asked the other woman, 'What's your name?'

She eyed Kristy suspiciously, but her gaze lingered on Nish. 'Francine Pearse. And you?' She tilted her nose upward. Kristy held up her warrant card, and so did Nish.

'I'm afraid we have bad news. Charlotte Winspear was found dead on Friday.'

Both women paled visibly. Taby's jaw fell open. Francine stared at them wide-eyed.

'Shall we sit down?' Nish suggested. The women did so, and the two DCs explained the situation.

'Where is she now?' Taby asked. 'I mean...'

'Her body's at the morgue,' Kristy said gently. 'Her parents are there to identify it.'

'Did you two attend the Piers Gaveston party?'

Both women stiffened, and they glanced at each other nervously. Kristy watched them and saw Nish nod at her.

Kristy leaned forwards, 'If you were there, we need to know. Please don't lie to us now, as it will look much worse later. I need to tell you this is a murder investigation. Charlotte was strangled to death.'

The two shocked students couldn't speak for several moments. Kristy waited patiently.

Taby was the first to answer. 'Yes, we were. And yes, Lottie was there as well. We all went on the same bus.'

'Francine, what about you? Did you see Charlotte that night?'

'Yes. I did. Like Taby said, we went on the same bus. It was a secret location, and we didn't know where we were going.'

'Was Charlotte with her boyfriend, Benjamin Henshaw?'

The two women exchanged glances. Taby looked down at her lap, and Francine stared at the window. Shafts of sunlight illuminated the carpet, and dust motes danced in the rays.

'Yes,' Taby said. 'But we didn't see much of him. He's one of the party organisers, so he was already there.'

'I see. Francine, what about you? Did you see Benjamin that evening?'

Francine cleared her throat. She was taller and looked more in control than Taby, who was clearly still upset. The tip of her nose was red and she sniffed loudly. Francine, on the other hand, had got over her initial shock quite well. She shook her head.

'No. I didn't see him much either.'

'But you spent time with Charlotte at the party? You were all there together, correct?'

Francine answered. 'It was a big party and there were lots of people. We mingled, as you do. Also, we did get quite drunk.' She spread her hands. 'It was a party after all. I can't remember seeing Charlotte after the first few minutes.'

Kristy turned to Taby. 'What about you?'

Taby didn't speak for a while. Finally she dragged her red-rimmed eyes to Kristy. 'We drank some cocktails, then we went from room to room. It was a big country house and there was all sorts of activities and...' Her voice trailed off.

'Live sex shows?' Nish asked awkwardly, but shut up when Kristy frowned at him. Nish shrugged and raised his hands.

'Was there any drug-taking going on? That's what happens at these parties, right?' Nish asked. Neither girl said anything.

Nish repeated his question. Only Francine replied. 'No comment.' Taby looked at her friend, and Francine wiggled her eyebrows. Kristy saw the exchange but didn't say anything.

Taby spoke. 'No comment.'

'So neither of you saw much of Charlotte that night,' Kristy said. She focused on Taby. 'You spent more time with her, it seems. Did you see her talking to anyone?'

Taby gulped. 'I mean, she was speaking to a lot of people. It was a party so...'

'But was there anyone in particular that she spent time with, or that you saw her with?'

Taby's eyes widened a fraction, then she shook her head. 'No.'

'When did you lose sight of her?'

'I can't remember. We got there around seven p.m. Maybe after a couple of hours?'

'And neither of you saw her after that?'

The two girls looked at each other. In unison, they shook their heads, and then looked down to the floor.

The sound of creaking floorboards came from upstairs. Kristy pointed up. 'Who's there?'

'Vicky, our other housemate.'

Kristy rose. 'I'll go and get her, shall I?'

Francine was up as well. 'No need, I'll give her a shout.' Without waiting for an answer, Francine ran upstairs. More floorboards creaked and there was a sound of hushed voices whispering.

Francine came down the stairs, followed by a shorter, red-haired girl. 'I'm Victoria Davies.' Her cheeks were pale, and the shock was clear on her face. 'Is it true? Lottie's dead?' She frowned.

'I'm very sorry, yes.'

Francine and Victoria hugged each other.

'We were asking your friends about the Piers Gaveston ball,' Kristy said. 'Did you go?'

Vicky dried her eyes and took some time to compose herself. 'No. I wasn't invited.'

'What did you do last Thursday evening?'

'I went to the pub with my boyfriend.'

'What's your boyfriend's name; which pub?' Kristy asked.

As she relayed the information, Vicky became stronger.

'Can you tell us anything else?' Kristy asked all the girls, while Nish noted the details. 'You share a house, so did any of you take the same classes as Charlotte, for example?'

Vicky's eyes narrowed. 'As it happens, Lottie and I had the same tutor for one of our courses.'

Nish asked, 'What's your tutor's name?'

'Greg Keating.'

# TWENTY

Beatrice watched from the window as the two detectives got in the car and drove away. She was gripping the heavy drapes tightly, like she needed support to stand. She let go and leaned forward with both hands on the windowsill. Her eyes closed as the words just uttered by the detectives reverberated around her skull. It still seemed unreal. Impossible. She didn't want to accept it. But they had just returned from the morgue, and there was no getting past it.

She walked away from the window and went up to her husband's study in the eastern wing of the house. It was more of a library with bookshelves up to the ceiling. A large mahogany desk occupied one corner, and large bay windows looked out into the rear garden. Dark wood panelling covered the walls, matching the maroon leather sofas.

Jacob was at his desk, and he looked up when his wife entered. Beatrice sat down on one of the armchairs opposite the desk. She simply looked at her husband in silence, till he looked away. He put his pen down and leaned back.

'What have you done?' Beatrice asked in a calm voice.

Jacob frowned. 'What sort of a question is that? I don't know what you mean.'

'I know you disliked her, Jacob.'

He put his hands on the table and stood. His mouth was working, and his eyes blazed at her. 'She was my daughter. Our daughter. How dare you say such a thing?'

She looked at him, her gaze sad and worn down with exhaustion. 'When I first came to this family, all those years ago, your mother said something important. She said you love winning so much you always cheated in games. At school you got into trouble for that. With your sisters at home, you hid the Monopoly cards and revealed them at the end of the game.'

Jacob stared at her, confused. 'What on earth are you talking about?'

'It's who you are, Jacob. Your mother was right. I've seen it time and time again. You always have to be right. It has to be your way, or there's no way.'

'I can't believe you're coming up with this nonsense.' Jacob slumped back on his chair. 'Our daughter's just died and you're talking crap. What's the matter with you?' His eyes narrowed, and then his features softened. 'Look, are you all right? I know this is a shock, to both of us. But we have to hang in there.'

'You hated the fact that the family inheritance now passes to the first born.'

Jacob's eyes widened.

Beatrice shook her head. 'When your father died, I remember how upset you were. How you couldn't stop talking about it for days. It annoyed me at the time. Remember our arguments?'

Jacob screwed his eyes shut and touched his forehead. 'Not this again.'

'You accepted it because you had no choice. But you didn't want it. And when things with Lottie started to turn bad, you...'

Jacob's mouth was open and he looked like he couldn't

breathe. 'I hope you're not going to suggest what I think you're trying to say.'

Beatrice suddenly felt helpless. 'What am I trying to say, Jacob? Do you know?'

Jacob's voice was a strained whisper. 'That I had something to do with Lottie's death? That I... I killed her? Is that what you're trying to say?'

Beatrice felt a terrible pressure on her chest, suffocating her words. 'Did you?'

Jacob's face cracked like a mirror hit by a hammer. 'How could you? I know I've not always been the model father, or husband... but to accuse me of this...' His head hung down, and his shoulders shook.

Beatrice was unmoved. 'You told Charles to keep an eye on Lottie. She told me she saw his car outside her house. He followed her to the Labour Party meetings.'

Jacob lifted his head. 'So what? I can't keep an eye on her? I can't be concerned that she's turning into a communist?'

'You show concern by asking Charles to follow her around? Do you know how freaked out she was after that? I told her initially that she was mistaken, but she wasn't.'

Jacob stared at his wife, unblinking. Beatrice said, 'What else did you do?' Her jaws clenched together. 'With Lottie out of the way, Rupert becomes the sole inheritor. That's what you wanted, right?'

Jacob smashed his palm on the desk, scattering pens, eyes bulging, blood mottling on his face. 'That's enough! Get out of my room. And listen.' He came around the table and wagged a finger in her face. 'These are vile and despicable lies. I think you're in shock and you don't know what the hell you're saying. You need to be in bed. I need to call a doctor.'

Beatrice stared at her husband calmly, like she was admiring a million-pound painting. 'The best lie is the closest approximation of the truth.'

'What?'

'You told me that, after you went into politics. Tell me, Jacob, if Charles was following Lottie around, how come he doesn't know what happened to her on Thursday night?'

Jacob looked to the admittedly wonderful ceiling, with its decorative cornices. 'First of all, Charles is my campaign manager, not a private detective. And yes, I did ask him to monitor her communist activities. Secondly, I don't think I did anything wrong. I was concerned about her. I felt these people were leading her astray.'

'She was a grown woman, Jacob. What would you have done next? Decide who she gets married to?'

Jacob flapped his arms wide. 'Come on.'

Beatrice stood. She was taller than her husband. 'I've ignored your whoring around. All the time you spend in Witney and London, barely coming home. With the children gone, I've been lonely, but I've not cheated on you. But this...'

She took a deep breath to still her shaking voice. 'If I find out you did anything to Lottie, I will never, ever forgive you.'

Jacob pressed his lips together and stared at her with daggers in his eyes. 'What will you do?'

She smiled. 'More to the point, what will you do, Jacob? Kill me? Go ahead. Have your own way. I'm not scared any more.'

# TWENTY-ONE

Twenty-two years ago

It was a cold, freezing night, and Danny woke up, shivering under the thin sheets. He heard a thump again, then a scream. He went out in to the dark corridor. At the end, there was a window, overlooking the rear of the tall apartment building. His heart froze when he saw the small figure straddling the windowsill. It was Molly. Her hair moved in the frigid wind, and her little body shook.

Fear paralysed Danny. He got closer, and spoke to his sister. 'Molly, get off the window. Now.'

Molly was staring at him, her face partly illuminated in the yellow streetlamps far down on the street. He could see the dried tears on her cheeks. His heart ruptured in sorrow, and the pain almost drove him to the floor.

'Please, Molly, come here. We'll get out of here, I promise. Please don't do this.'

Molly looked at him without any expression. Then she looked far down below.

'I want to see Mummy,' she whispered. 'Where is she?'

Emotion shook Danny's voice. 'I'll take her to you. Come here.'

Molly shook her head once. With a calmness born of someone who has made her mind up, she lifted one leg, then slipped off the window ledge.

'Molly!' Danny rushed to the window. He saw Molly's body sailing to the street far below, falling like a wounded bird without wings.

* * *

Danny woke up with a start, sweat pouring down his face, pyjama top sticking to his chest. It was the same nightmare that haunted him every evening. He felt the tears choking his throat. He'd never see his sister again. He'd let her down. He couldn't stop her falling from the window; and he couldn't stop the bad things that happened to her. His tears began to dry as the anger rose up inside him. The pain was a part of him, cloaking his heart in a steely lair. He felt heavy, like you would never get out of the bed. Mornings like these he wished he didn't exist. Then the pent-up fury slowly began to seep out of him, and his hands became claws and dug into his legs. He wished he could draw blood sometimes. He wished he could make everyone bleed, make them feel his pain.

Danny glared back at his foster mother. It was 8 a.m. and they were getting ready for school.

'The cereal has gone soft,' he said. 'Can I have some eggs, please?'

Julia sneered at him. Her cheeks were red, hanging loose on both sides of her fleshy face. She used a large hand to wipe the moisture from her forehead. 'What do you think this is, a hotel? Eat what you're given.'

'Yes,' Gary, his foster father added. Gary was tall, and thin as a reed, his physique almost the opposite of his wife. But they bore the same amount of hatred for him, which he could never fathom. He knew the council paid them well to look after him. But he always went hungry, because they threw him the scraps. He didn't get much lunch money for school either.

'If you don't like it, then just starve,' Gary said.

Danny knew arguing never got anywhere. He had been clipped around the ears a couple of times. Julia was scarier than Gary, and she had a fast hand to go with her sharp tongue. But she was careful never to hit Danny where it might leave a mark. Danny knew they didn't want him to call the social services; it was they who paid his foster parents the allowance for his upkeep.

Feeling the hunger pangs in his stomach, he trudged upstairs to his tiny box room.

'Don't be late for school,' Julia screeched from downstairs.

Danny didn't reply. The carpets were threadbare, and the floorboards creaked under his feet. He went into the bathroom, and then back into his room. He stayed there for a while. His room had just enough space for a single bed and a tiny desk and chair. He had barely any room to move around. A window looked into the small front garden and the street where they lived. Every house looked the same, a bland, poorly maintained council house that was funded by the state. Danny waited for a while, then crept out into the landing, in his bare feet. Taking care not to make any sound, or as little sound as possible, he nudged the bedroom door of his foster parents.

The door fell open. Danny went in swiftly and had a look around. Behind the door, Gary had hung his trousers. He worked as a builder, and these were his work clothes. Swiftly, Danny put his hands inside, checking for a wallet. He found some keys, and then his fingers brushed against paper. He pulled it out and found a bunch of £20 notes. He peeled off two notes, stuffed them in his pocket, and put the rest back. He was about to get out, when he heard heavy steps coming up. He froze and put his eyes at the crack of the door. His heart sank. Gary was coming upstairs.

Danny knew he was trapped. He managed to get under the bed just as Gary came in. He heard Gary rummage around in the drawers and take something out of his pocket. Then he left, shutting the door behind him.

Danny waited until he heard Gary go downstairs. Then he stood and checked the landing again, by opening the door a fraction. It was empty. He snuck out as quickly as he could, and then went back into his room.

He took his schoolbag and went downstairs. As he was putting his shoes on, Julia appeared, hands on her hips. Her large, reddish face was ugly and spotted with acne scars.

'You still here, you stupid prat?' she hissed. 'You're going to be late for school.'

'I'm going,' Danny replied sullenly, and stood up. He slammed the door shut loudly as he left and, to his satisfaction, heard Julia shout out a curse. When he was halfway down the road, he stopped and pulled out the crumpled piece of paper he always kept in his pocket, whispering the familiar mix of letters and numbers to himself. It was time.

# TWENTY-TWO

The morning at school went by swiftly. When the bell for lunch rang, Danny shoved his exercise book inside his bag and got up quickly. The hallway was full of kids running around, or chattering to their friends near their lockers. Danny was a loner; he had no friends. He got a sandwich from the canteen and walked to the playgrounds, where he knew a quiet spot under the trees. He stopped when he heard a voice behind him.

'Hey, weirdo. You've not paid me yet.'

It was the school bully, Fat Simon. The boy came around and stood in front of Danny, two of his mates on either side. Peter and Alex, both just as wide as Simon was. They picked on Danny; they took his food at the canteen. He tried to walk past them, but they blocked his way.

'Let me go,' Danny whined. Simon laughed and smacked him behind the head. Then he grabbed his sandwich and Danny kicked his shin bone, hard, and Simon whined, then his face turned red.

'How dare you hit me, you bastard,' he hissed. With his two

friends, he pushed Danny to the floor, then they kicked him, taking turns. Danny turned himself into a ball, tucking his head into his neck to shelter himself from the blows. Pain pulsated in his back and legs as he was kicked repeatedly. Then the bullies stopped. Simon spat on him and sneered.

'Don't try that again, you dumb idiot.'

Danny got up and brushed himself off. He dried his tears and pressed on his right elbow, which was bleeding. A black weight pressed against his throat and the sunny day had turned poisonous and rotten. The rays of light seemed like barbs that dug into his skin.

He started the long walk back to the school building. As he walked past a bush, he heard the tweet of a bird. It wasn't an ordinary sound: this bird was screeching, like it was in pain. Danny stopped and looked inside the bush. A sparrow lay at the bottom, a wing turned into an awkward angle under its body. The sparrow was trying to fly, but its wing wasn't opening. Danny stared at the bird, then reached out and grabbed it.

He held the bird in his fist, staring at it. Its little brown beak was open, and he could see a small tongue. He realised the bird had broken its wing somehow, and it was in pain.

Pain and hurt like he felt now. The pain never left him; it kept coming back. Danny's hand tightened around the bird. The sparrow screeched and struggled. Danny stared at it, his eyes bulging. He wanted to end the bird's suffering. His grip tightened remorselessly and the bird now fought, tried to peck Danny's hand. It's little beak hammered against his hand, but Danny didn't let go. He squeezed until the wings cracked under his grip, and the bird stopped moving. Its eyes closed, and the head hung sideways. It was dead. Danny didn't let go, but he relaxed his grip. He stared at the dead creature with wonder in his eyes.

He had done something useful today. He had ended the

suffering, the hurt and pain. He wanted to do this again, inflict his own control over the world, heal it in his own way.

He stuffed the dead bird in his pocket and walked away. His heart was lighter, and there was a spring in his step.

\* \* \*

When school finished, Danny was out quickly. He ran to the bus station and rode into town. He had looked in the *Yellow Pages*, and got the address for the local DVLA office. He walked inside, and the people sitting there gaped at him. He was wearing his school uniform, and he was the only boy there. People queued up, waiting their turn. Danny was tired after his day at school. He was also hungry and thirsty. He took the heavy bag off his shoulder and dragged it on the ground. His water bottle had a few drops left, and he sucked it dry.

Eventually, his turn came. The woman at the counter stared at him, too astonished for words.

'Hello, how are you?' Danny asked.

The woman merely blinked. Then she cleared her throat.

'I, uh, what do you want?'

Danny slipped the piece of paper with the car's registration number on it. 'I want to know who owns this car, and the address where it's kept.'

The woman looked at the paper, then back at Danny. He smiled at her. She tried to smile, but failed.

'Why do you need the owner's contact details?'

Danny had thought of a lie already, but he wasn't sure if it was a very good one. 'It's my uncle's car, and I haven't seen him for a long time. I just want to know if he's still around.'

'You don't know your uncle's name?'

'His name is Harry, but that's his nickname. My parents are both dead, and I have no other relatives.'

The woman's face softened. She stared at Danny for a little

longer, then she looked at her computer. She entered the car's registration, then pressed a button. A machine whirred, and a piece of paper came out of a printer.

'That will be two pounds please.'

Danny counted the money out and gave it to the woman. Eagerly, he read the man's name and address.

'I hope you find your uncle,' the woman said with a smile.

'Thank you. So do I.'

# TWENTY-THREE

Nikki wound the window down, letting the warm air onto her skin. She took out her phone, glancing at Monty.

'Do you mind taking a detour?'

He shrugged. 'Not really. Where to?'

'It's on the way back. Town called Wharton.'

'Yes, I know where that is. Whose house we going to?'

'Thomas Armstrong, AKA Tom. My sergeant. That's where he lives now.'

Monty raised an eyebrow. 'Something to do with him not turning up at work?'

'Yes, and also not answering his phone. He recently changed address as well. I need to find out what's going on with him.'

'Good of you to check up on him.'

She eyed him. 'Wouldn't you do the same for your team?'

'If I was worried about them, yes I would.'

Nikki was quiet for a while. She knew Monty well enough now to tell him things she normally kept to herself.

'He preferred working under his previous boss. He had

hoped to make the DI grade. Not only did he not succeed, but then he had to work with me. He's accepted it now, but recently he's been off.'

'Drink or drugs? Or problem at home?'

Nikki thought for a while. It wasn't unusual for police officers to fall victim to alcohol and recreational drugs. They didn't deal with stress well, and mental health issues were common.

'I don't know,' Nikki said. 'He's never seemed to be under the influence when he's at work. But I guess you can never be sure.'

'Does he know you're coming?' Monty asked as he took the exit for Wharton. Nikki shook her head.

They drove in silence through light traffic. Wharton was a nondescript town, a plain high street, a school and a couple of doctors' surgeries pretty much made it up. It was a far cry from the more picturesque Cotswold villages, where the original inhabitants had sold up for hotels to be built on the land, or converted their homes into hotels.

Monty parked on a residential street. The houses were small, squat terraces, all made with the distinctive limestone building blocks that characterised Oxfordshire. Monty stayed in the car, while Nikki knocked on the door and waited.

A light was on in the living room. The curtains twitched once. Then the door opened. Tom stared at Nikki for a while, then at the car on the other side of the road. He was wearing jogging bottoms and a T-shirt, and he hadn't shaved. There were black circles under his eyes, and the lines on his face were deeper.

He opened the door wider for Nikki to step in. The small hallway opened into the living room, where a silent TV sat in front of a pair of sofas. Pictures of children were on the wall and on the bookshelf.

'You have a boy and a girl?' Nikki asked.

'Yes,' Tom said shortly. He remained standing. 'Do you want a cup of tea or coffee?'

'No, thank you. What's going on, Tom? You're not turning up to work, and the sick note you've submitted is a sick certificate that says flu.'

Nikki folded her arms across her chest.

Tom rubbed his cheeks and pointed to the sofa. Both of them sat down.

'I'm getting divorced, guv. Lost the house and the kids. Well, I moved out. I didn't do anything bad. Never touched her. But we were arguing, and I left before it got bad.'

'I'm sorry to hear that. Why didn't you tell me?'

Tom spread his hands. 'What's there to tell?' He went quiet, looking out the window.

'I went through it as well, as it happens,' Nikki said. 'A long time ago now, when my daughter was little. Time is the best healer in these situations. Remember that.'

Tom grimaced. 'That's what everyone says. Look, I did nothing wrong. Our relationship hadn't been working out for years. This year I met someone else and decided to move out. I told her, and she went totally bat-shit crazy.' He shook his head. 'It's my fault for not ending it years back. I'm paying for it now.'

'Are the courts involved?'

'Yes. I didn't want them to be. But she wants the whole house for herself. Doesn't want to give me any custody of the children. She tells them all sorts of lies about me. I don't have a choice, guv. I can't really afford the rent and the court case, too.' He held eyes with Nikki. 'But I'm not giving up on my children. They need me.'

Nikki nodded. She couldn't get involved; these matters were personal. She had been lucky; she had reached an amicable settlement with her husband, and they had decided to share Rita's custody. Tom seemed to be facing an uphill battle. His mood swings made a lot more sense now.

'How long has this been going on?'

'One year now. The courts are unbelievably slow. I could be waiting months for the next hearing date.'

'Do you feel like coming back to work? Might even help.'

Tom shook his head. 'You know what our work is like, guv. I don't feel like seeing dead bodies, or chasing armed robbers right now. Might end up doing something stupid.' He smiled sadly. 'I'm sorry.'

'Don't be.' Nikki felt bad for him. 'Keep yourself occupied though. Are you seeing the children?'

'I'm renting this house for them, even though the rent is killing my savings. But they only come every other weekend. We have a great time when they're here. I'm trying to get more custody. It would help if their mother stopped badmouthing me.'

'And your partner?'

'Yes, she comes as well.'

'Okay. Look, just call me if you need any help. I've been through it, and I know what it's like. Feel free to shout out.'

Tom smiled. 'Thanks, guv. Appreciate it. By the way, did DI Sen bring you here?'

Nikki had forgotten that Tom and Monty knew each other. They had worked for TVP for a long time.

'Yes. He's helping out with the case in your absence. Don't worry, though: he won't take your spot. He's got his own team, anyway.'

'No problem. I'm glad you've got a spare pair of hands. He's got a good reputation as well. Decent copper. He won a Policeman of the Year award a couple of years ago, along with a medal for bravery during an armed robbery raid. He was getting shot at but went out in the open to pull two injured DCs back to safety. He saved their lives.'

Nikki blinked in surprise. 'Did he now?'

'Yes. Tell him I said hello.'

'I will.' Nikki rose, wondering at Tom's revelation. Monty had kept that quiet, but then again it wasn't the kind of thing she expected him to talk about.

'Take care of yourself,' Nikki said.

Her phone buzzed when she reached the road. It was Kristy, giving her a sit rep.

'We got details of a lecturer who was tutor to Charlotte and one of her housemates. His name's Greg Keating, and he's in the college now. Do you want us to go see him?'

Nikki pondered for a few seconds. She wanted to get a feel of Charlotte's life, and her tutor would be a good place to start.

'I'll go with DI Sen. Send me his details, please and let him know. Can you round up the rest of Charlotte's friends, too? And where are we on finding the boyfriend? Good work so far, by the way.'

Monty glanced at her as she got in the car. 'All okay?'

She told him about Tom, and he clicked his tongue against the roof of his mouth. 'Shame. Guess we know what it feels like, right?'

Nikki nodded. She knew Monty had been through it as well. He was close to his daughter, and that was good to know. He studied her seriously, and her heart lurched suddenly. His eyes could definitely hold her captive. She drummed her fingers on her thigh, feigning nonchalance, aware that he was observing her.

'Shall we head back to the nick? I mean to Merton College, sorry.'

When she looked at him, he was grinning and that brought a tinge of warmth to her cheeks.

'What?' she demanded, hoping she didn't sound too flustered.

'Have you made up your mind about where we're going?'

'I just told you. Merton College. The victim's tutor is there.'

'Jolly good.' Monty's large hands gripped the steering wheel, skin stretching across the knuckles. He swung the car around and they went back to the motorway.

# TWENTY-FOUR

Nikki and Monty drove into the porter's lodge of Merton College. Dating from 1264, Merton is one of the oldest colleges; it is also one of the larger colleges in Oxford. The grounds are large in comparison to most Oxford colleges, though they are dwarfed by the nearby Christ Church Meadows; Christ Church being, beyond any doubt, more of a palace than an academic institution. Like its neighbouring college, Merton has a chapel, built in medieval times.

Monty was looking at the map as they followed the porter to the tutor's rooms inside the college. The grounds were huge, and here an ancient quadrangle of buildings converged around a pristine lawn.

'Look at this,' Monty said. 'The road that separates the college from Merton Field is called Deadman's Walk.'

'How interesting,' Nikki said dryly. 'Wonder why it's called that.'

The porter showed them up to the second floor; he knocked on a door that bore the name – *Gregory Keating MSc*.

The door was opened by a man with a mane of dark hair; he wore square-rimmed glasses. His dark eyes had a gleam of curiosity as he looked at Nikki and Monty. He was average height, slim-shouldered, and he wore a waistcoat and a tie that marked him as an Oxonian academic at work.

'Please come in. I spoke to your juniors.'

Nikki was surprised at how young he was. He couldn't be any more than in his early to mid-thirties. His body was athletic, but sparsely muscled, and he moved quickly, turning on his black shoes.

'Can I get you a tea or coffee?'

'I wouldn't mind a coffee, actually,' Nikki said.

Monty nodded. 'Me too. Milk, no sugar.'

'Certainly.'

He came out of the desk area and went past another table stacked with books and papers. The entire room in fact looked like an academic's library. Dark-panelled walls rose up to waist height, then the old stone walls took over, till they reached the wooden-beamed ceiling. In front of the bay windows, there was a table with a coffee machine and teapot. Under the table, Nikki could see, there was a discreet drinks cabinet. Wine bottles were laid out in a rack on the sides. The wine cellars of the Oxford colleges, she knew, held some of the most expensive collections in the world.

She looked around the room as the lecturer made the coffee. On the mantelpiece she saw photos of a young man holding a rowing oar and smiling with a medal. In another, smaller, photo there was an older man, shot from the side when he wasn't looking at the camera. Nikki leaned closer as she thought the man looked familiar. Recognition was difficult as the photo was only of the profile.

Greg carried a tray with three cups back to the table. Nikki and Monty took their cups with a murmur of thanks. Nikki watched as Greg made space on the table. He didn't have a ring on his fingers. He wasn't a smoker either; his nails were free of even the faintest of yellow nicotine stains. The hands were large and the palms calloused – unusual hands for an academic. Then she remembered the rowing photo on the mantelpiece. Greg settled in his chair and focused on them.

'Is it actually true?' A deep frown crossed his face. 'Charlotte's... dead?'

'I'm afraid so, yes.' Nikki consulted her notebook. 'You were her tutor for the whole of this year, is that correct?'

'Yes.'

'A friend of hers was also your student – Victoria Davies. They both studied PPE.'

'Yes. I saw them both recently.' He thought for a while, frowning. 'Before the May exams, around the fifteenth of May, I think. Final exams were at the end of May.'

Nikki wrote this down. 'That was the last time you saw Charlotte?'

'Yes. We exchanged emails a few times, during and after her exams. I do that with all my students. You will find that's quite common between students and teachers in Oxford. We run on small group-based tutorials, after all.'

'But in your group there was only Charlotte and Victoria?'

'In the final year, students specialise in one topic of their chosen subject. As each student has a narrow focus, it's difficult to have a large group.'

'So you have several small groups like these? For the final-year students, I mean?'

'Yes.'

Nikki scribbled in her notebook, and Monty took over. 'Did anything seem amiss with Charlotte when you saw her last?'

'Not particularly. She was stressed with the exams obviously.' His head lowered and he seemed to focus on a point under the table.

'There was something, actually. When the tutorial finished, I heard her voice outside my window. I looked down at the quadrangle and saw her with her boyfriend. They were having what seemed to be an argument. Raised voices and waving hands. Charlotte stormed off and left him standing. He followed.'

Monty said, 'How did you know it was her boyfriend?'

'I've seen them together in the past, in the great dining hall. Charlotte introduced him to me. Benjamin, I think his name was.'

'Do you know much about him?' Nikki asked.

'Only that he's at Somerville, also studying PPE. I don't know a great deal more, I'm afraid. But I do have friends at Somerville, some of the lecturers. I might be able to speak to them, if you like.'

Nikki thought that was helpful of him. 'Thank you, that would be useful.'

There was a guarded look in Greg's eyes all of a sudden. 'Do you have any idea who might've done this?'

'It's a fast-moving investigation, and we are keeping all channels of enquiry open.' It was a fobbing-off answer, and Greg seemed to know that, but his face remained impassive.

Monty asked, 'Do you know about the Piers Gaveston Society?'

'The drinking club? Yes, of course. There's a number of them in Oxford, as you must know. What about it?'

'Charlotte was last seen at their summer ball, last Thursday. We don't know where it was held, but of course, we will make our enquiries. Would you happen to know anything?'

Greg shook his head. 'I don't get involved in these matters. Sorry.'

'Do you socialise much outside the university?' Monty asked. 'I was under the impression most academics' social lives revolved around the college.'

Greg blinked once and his demeanour changed a fraction. A slight hardening of the jaw. 'I don't socialise with students, if that's what you mean. But yes, the dinners in the Senior

Common Room and drinks with the college dean do occupy many of my evenings. I also attend mass at Christ Church Cathedral.'

'So you mix with the academics? At college, or the university?'

'Mostly the college, but also at university. Sometimes there are musical events as well, not to mention talks by experts in their fields.' He smiled, his easy manner returned. 'There's always something going on in Oxford.'

'Something highbrow, you mean,' Nikki said.

'Something for everyone if you ask me. Academics do know how to have fun, believe me.' He became serious. 'Is there anything I can do to help at this stage?'

'Yes,' Nikki said. 'Do you know of any groups or societies that Charlotte belonged to?'

Greg's forehead creased as two fingers touched his chin. He was deep in thought. 'We used to talk about matters outside coursework as well. Once we discussed student interviews, and I talked about Oxford admitting more state school students. Both Charlotte and Vicky were adamant it wasn't enough. The talk turned to politics, and Charlotte was clearly an outspoken left-winger.' He smiled. 'I have some sympathies, I must say. In my younger days, I used to debate higher taxation at the Fabian Society.'

Nikki frowned, not recognising the name.

Monty said, 'You mean the youth-level Labour organisa-tion? Where younger left-wingers air their views and so on.'

'Yes.' Greg nodded. 'It's like a forum for young people inter-ested in socialist and communist ideas. It's harmless actually.' He shrugged. 'The discussions are mainly intellectual, and there aren't any party political tricks carried out, if you know what I mean.'

Monty said, 'The members of the Fabian Society are very powerful though, aren't they? Several prime ministers have come from their ranks – such as Tony Blair and Gordon Brown. And, if I'm not mistaken, the Oxford Fabian Society has a long history, several hundred years old.'

Greg smiled at Monty. 'You seem to know a lot about them.'

'I just read a report about them in the papers, when Tony Blair came to give a speech. It was many years ago. I was in the security detail for the area.'

'Getting back to Charlotte,' Nikki said, looking at Monty, then back to Greg. 'Do you know how involved she was with her politics?'

Greg appeared lost in thought again. 'Quite deeply, I think. She was passionate about it. She certainly attended the Fabian Society talks in Oxford.'

'Did you ever attend the Oxford Fabian Society?' Monty asked.

Greg shook his head. 'I'm actually a reformed capitalist, if there is such a term. My political views are different now that I'm older. I don't believe in high taxation and income

redistribution. That redistributed income goes into the wrong pockets and gets wasted. Ultimately, it kills the very social mobility that money is supposed to create.' He stopped and smiled sheepishly. 'Sorry. Rant over.'

Nikki was interested. Underneath the cool exterior Greg was clearly a passionate man. He knew he had revealed more of himself than he was perhaps prepared to do, and he looked a little embarrassed.

'Did Charlotte ever speak about her friends in the Fabian Society or in the socialist circles in Oxford?'

'Yes. She was the head of the Student Labour Union. It is part of the university, but I believe they get funding from the Labour Party as well.'

Nikki scribbled on her notebook. Monty said, 'Did she mention any people she met at these places?'

Greg was thoughtful again. 'Nothing that comes to mind. Her friends might know.'

'We have spoken to her housemates. Can you think of anyone else?'

Greg shook his head. 'Students have their own lives, as you can imagine.'

'We also want to speak to her boyfriend, Ben Henshaw. If you hear where he might be can you get in touch?' Nikki passed him her card, and Monty did the same. 'If you think of anything else, please let us know.'

As she followed Monty out of the room, her thoughts remained on Greg. He clearly knew Charlotte well. She didn't think he was hiding anything. His posture was easy and relaxed, and he seemed keen to help. But still, Nikki knew she had to keep an open mind. Greg Keating, like the others who had known Charlotte, wasn't out of the woods yet.

# TWENTY-FIVE

Monty and Nikki walked outside. Sunlight was angling in through the clouds, and Nikki turned her head up to it. The towers of Merton College blocked some rays, but the sun glided out of the clouds, suddenly basking the quadrangle in sunlight. It was quiet all around the medieval building, silent minds cogitating inside, like they had for millennia. At moments like this, Nikki often felt Oxford had an atmosphere entirely of its own.

'Where to now?' Monty asked. He, too, was gazing around at the hushed and beautiful quadrangle buildings.

'I want to see Charlotte's housemates again.'

The drive to Cowley didn't take long. Monty parked the car, and they walked through Cowley's colourful main street, then took a right down one of the roads. Monty pressed on the buzzer and they heard steps from inside. Monty held up his warrant card and introduced himself.

'Two different policemen came last time,' the tall woman said. She was almost up to Monty's shoulder height, and he was comfortably north of six feet. She was a brunette, with a bunch of freckles on her nose, and wide shoulders. Nikki wondered if she was a rower.

'And you are?'

'Francine Pearse.'

Nikki came forward. 'I am the senior investigating officer in charge of the murder enquiry into Charlotte's death. I know you have spoken to my detective constables, but there are a few things more I need to know.'

Francine let them in. The living room was empty except for scattered plates of food; and the TV was on, showing some irrelevant game show.

'Who else is here?' Monty asked.

'Taby's gone out shopping, but Vicky's around. Shall I call her?'

'Yes, please.'

Victoria Davies came downstairs, stopping at mid-stairs to stare at the strangers. Nikki noted she was smaller, plumper than Francine, who had a certain glamorous air about her, despite being in jogging bottoms and T-shirt, *sans* make-up. Vicky had short, curly red hair and rosy cheeks that were paling swiftly.

Nikki introduced herself and Monty, and asked Vicky to take a seat.

'How long have the two of you known Charlotte?' Nikki asked.

Francine pointed at Vicky. 'Vicky's known her the longest. They go to the same college.'

Vicky spoke to her friend. 'Yes, but you've known Lottie from the first year as well. That's when all three of you joined the PG society.'

'Piers Gaveston? The drinking club?'

Francine looked at her nails but Vicky said, 'Oh, it's much more than just a drinking club. They organise dinners, balls, fox hunting trips for selected members, even...'

'The society has changed a lot in recent years,' Francine interrupted, glaring at Vicky. 'It's not like it used to be in the old days. Only the members would know that.' She smiled sweetly at Vicky, who looked irritated at the interruption.

Nikki watched the exchange with interest.

'So you're a member of the society, I take it?' Nikki asked Francine.

'Yes, and I can tell you what you read in the media is not the truth.'

Vicky laughed. 'Is that why you have to leave your phones at home and guests have to sign a non-disclosure agreement?'

Nikki was astonished. 'Is that true?'

Francine shook her head like she was admonishing a baby. 'That's complete bollocks, Vicky, and you know it.'

'Anyway,' Monty interjected. 'Let's get back to Charlotte.'

Nikki picked up the thread. 'Yes. Vicky, you had tutorials with Charlotte. Is that correct? With Mr Greg Keating?'

Vicky nodded.

'Do you know the names of any other tutors Charlotte had this year?'

'Yes. For politics she had Dr Baden Powell.'

'She studied PPE?'

Vicky nodded. 'I did pure Economics, and that's why we had joint tutorials with Mr Keating. I know what tutors she had because she pointed them out to me during lunch at the great dining hall.'

'Is it actually called the great dining hall?' Nikki asked.

'Yes.' Both Vicky and Francine smiled. 'The masters sit on a raised platform as well, and they have to sit down first before we take our seats.'

'Okay,' Monty interjected. 'Francine, did you have any joint tutorials with Charlotte? What about your other housemate?'

'Taby? No, both Taby and myself went to Somerville. Vicky and Charlotte were at Merton.'

'Was Ben Henshaw in any of your tutorials at Somerville?' Nikki asked.

They shook their heads.

'And you ran SLUTS as well,' Vicky said pointedly, looking at Francine. The woman flushed, glaring at Vicky.

'How is that relevant? We're talking about Lottie,' she said, her cheeks crimson.

Monty and Nikki exchanged a glance. The tension between these two was obvious. There was a sound at the door, and Taby walked in with a shopping bag. She put it down on the floor and gaped at them. Nikki and Monty showed her their warrant cards.

Taby was a pretty girl, with shoulder-length chestnut hair and large grey-blue eyes. Nikki noted that Taby and Francine were different from Vicky, who was shorter, plumper and more nerdish.

Taby was a bit breathless having carried the heavy bag. She tucked one of her braids behind her ear. 'I thought we told the police everything.'

'You spoke to my colleagues,' Nikki said, 'But I needed a little more information. Have a seat, please.' She turned to Francine. 'What is SLUTS? Is that the right name?' She arched an eyebrow.

Francine seemed uncomfortable. 'It stands for Somerville Ladies Ultimate Tequila Drinking Society. There's a D in it as well. Most students in Oxford are men. There's hardly any girls-only drinking societies. So, we, uh, decided to come up with one.'

Nikki smiled at her. 'Who's we?'

'The ladies at Somerville, as the name suggests.' Francine grinned, then her face became serious. 'We got together and decided to start the club.'

'Was Charlotte a member?'

Francine and Taby exchanged a look, and something appeared to pass between them. Nikki noticed it.

'Yes, she was. Although she went to Merton, anyone can join SLUTS if they pass the drink test.'

'Which was?' Nikki was intrigued. This sounded like the kind of club she would've joined in her admittedly wild student days. Not that she ever went to Oxford.

'A shot of tequila every ten minutes for the first hour, chased by a double rum and Coke, and then repeat. Once the applicant passes the test, they are invited to drinking games that start immediately after.'

'I see. And how many members did you have?'

'Quite a few. As of last week, the number stood at forty-five.'

Monty asked, 'When did Charlotte last join a meeting of... your drinking club?'

Francine and Taby exchanged a glance. Taby shrugged. 'The last social was end of term, two weeks ago. She didn't turn up.'

'But she did previously? She was a member, after all,' Monty persisted.

Francine and Taby looked uncomfortable. 'She has in the past, yes,' Taby remarked. Francine stared at her friend, and Nikki knew by now there was an undercurrent of secrets here that she needed to understand.

'Francine, were you on good terms with Charlotte?' she asked.

The woman seemed shocked by the question. She blinked a couple of times. 'Yes, I was. Why do you ask?'

Nikki stared at her for a while, then at Taby. Neither broke eye contact with her. 'No reason. Just asking.'

'Lottie was our friend. We lived together. To be honest, I can't believe this has happened.' Taby's lips trembled, and Francine held her hand. Tears brimmed in both their eyes. Vicky's head lowered to her chest, and a sob escaped her lips.

Nikki noticed neither Taby nor Francine comforted Vicky. She gave the girls some time.

'Vicky, if you don't mind me calling you that,' Nikki said, 'when was your last tutorial with Charlotte and Dr Keating?'

Vicky wiped her eyes and sniffed loudly. 'That was before finals week. So about three weeks ago. Lottie seemed her normal self.'

'And she was fine after that?'

'Yes. As far as I could tell anyway. She didn't say anything was wrong.'

Nikki looked at the other two girls, who also shook their heads. She stood. 'Can one of you please show me Charlotte's room?'

Francine, who was the natural leader, stood, but Vicky was quicker. She went for the stairs. 'I'll show you her room.'

Monty and Nikki followed the woman upstairs. The floorboards creaked on the narrow staircase and the brown carpet had definitely seen better days. It was tattered in places. Clearly a student joint, Nikki thought, and she was surprised these four women lived in such squalor. The condition of the first floor wasn't much better. It had two bedrooms, a bathroom, and another flight of stairs went up to the converted loft which had two more bedrooms. Charlotte had one of the rooms in the loft.

Vicky opened the door to the first bedroom in the loft and went inside. It was definitely a student's room. There was a table by the window which overlooked the garden and the back of the house. There was a corkboard to one side with various notes pinned on it. Nikki saw a Merton College lectures timetable and various others for Student Union events. There was a prominent card in the middle for a Fabian Society dinner in a week's time.

Monty looked around the table while Nikki opened the wardrobe. To her surprise it was mostly empty, bar some shoes at the bottom. She bent underneath the bed, and, with gloved hands, pulled out a suitcase. She popped it open and found it full of packed clothes.

'She was moving back to college accommodation,' Vicky said, from the door. 'Colleges allow us to go back when we want to.'

'She wasn't going back home to stay?'

Vicky didn't say anything. Nikki stood and went closer to the girl.

'You and Lottie were close, right?' she asked softly.

Vicky stared at her for a while, then nodded. 'We weren't at first. But over the years we got closer.'

Nikki could see why they weren't close at first. Charlotte was probably a popular girl, and she would have hung out with the *cool girls*, like the two downstairs.

'Were you worried about Lottie?' Nikki asked.

Vicky thought for a while, then shrugged. 'She didn't say anything. But I know she didn't want to go back home; she wanted to stay in college till she started her internship.'

'Why didn't she want to go back home?'

Vicky sat down on the bed. Nikki pulled up a chair, and Monty leaned against the wall.

'She didn't get on with her father. They argued about her joining the Labour Party. The statue thing made matters worse. She said she argued with her dad about that. He wanted her to stop participating in the campaign.'

Charlotte's parents had told her nothing, Nikki realised. It made sense. Jacob Winspear must've been horrified by his own daughter's dalliance with the left. She didn't like the man. He was hiding something, she was sure. Not just his poor relationship with his daughter; there was more.

'And did she stop?'

'No. That was the thing about Lottie. She was obstinate like a mule. Her father's disapproval meant nothing to her. She wanted to make her own way in life.'

'She was a problem for him,' Monty murmured from the wall. 'What about her boyfriend, Benjamin?'

'What about him?' Vicky looked up at Monty.

'Was he a left-winger as well?'

Vicky shook her head. 'No. He was very much a Tory. He hid it under a liberal attitude and so on, but definitely a capitalist.'

'Were they close as a couple?' Nikki asked.

Vicky inspected her nails. 'I think so. But of late...'

'Go on,' Nikki urged.

Vicky looked unsure of herself, then seemed to make her mind up. 'Lottie told me there was another man in her life. But she was very coy about him. Wouldn't tell me who he was. She made me promise not to tell anyone.'

'Was he a student?'

'I assume so. She really wouldn't tell me much more.'

Nikki considered this. 'So, she was cheating on Benjamin?'

Vicky looked anxious. 'I'm not going to get into trouble for this, am I?'

'Not at all. Please don't worry.'

'Benjamin and her were going through a rough patch. He invited her to the PG ball and so on, and I think he wanted to rekindle their romance, but she wasn't so sure.'

'Vicky, this is very important. Do you have any idea who this new man in Charlotte's life might be?'

The girl looked helpless. 'I'm sorry. I've racked my brains trying to think ever since I heard about what happened. But she didn't tell me anything about him. Only to not tell anyone. Believe me, if I knew who he was I'd be telling you right now.'

Vicky's cheeks were red and tears threatened again. She dabbed her eyes with the back of her hands.

'I remember one thing. She said she'd known him for a while. That pretty much ruled out a first-year student.'

'It had to be someone who was already in Oxford,' Nikki said, and Vicky nodded.

From behind, Monty added, 'But not necessarily at the university.'

Vicky said, 'Lottie did have friends outside the college. She went to the Labour Club meetings and was a member there.'

'Thank you,' Nikki said. 'Do you have any names at the Labour Club?'

Vicky shook her head. Her hands twisted on her lap. 'I should tell you something about Lottie.'

Nikki and Monty waited. Vicky said, 'Lottie liked...' she paused, her voice faltering awkwardly, 'you know...' She looked at Nikki, and Nikki knew what she meant.

'She slept around?'

Vicky's eyes flickered down to her hands. 'I don't know details. But I don't think Ben or this new guy were the only men she was intimate with.'

'Did she tell you about any others?'

'She told me about a couple of men she met at bars and nightclubs. They were all older. To be honest, she preferred older men. They were sexier, she once told me.'

Nikki digested this in silence. She sat down next to Vicky. 'Look at me,' she said. Vicky raised her head. 'You won't get into any trouble. But I need to know because it could be important.' She paused. 'Was Lottie with a married man?'

'She never said that. But I know there was another man, in his thirties. She said it was casual, and she saw him now and then.'

'And that man wasn't the one you just mentioned?'

'No. Sorry if this is confusing.'

'So, Lottie had two other men on the go, apart from Ben. Correct?'

Vicky nodded, looking miserable. 'I feel terrible spilling all her secrets. But it might help you.'

Monty said, 'It does. I want you to think carefully. Are you sure you never saw Lottie with either of these two men?'

'She kept it very quiet. No one else knew but me. No, I never saw her with them.'

'She never dropped a hint, or clue as to who they might be?'

'I'm sorry.'

Nikki gave the girl's hand a squeeze. 'Thank you. If you think of anything else, let us know.'

She resumed searching the room. Monty found a laptop in the desk drawer and a couple of drives. Neither of them found a phone. Nikki took some of her dresses for DNA samples. From the bathroom downstairs, she already had Charlotte's toothbrush.

'I know where the ball was held,' Vicky blurted as they turned to leave.

'Go on,' Nikki prompted. 'Anything you tell us will help us catch who did this to your friend.'

'Bloomfield House. That's all I know. I heard them mention it when they were getting ready to go out. But I don't know where it is.'

'Thank you.'

Nikki and Monty descended the stairs, their hands full of specimen bags.

The women were sitting in silence.

'Please call us if you think of anything else – it doesn't matter how small or insignificant.' She gave them her card, and so did Monty. All three of them looked worried.

'There will be a police car outside for the next few days. You can ask them as well if you want to contact me.'

Nikki nodded at the trio, and followed Monty out the door. Her lips were pursed as she stared down at the pavement, her mind clicking as it changed gears softly. She felt Monty's eyes on her and appreciated his silence. He didn't start the car after they got in.

Nikki glanced at Monty. "Two other blokes? Charlotte was a busy girl."

"You don't believe Vicky?"

"Vicky has no reason to lie. It took her guts to open up to us. The dynamics between those girls is a bit strange. I think Charlotte was close to Francine and Taby before, but then they fell out. That's when Charlotte got closer to Vicky."

"But Charlotte still didn't tell Vicky who this new man, or men, were. If they were older, that doesn't really matter." Monty smiled at Nikki. "I'm no expert, clearly. But women often have relationships with older men. I think there's something else about these men. That's why Charlotte kept their identities a secret."

Nikki looked closer at Monty, and read the answer in his eyes. "Student teacher relationship?"

"Like the tutors she spent time with?"

"Vicky was there as well, though. Some of the time, anyway."

"All the more reason not to tell her."

Nikki frowned, tapping her lower lips with her index finger. "Or it could be a boyfriend, or ex of the other two girls. Maybe that's why she fell out with them in the first place."

Monty started the engine, and the car nosed into the traffic. Nikki said, "The girls don't have a police record, do they?"

"None whatsoever."

"Regardless, let's keep an eye on them. I also want a closer look at the tutors."

# TWENTY-SIX

Nikki and Monty walked down the quadrangle of Merton College for the second time that day. They went up the two stone steps leading to the ground-floor platform that encircled the Mob Quad, as it was known. They followed the porter, who walked past the pristine lawn, and entered one of the arches in the Gothic stone building. Mob Quad was reputedly the oldest quadrangle in Oxford, and the building, although beautifully preserved, showed its age. The stone surface gave off a chill that Nikki felt in her bones. She wrapped her arms around herself. The narrow opening led to a similarly narrow staircase, space only for single file traffic. There were two rooms on the first floor, and one of them had *Dr James Baden Powell* written on the old wooden surface. The porter knocked on the door, and the lecturer appeared. He was young, no more than mid-thirties, and strikingly handsome. He was tall, but shorter than Monty, who towered above most men. He had to duck as James held the door open for them to enter.

'Horrible situation, this,' he said, once they sat down. 'I cannot begin to get my mind around it.'

'When did you last see Charlotte?' Nikki asked.

'Three weeks ago, at her last tutorial. I taught her politics.'

'How did she seem when you saw her?'

'Her normal self. Nothing out of the ordinary. She was tired of working. The last term in Oxford can be stressful for students. Her thesis on Karl Marx was well done, however; she had done herself proud.' He became lost in his own thoughts. 'She would've got a First if...'

'Do you know if she had any enemies?'

The question seemed to startle the lecturer. 'Enemies? Sorry, I wouldn't be aware if she did.'

'Did you have any other students at the tutorials?'

A guarded look came over his face for a few seconds, then vanished. 'Yes, we did. Politics is a popular subject, and I normally had two or three students.'

'Can you tell us their names?' Nikki asked.

He looked doubtful. 'I can have a look in my diary, and let you know.'

'That would be very helpful. We're trying to find out as much as we can about Charlotte. How long had you known her?'

'I've been attached to the college for the last two years. I've known Charlotte since her second year.'

'So you knew her well?'

Again, the guarded look flashed across his face. He was different from the distant but relaxed Greg Keating, Nikki thought. Greg didn't seem defensive like James was. She wondered why.

'Not really.' He smiled, but it was forced.

'She was into her left-wing politics,' Nikki stated, not believing what he'd just said. 'Did she talk to you about that?'

He coughed into a fist, then cleared his throat. 'Yes. I know she was a member of the Fabians and the Labour Club.'

'She attended meetings there. Did you ever go with her?'

He shook his head. 'Do you have any idea who might have done this?'

Nikki let his question hang in the air for a while. She stared at him. 'That's why I was asking if you thought she had any enemies, or was in any kind of trouble.'

'I'm sorry, Inspector. Can't help you there.'

Monty said, 'Did you know Charlotte was coming back to stay in the college?' They had spoken to the porter, who had checked his books to confirm. Charlotte had a room booked for the summer.

He raised his eyebrows. 'Sorry, I didn't know that.'

'She had a room overlooking the Fellows' Garden. Quite a nice location. Where do you live, Dr Baden Powell?'

'James, please.' He flashed them a winning smile. Perfect set of white teeth, Nikki noticed. 'I live in Summertown, north Oxford.' He glanced at his watch, then at the paperwork on his desk. 'I hate to rush you, but I need to get a move on with my stuff.'

Nikki and Monty stood. They gave James their cards, and then left.

As they walked back to the car, Monty spoke under his breath.

'He's hiding something.'

'I know. I was in two minds whether to ask him for a DNA swab. I guess there's always a second time,' Nikki said. They walked slowly back; Nikki stopped under the shadow of a large oak tree.

They hadn't found anything that would give them a lead. Neither her home computer nor the laptop from her rented house had shown anything of value to the investigation. Photos of her friends, and her university coursework. While updating on the tech search, Will had reported no further activity from Night Crawler. It was a dead end. She looked around the grounds. Charlotte had been a complex woman. She was promiscuous, vivacious, intellectually voracious. She wasn't afraid of the world; she wanted to take it full on. And the man who strangled her to death knew her well. He knew she would be outside in the grounds of that country mansion, that fateful summer evening.

# TWENTY-SEVEN

The dry leaves crunched underneath Nikki's boots as she walked down the extensive grounds of Bloomfield House. The house belonged to a French publishing magnate, D'Arcy. He had bought it from Viscount Bloomfield, who couldn't tolerate the huge costs of the upkeep. Nikki stopped and turned around. The building was in front of her. Behind, and all around, the sweeping, gently rolling hills of the Cotswolds undulated in myriad shades of green. The fading sun was out in all its glory, lighting the horizon with red and gold swathes. It was a beautiful sight, and she wished she had the frame of mind to appreciate it.

Monty was talking to one of the groundsmen, near the edge of the house. The magnificent baroque building was made of yellow limestone brick like most of the Cotswold stately homes. It had twenty-two bedrooms, and the ground floor was the size of a football pitch. That's where the PG party was held, and apparently, this venue was popular with members of Oxford's secretive drinking clubs. The groundsman had just imparted that golden nugget to Monty, and hence he was now in deep conversation. Nikki had wandered on, not because she was

142

uninterested, but she sensed something pulling her on. She couldn't explain it. She felt restless, like she needed to do something.

As she walked down the slope, the grass grew wild, and weeds came up to her knees. The air was hushed, and it was sticky hot. Fat flies buzzed around her, birds called out in the trees. Nikki remembered Thursday. It had been hot like this. And where was Charlotte? Somewhere here. She stopped to get her bearings. She couldn't see Monty any more, the bulge of the land in front obscured her view of the house.

The grounds covered fifteen acres, and there was no hope, even with a full team, of scouring the whole place for any clues. Nikki felt a little foolish all of a sudden. She didn't know what she'd expected to find. But she did feel Charlotte had died here.

She walked around for a while, keeping her eyes on the ground, but didn't find anything of interest. There was a lake up ahead, and the waters were still, reflecting the sky. She watched for a while, then made her way back. Monty was still speaking to the groundsman, and another man had joined them.

Monty introduced them. 'This is Mr Vardy, the housekeeper. He lives in the bungalow on the other side.'

'You can't see it from here,' Mr Vardy said. 'It's round the corner, and a few minutes' walk from the main house.'

'Were you here the night of the Piers Gaveston summer ball?' Monty asked.

'Yes, of course. I don't get involved with the party obviously. But I have to be on site in case there's a medical emergency or like a fire breaks out. There's security in place for that as well, but I too have a job.'

Nikki asked, 'On the evening of the party, did you see anything that might cause you concern?'

Mr Vardy gave Nikki a sardonic grin. 'All of us have to sign a non-disclosure agreement to say we won't reveal any details of what happens here. But I know about that poor girl, and we have to make an exception.

'You might not believe this,' the housekeeper went on, 'but anything and everything is allowed. I've heard that drug dealers actually set up stalls inside. There's live sex shows, circus shows, all sorts, but no cameras are allowed. I've never ventured inside. The less I know, the better.'

'What about outside?' Nikki asked. 'Did you go around the grounds?'

'At the gates there's security.' Mr Vardy raised a hand in the direction of the undulating fields of the property. 'As you can see, the boundaries are rather far off. The organisers can't put security everywhere. And the youngsters get up to all sorts in the grass, I can tell you.' He smiled and shrugged. 'Not my job to be their guardian, sorry.'

The housekeeper added, 'They're all in their twenties. Young, but they should be able to take responsibility for themselves.'

Monty asked, 'Do lecturers also attend?'

'Maybe. We don't see the guest list.'

Nikki decided to be direct. "Really, Mr Vardy? You're the housekeeper, you know about the drug dealers and circus acts, but you don't know who attends?"

Mr Vardy flushed. "Not really."

"The NDA you signed is now invalid. There will be a clause in it for acts like death. Or murder, as happened here."

Mr Vardy scratched his neck. "Yes, I accept that. But believe me, it's the security personnel who have the guest list for the night, and that list is strictly controlled by the members of the drinking society."

"You're here when these things happen. You don't know if older men from the University attend?"

Again, Mr Vardy looked uncomfortable. "Alright," he said

after a pause. "Yes, some older men do attend. Not very old, by which I mean, they're probably in their mid-thirties to mid-forties. I've never seen a sixty-year-old man come for one of these parties."

"Do you recognise any of these men? Have you seen the same older man come every year?"

Mr Vardy frowned as he tried to recall. "Maybe. I don't pay much attention to this, you understand. I could even lose my job for talking to you about this."

Monty said, "This will remain confidential, don't worry. Anything else you recall, specifically that night?"

Mr Vardy inspected his toes. Nikki observed him, then exchanged a look with Monty. They both knew this could be an important moment. Her eyes drifted down the waving, summer scented grass. The lake caught her eyes again, glinting in the sunshine, as if calling her. Nikki frowned, a slow rush in her ears, like the wind moving through the huge oak tree overhead. The ends of Charlotte's dress had mud on them. So did her shoes, and feet. She remembered that from her first sight of the body. She had assumed that happened when she was laid down on the hillside.

But what if...Nikki's feet were moving already. She took a step forward, then stopped as Mr Vardy spoke.

"They go out, often," Mr Vardy said. "The students, I mean. They come out here, and wander around, and get up to the usual things that young people do."

"Do they go near the lake?"

"There's a reason why the lake is further out. The waters are deep, so we don't encourage it."

"Come on," Nikki motioned to Monty. He had clearly read the look on her face. Together, they walked through the wild grass. Monty found a path that skirted around the edges of the knee-high vegetation, and they got to the lakeside quickly.

Nikki kept her eyes glued to the earth, treading slowly. She took photos with her phone, to note the layout of the ground, the surroundings, the wetness of the earth. She would use the photos later to reinforce her mental image of this place. It helped her to imagine the victim's final steps.

She walked around the edges of the grass, where it slowly started to get muddy. She heard Monty up ahead shout. He had something in his gloved hand, and he was holding it aloft.

As she neared him she saw what it was. The white beads of a pearl necklace rested on his large palm. It was torn, and only a few beads remained, but it was clearly a necklace.

# TWENTY-EIGHT

Monty drove back from Bloomfield House. His mind was busy trying to dissect what they had uncovered during their visit. Finding the necklace was important. They had searched till the light began to fade, and Nikki had called for help. A nearby squad car responded, and two uniformed constables had joined them. They found nothing else, but from tomorrow, more units would comb the grounds.

"We can get prints today," Monty said, his fingers drumming on the wheel. "DNA will take a couple of days to come back."

"If we have a match with Charlotte, that only tells us she was there, and probably assaulted." Nikki pursed her lips in thought.

"We didn't see any other signs of assault, but it's difficult to confirm that because the wild grass." Monty said slowly. "I wonder why the killer left the necklace. That was careless. He was in a rush to get the body out of there."

"Or maybe it was dark when he came back for the body, and he missed it."

Monty thought to himself. Nikki made eminent sense, as usual. "Yes, possibly."

The night of the PG dinner was a wild party, and he wondered if there had been more casualties that night, albeit not a death, like in Charlotte's case. The wealthy kids who came to these parties probably had enough clout to keep any adverse incidents a secret from the media.

He glanced towards Nikki, who was staring out the window, her lips pressed together, an intense expression on her face.

'Penny for your thoughts,' he said. She turned to look at him, her jaws set together.

'Maybe Charlotte met someone she had planned to, or a new person.".'

'Makes sense. But we'll have trouble finding witnesses, or anyone to talk to us.'

'Apart from her housemates,' Nikki said. She looked at the side-view mirror.

'Have you seen that black Toyota van behind us?'

Monty looked at the rear-view mirror. The van was three cars behind, on the left lane, and a man was visible in the front seat. He wore black shades, and Monty couldn't see him properly.

'He's been following us since we left Bloomfield House,' Nikki said. 'Have you seen him before?'

Monty frowned and shook his head. 'Have you?'

'Yes,' Nikki said, pulling out her phone. 'Once, when I was driving to the nick. Sure it was the same car. I didn't take the registration then.' She called Switchboard on her phone.

'DI Gill calling Control. Can you put me through to Traffic, please?'

'Control connecting DI Gill to Traffic. Hold on, please.'

When the duty sergeant for Traffic answered, Nikki gave them the car's details. Monty noticed the car had changed lanes and was now directly behind them, still staying three cars behind. Nikki gave them the registration details.

'It's owned by a car hire company, guv,' the traffic sergeant said. 'The vehicle was hired last month, by a company whose name isn't disclosed. I can ring the rental company and ask for it.'

'See if you can, please, and call me back. Thanks.'

Monty glanced in his rear-view mirror again. The black van had fallen back further, as if aware he was now under watch. Monty could see him, about six cars back now, in the same lane.

'When did you see him?' he asked Nikki. He felt a spike of worry in his guts. Nikki lived alone, and, if this weirdo was keeping an eye on her, that wasn't good news.

'When I was driving to work, day before yesterday. Pretty sure I saw him around the station last night as well. Twice can't be a coincidence.'

'True that.'

Monty changed lanes, keeping his eyes peeled for the black Toyota. He couldn't see it anymore. He reduced speed and made sure it had gone. They had gone past two exits, and the Toyota could've taken either one of them. He cursed himself. He should've noted which exit they took. He told Nikki.

'Don't bother yourself too much,' Nikki said. 'Now we know, we can tell the others as well to keep an eye out for him.'

Nikki stifled a yawn and rubbed her face. 'Been a long day. Anything to catch up on at the nick?'

'Nothing new as far as I know. Shall I drop you off home?'

'If you don't mind.'

Monty nodded, then he felt Nikki's eyes on him. He glanced at her, askance. 'What?'

'You still living alone?'

Monty frowned. 'You know that. Why're you asking?'

He took the exit for Kidlington. Nikki said, 'I was just wondering if Emily might have moved in.'

Monty sighed. His relationship with his only daughter was fraught at the moment. She was sixteen and becoming rather rebellious. Her mother, his ex-wife, Josephine, didn't help matters. Emily stayed with him every other weekend, and it was from Thursday till Monday. He had close to fifty per cent custody, as Emily spent half her holidays with him as well. Monty lived in Headley, not far from Josephine, which helped.

'When she comes, she goes out half the night. She stinks of fags when she gets back, and I can tell she's been smoking cannabis.'

'Like you did when you were her age?' Nikki said in a teasing voice.

'I was into heroin actually, shooting up my veins.' Monty raised his eyebrows.

'Good job your daughter's nothing like you. But seriously, have you asked her where she goes? You must know who her friends are.'

'That's the problem. I don't and neither does her mother – at least that's what she's telling me. These are new friends, who have just joined her school. I'm worried she's getting into the wrong crowd.'

'You need to talk to her.'

Monty shook his head. 'Believe me, I've tried. Her mother doesn't tell me much, which doesn't help either.'

Light was getting scarce in the sky as Monty drove. By the time they arrived at Nikki' house, shades of blue were deepening across the horizon, and yellow lights were glowing in houses.

'Would you like to come in for a coffee?' Nikki asked lightly. She had never invited Monty into her house before, although he had been inside once when he came to pick her up for work.

Monty paused a beat before replying. 'Yes, sure.'

He got out slowly and followed Nikki. She entered and turned the lights on. Monty shut the door behind them. Then she turned to him. Her eyes were bright, no trace of the tiredness she had just complained about. She headed into the kitchen, and Monty followed, after taking his shoes off.

Nikki offered Monty a coffee, which he accepted with thanks. The kitchen was clean and orderly, he noted. He complimented Nikki, at which she laughed.

'Living alone means I make minimal mess, and half the time I get takeaways, anyway.' She patted her sides, above the waist. 'That sticks here.'

Monty didn't agree. Nikki was in good shape. She was in her forties, and he suspected her diet was good, because as she had mentioned several times – exercise wasn't her thing, though she went running. He knew she had passed her fitness test easily, which was an annual requirement in the force.

'You're in fine fettle, Miss Gill, and I'm not just saying that to please you.' He grinned. 'Well I might pay more compliments if you get dinner.'

'Thank you. But you'll have to work harder to get dinner tonight.' She grinned and put a cup of steaming coffee in front of him. She sat down opposite, at the kitchen counter.

'Now tell me. You're talking to Emily, right? With teenagers, you need to get the time right. And just trust me on this, make sure she's not hungry.'

Monty sipped on the coffee, and then wiped the foam from his lips. 'Hungry? Surely she's old enough to feed herself?'

Nikki had seen Emily once, when she stopped by the station, to get a lift from him. The memory made him smile. Nikki had got on well with Emily, even within the confines of the work place. They had a chat in the car park as he brought the car around. Emily told him later she liked Nikki.

Emily was on the thin side, but not because she was dieting. She had always had that body shape.

'Point noted. I'll make her a fry up before I grill her about the social life.'

'She doesn't like fry ups.'

'How do you know? OK, so that's correct. She doesn't like meat, to be honest. I don't mind that. It's a good habit, I think.' He paused. He loved his little girl. She meant the world to him. He had been worried after the divorce. Emily was eleven then, and she didn't take it well. Perhaps not having siblings made it harder. But he had tried his best to provide her with a home – her own room and space in his new house. Over the years, Emily had blossomed into a beautiful girl, who did well at school; and it filled his heart with warm sunshine. The only cloud in his parenting horizon was her recent social life.

'I don't want to get all police detective with her,' he said. 'It might make her more rebellious.'

Nikki's dark eyes twinkled. 'Admit it. You've been following her around.'

He raised both hands. 'Guilty as charged. I'm the weird old man in the nightclubs, getting stopped by the bouncers on suspicion of selling drugs to teenagers.'

Nikki smiled. 'That's you, definitely.' She cupped her chin in her hand, and for some reason, she looked different but just as beautiful. Breath caught in his chest, and he opened his mouth to breathe.

'You're a good father,' Nikki said softly. 'Girls need their dads.'

'Yes. Josephine had a poor relationship with hers, and that affected the way she views men. I couldn't help but think all her anger towards her dad ended up being directed at me.' He raised a hand. 'Sorry. Old history, water under the bridge. I just wanted to make sure I'm there for Emily when she needs me. That can only be good for her, correct?'

'Absolutely. Do you know if she has a boyfriend?'

Monty thought about it for a while. It didn't bear much

thinking about, to be honest. He didn't like the idea. His personal nightmare was that Emily had a druggie boyfriend, leading her astray. And it was possible, considering how secretive Emily had been about her recent activities. He explained it to Nikki.

'Not necessarily. I mean, if she had a boyfriend she'd keep it a secret from both of you, but her mother would know before you did. I suggest you sit down and tell her of your concerns. She's a sensible girl, from what I could gather. I'm sure she'll listen.'

Monty drained his coffee. 'I hope so.' Nikki rose and went to the fridge. She pulled out a couple of pots and put them on the hob. Monty watched her back as she worked. Then she turned to him.

'Stay for dinner?'

He checked his watch. There was a turmoil in his heart he was trying to disguise. He knew it had taken Nikki courage to ask him to stay. He didn't want to let her down, but neither was he ready to let one thing lead to another.

He stood and walked slowly to her. Her eyes widened a fraction, and he noticed her hands tighten on the kitchen counter. He stopped, and their eyes held each other captive.

'Thanks, and I'd love to stay,' he said, and meant it, 'but I promised Emily I'd take her to netball practice tomorrow morning. That starts at 7.30, which means I have to be up early to pick her up. I'm sorry.' Again, he meant the last two words.

Nikki's eyes bore deep into his, and he saw desire, but caution, too, running through like oil on water. He read the silent message.

*This is between us. Don't betray me.*

He felt exactly the same way. He forced himself to smile, then exhaled. 'See you tomorrow?'

She nodded and, together, they walked to the door.

# TWENTY-NINE

Twenty-one years ago

Danny was fourteen years old, and although he was skinny, he was starting to get taller. He had also made friends with a couple of boys who smoked weed and drank beer. Smoking weed made him sleepy, but it also relaxed him. He had some little pocket money saved up, so he had bought a small amount for his friend, Paul. He had been at Paul's house, smoking, and as he trudged back home, he knew he was late. He also knew his foster parents would be at home, probably drunk and watching TV. They didn't really care what time he got back home, but Julia liked to make a fuss about it. He was their meal ticket after all, and she wanted to be sure he was back in his room, and she didn't have to go out to search for him.

He opened the door and stepped inside. As he took his jacket off, Julia appeared in the doorway. 'Where have you been?' she demanded.

Danny didn't reply. He had his back to her and started taking his shoes off. Julia came up to him.

'I asked you a question, you toerag.' She raised her voice.

Danny still ignored her. He tried to brush past her and go up the stairs. She pulled on his arm and shoved him back against the coat rack.

'I got a message from your school. You're turning up late and not doing homework.'

Danny frowned at her. 'Since when do you care?'

Julia narrowed her eyes and leaned forward, sniffing his clothes. 'Why are your eyes red? Where have you been?'

'None of your concern,' Danny said, and he tried to go upstairs again. This time Julia smacked him on the shoulders, and then shoved him back against the wall.

'Don't you dare talk back to me. I'm your guardian, do you hear me?'

Rage spiked in Danny's veins. He got up, and his lips bent into a snarl. He thought of the times he'd gone to bed hungry and been treated worse than a dog.

'You're not my guardian. You're nothing to me. You're just a filthy piece of fat shit.'

Julia's eyes popped open, and her lips twisted in anger. 'How dare you talk to me like that?' she screamed. She raised a hand to slap him, but Danny was quicker. He shoved her back with both hands, and she lost her balance and fell against the radiator.

Slowly, she tried to pick herself up. 'Gary!' she screeched. 'This miserable toerag is beating me up!'

Gary appeared at the doorway, his eyes hooded; he was bent forward slightly. He was either high on drugs, or he had been drinking. 'What's going on here?' he slurred, stepping forward. He tried to grab Danny as he walked past. Danny pushed, and they started to fight.

Gary was strong, but Danny suddenly had a new ferocity in his limbs. He spat and snarled, then his teeth sank on Gary's forearm. He bit down harder and tasted blood. Gary screamed and let him go.

Danny ran into the kitchen. Julia was up, and she came after him. There was a pot of boiling water on the cooker. Without thinking, Danny took the lid off and picked up the pot. He hurled it on Julia, the scalding water burning her skin. Julia had no time to react or save herself. She howled in agony as her skin turned beetroot red. She slipped on the floor and fell down again.

Adrenaline was bubbling in Danny's blood now. His hands gripped the pot tightly, and he raised it above his head. He brought it down with savage fury on Julia's hateful face. For a split second he saw her eyes meet his, and he saw fear in them. That made him feel good. It made him feel powerful and in control. He felt like that moment when he squeezed the life out of the sparrow.

He hit Julia hard with the pot, and he heard her cheekbones and nose crack. She screamed again, but Danny didn't stop. Julia had her arm raised, but Danny hit her repeatedly with the pot. He saw a shadow rush at him, then Gary smacked into him hard, propelling him backwards against the kitchen counter. Gary was stronger, and he pinned Danny against the counter, trying to hold his head down over the sink.

Danny twisted sideways, and he saw a knife on the counter. He picked it up quickly and stabbed backwards, catching Gary in the chest. Gary tried to move, but he slipped on the water on the floor and fell down. Before he could get up, Danny was on him like a flash, stabbing him in blind fury. Gary fought back, but Danny was faster, the knife blade hitting Gary in the face and neck. A stream of blood sprouted up, its flow warm against Danny's hands. He stabbed Gary in the neck again, till the man stopped moving.

Then his eyes fell on Julia. Her mouth was open, face frozen in shock. Red, burning flesh scarred her cheeks. She tried to move away, but Danny seized her.

Julia gasped. 'No, no. Please let me go. Please don't do this.'

Danny smiled. 'As you sow,' he murmured, 'so you reap.'

He felt that aura of invincibility again. He had the power to control the world around him. Without a word, he stabbed Julia in the neck. He kept stabbing till warm blood pulsed out, making a halo around her head, joining the crimson tide leaking out of Gary's prone body.

Danny stood, feeling perfectly calm, although his heart was beating like mad, a drumbeat in his ears drowning out all other sound. He took a kitchen towel and wiped the blade, then wrapping the kitchen towel around the blade, he shoved it down his trousers. He looked in the cupboards, till he found the bottle of cooking oil. He stepped over the bodies and went into the living room, where he found a cigarette lighter. He came back, and then splashed the oil over Julia and Gary. Then he lit the lighter and chucked it on the slick of blood and oil.

He stood and watched the flames lick higher. He smelled the burning flesh, and it was a strange new smell, something he would never forget. As the fire spread around the kitchen, he went out the back door. He had remembered the key, and he locked the back door to make sure no one could enter. He climbed the back garden wall, coming out into the alley, then sprinted down it, escaping his sordid life.

He knew he had to get away quickly. Problem was, he had no idea of where to go. It was too late to go back into the house and get the few clothes that belonged to him. He walked rapidly to the end of the street and turned the corner. When he looked up, he could see black smoke rising in the sky. He looked around him. There was only one option: he had to find the man who drove the silver BMW and knew his mother.

# THIRTY

Twenty-one years ago

Danny was shaking like a leaf. He had to calm himself down. He went to the park opposite his school and bought himself a drink from the corner shop. He sat down on a park bench. He needed to make a plan. He had less than twenty pounds in his pocket. That would buy food for a couple of days, then he had nothing. He didn't want to go back to social services. Those idiots would put him in with another abusive family. To these foster families, he was just a meal ticket. He would rather be on the streets.

He went to the post office and bought paper, envelopes and stamps. He looked up the man's phone number in the directory, then called him from a phone booth. A woman answered. Danny asked for the man by name, and he said it was urgent. A few minutes later, the man answered.

'I'm Danny, Janet's son. Do you want me to tell your wife that you slept with my mother?'

There was silence. Danny could hear the man moving around, and then he heard a door shut.

'Listen, you little prick,' the man whispered, 'you'll end up dead if you carry on like this. Do you understand?'

'I'm going to the police to tell them who you are.'

There was a gasp of disbelief on the other end of the line. 'If you dare... I'll find you. I swear.'

'I need money and a place to live,' Danny said. 'Let me tell you how this will work. You will put five thousand pounds in cash in an envelope and leave it at an address that I will give you. If you don't, then I will go to the police and tell them everything. If you hurt me, I have told one of my friends who you are, and I've written everything down. My friend will take my story to the police if I don't call him every day. Do you understand?'

Danny cupped a hand over the receiver and breathed fast. His heart was going wild in his chest. He had thought this through, having read about this plan in a crime thriller. It was a good job he liked reading so much. It gave him ideas he would never have otherwise.

The man was silent for so long Danny thought he had hung up. 'Hello?'

'I'm here,' the man said. To Danny's surprise, he gave a short laugh. 'You're a good one, you know that?'

'Yes, but I can be really bad for you. Do you agree?'

The man let out a long sigh. 'I should've known this might happen. Listen to me good, kid. I will find you. And your friend. No word will get to the police. You can do what you like.'

He didn't hang up. Danny said, 'Fine. I'm going to the police now. Okay?'

Neither of them hung up. Both waited in silence. Finally, again to his surprise, Danny heard the man laugh.

'What's the address?'

Danny's heart did a crazy somersault. He felt like punching the air and screaming. His plan had worked.

'It's the Dodington Parkway train station lockers. The

second left from the bottom will be open. Put the money in there. Just leave, and don't look back.'

After a pause, the man spoke. 'I'll put ten thousand in cash. Can you keep that money safe?'

Danny frowned. 'Why are you giving me more?'

'I asked you a question. Can you keep that money safe?'

'Yes.'

'Good. Make sure you go to school. When you run out of money, call me.'

That had been Danny's plan, but he was confused now. Why was the man helping him all of a sudden? He felt a tinge of pride, a new emotion for him. He really had managed to scare this guy. What more could he get out of him? Time would tell. For now, it was best not to be too greedy. He also had to make sure he didn't make any mistakes and let the man find him.

'Don't worry, I will call you.'

# THIRTY-ONE

Benjamin Henshaw was pacing the narrow confines of his bedsit. He wondered what Brian was doing. He was in police custody, that he knew for certain. He hadn't tried to call him, just in case the cops tracked his phone. Ben's main worry was the car now. He needed to get rid of it before the cops found it. He had a plan, and it didn't involve Jacob.

Ben had been to the locker at the station and found the money. To his relief, it was all there. Jacob had delivered. Now, he had to put his own plan into gear. His phone beeped; it was a text from Jacob.

My man is five minutes away. His name's John.

And my name's King George V, Ben thought with a sneer. As if Jacob would tell him his man's real name.

The street outside was quiet, like the rest of Headington at this time of the night. Ben heard the noise of the car outside and parted the blinds. A balding man stepped out of a two-seater BMW. He didn't look like a gangster. For starters, he wore a tweed coat. In the streetlight, Ben could see his soft white hands and sloping shoulders. This guy looked more like an accountant than anything else. That made him breathe easier. He opened his door and slipped outside. There was a dark landing; the bulb that gave light was on the blink. Opposite there was a staircase. Ben left his door open, but turned off the light in his room. He stole up the staircase swiftly, his rubber-soled shoes not making a sound. He had a hammer in his hand, purchased earlier from a hardware store.

The man came up the stairs. He paused at the dark landing. There were only two doors for him to knock on, and only one that was open and also had the correct door number. It didn't take him long to go forward and knock on number seven.

Slowly, Ben uncoiled himself down the stairs, silent as a mouse. The man knocked on his door. Light from the street fell into the landing.

'Benjamin? Are you there?' the man said. He sounded nervous. He knocked on the door again, then stopped as he realised it was open. The time was now. Ben flew down the last couple of stairs and launched himself on the man. They crashed into his room, falling on the floor. Ben had the advantage of surprise. He was on the man's back, and he swung the hammer to hit the man on the back of his skull. He didn't hit him too hard; he didn't want him to die.

He punched him as well for good measure, and the man went limp. Ben shut the door. The other door across the landing remained closed. He turned the light on, making sure the man was unconscious, and frisked the man's pockets. He found a card holder with two credit cards and a driving licence. The man's name was Charles Topley.

'John my arse,' Ben muttered to himself. He put the card holder and the car keys in his pocket. He ripped off some bedsheets and tied Charles's hands and feet together. He opened his mouth and stuffed cloth inside it. He had packed his single holdall bag already. He shut the door, but didn't lock it.

He didn't want this guy to die. His ties were loose, and when he came to, he could get on his feet with some effort. When Ben took his pulse, it was strong.

He went out the door and stole down the stairs. He put his holdall in the rear of the BMW. The gas tank was full. He revved the engine of the Z4 once, enjoying the sound, then felt like an idiot immediately. He needed to make as little sound as possible, and he was doing the opposite. The clock on the dashboard said it was half past ten at night. Ben watched the street for a while. Headington was well known for being the town that had the John Radcliffe Hospital, but it didn't have much else. No one was around on the deserted high street, save a couple of people smoking outside a pub.

Ben pulled out and started to drive. He knew he had to get as far away as possible from Oxford. In many ways, the life he knew was over. And all for a few moments of madness. Remorse gripped him, twisting his heart. He had no choice but to go through with it now. At least he had some money, and he needed it. He thought of his parents once, and he could only guess the torment they were going through. He would contact them soon, with a burner phone, but to do so now would put them in a difficult position. The police would ask them if he rang them, and they would have to lie. His mother wasn't a good liar, and he didn't want his parents to be in that position. They had covered for him all his life. This time, he was on his own.

He took the M40 motorway towards London. Before he reached the capital city, he would branch off towards Dover. He had checked the ferry timetables and knew there wasn't a ferry at this time of the night. He would have to wait till the morning. It was risky, but so be it. Charles Topley would wake up soon and raise the alarm. Maybe he should've killed him, Ben thought, but immediately discarded the idea. He was in enough trouble as it was. No point in adding to the list.

Ben also thought Mr Topley might not report his assault

and his car as being stolen. To do so, he would have to explain to the cops what he was doing in a crappy bedsit in Headington in the first place. Jacob would tell his man to keep schtum. Ben hoped so, anyway. However, he had no doubt Jacob would try and hunt him down. Ben knew too much. Men like Jacob didn't like loose ends, especially those that could bite back in the future.

The roads were quiet, and the car was whizzing past the Waterperry junction. Ben thought of the hill where Lottie had lain and grief struck him again. He had a sudden, mad impulse to take the exit. For one last time, he wanted to see that place, like it was a shrine where he paid his final respects. The madness passed, and the car zipped down the road to Dover, and ultimately, France and Spain.

# THIRTY-TWO

Charles Topley couldn't breathe. He couldn't see anything either; he must be drowning. Hang on, he couldn't remember going anywhere near the river. He was driving... his memory flashed back, igniting the recent events. He tried to move, but the sudden pain in his head forced him to lie still. He panted through his nose, taking deep breaths. He was lying in darkness. It wasn't pitch black however, as there was some light. He shook his head, which was a bad move. A red-hot fireball of agony erupted in his skull, and his head collapsed back onto the dirty carpet. He screwed his eyes shut and focused on breathing for a while. His wife had taught him some Indian breathing exercises called Pranayama. It was yoga for the lungs apparently and helped to calm the mind by regulating breathing patterns. He did it now, concentrating on drawing in each breath and inflating his lungs. Something worked. He stopped struggling and visualised the air entering and leaving his body.

His tongue moved. He worked it to dislodge the horrible cloth stuffed in his mouth. He tried to move again, this time by using his legs. His feet and ankles were tied together, but he could move them. He scraped his legs backwards and was finally able to sit up, with his back to the bed. The pain in his head was unbearable, and the effort to sit almost made him pass out. He practised Pranayama again. Eight slow breaths in, and then out all the way till his lungs were empty. When he was done, he tried to move his hands. To his surprise, he wasn't tied that strongly. With some effort, he was able to loosen his wrists from the bedsheets that had tied them together. He blinked. It was early morning, maybe just after dawn.

His head throbbed, and his tongue was parched dry. Even the slightest movement sent pain crashing through his skull and made him nauseous. He managed to free his legs, then tried to stand but fell onto the bed. He patted his pockets. His phone, keys and wallet were gone. He touched the source of pain in his skull – it came away sticky with dried blood.

Did Benjamin do this to him? Charles had met Benjamin. He was from a well-to-do family, a typical Oxford student. Yet, there was always an edge to him. A watchful silence that used to make Charles wary of him. Something about the boy wasn't quite right. And after what happened to Lottie...

Jacob had manipulated the boy into watching Lottie, too. It had become Benjamin's obsession, which suited Jacob fine. Instead of getting a private detective, he used the boyfriend. He didn't care that Ben was strange in the head. Or was it Jacob who was messed up?

Charles touched his forehead. Bloody Jacob. He cursed the day he had agreed to work for him. They were friends from Oxford, and while Jacob managed the family business, Charles had gone to work in public relations, or PR. He did well for himself, rising to partner of his firm. Now, he rued he ever had agreed to become Jacob's campaign manager and use his old media contacts for that purpose. His wife had told him not to. She never liked Jacob, and she had been bloody right.

Charles licked his dry lips and stood. The room was bare – only a desk, chair and single bed, with an empty wardrobe in the corner. There was a sink on the wall, with a mirror. Charles splashed some water on his face; he gasped when he saw his own image. He looked pale, cheeks sagging; he seemed half dead.

Somehow, he manged to make it out of the door. He staggered outside and took in a few deep breaths of the morning air. Across the road, there was a phone box. There was a woman inside, and Charles waited outside impatiently. The woman came out and gaped at him. *Yes, I must be a sight for sore eyes,* he grumbled to himself.

He sagged against the phone box and dialled 999. He told the police he'd been assaulted on the street and left unconscious till the morning. He didn't mention the bedsit, but he did tell them he recognised his attacker. Benjamin Henshaw had taken his wallet, phone, keys and car. By the time he finished, the police said they were sending him an ambulance: help he was grateful for.

While he waited, he rang Jacob, who answered on the first ring.

'I've been calling your phone non-stop. What happened?'

Charles told him. There was silence for a few seconds, then Jacob exploded.

'He's a bloody kid. How could you let him do this to you?'

'He's less than half my age and twice as strong.' Charles raised his voice and felt sick again. His head was spinning circles. 'Anyway, I told the cops. I had to.'

'You did what?' Jacob was aghast. 'You called... why?' He spluttered in rage, unable to complete what he started.

'Because you and I are done, Jacob. Finished. I'm not the man to wash your dirty laundry. You can do that yourself.'

# THIRTY-THREE

Nikki was woken up by the buzzing of the alarm. She raised her groggy head, and then reached out a hand to shut the infernal device. It didn't work, and that's when she realised it was her work phone. She really needed to change the ringtone. She looked at it and saw Switchboard calling her. It was seven in the morning, and she should've been up by now. She sat up in bed and answered.

'Control calling DI Gill, do you copy?'

'Hello, Control, this is DI Gill.'

'Hold on, please.' There was a brief silence, then a male voice came on the line. It was Monty, much to her surprise. Why didn't he call her mobile? She reached for it on the bedside table. She had two missed calls from him.

'I heard just now. They called me, as I'm duty SIO for the week,' Monty said. 'Benjamin Henshaw assaulted Charles Topley, who happens to be Mr Winspear's campaign manager. Then he escaped with his car.'

Monty filled her in with the rest of the details. Nikki was up, shrugging into a bathrobe as she put him on the loudspeaker.

'I've put out an all-points bulletin. Mr Topley was assaulted in Headington, late last night. Benjamin's had the whole night to drive somewhere. He could be anywhere.'

Nikki thought for a while. 'He'll try to get out of the country. I wonder if he's got his passport? Check all the ports and harbours.'

'Kristy and Nish are trying to get hold of his passport and driving licence details. Once we have those, we can issue port alerts.'

'Thanks. I'll see you at the nick in half an hour.'

Nikki had a quick coffee and shower. By the time she got to work it was 8 a.m. Monty was in the room with Kristy and Nish. There was a tray of coffee and doughnuts on the table, and Nikki reached for her second cup of the morning, while eyeing the doughnut with longing.

'We're getting the CCTV images any time now from traffic,' Kristy said. 'That should give us some idea which direction he's headed.'

Nikki leaned back in her chair. She locked eyes with Monty, who was sitting opposite. She ignored the warmth that fluttered in her belly as he stared at her intently. She took a sip of coffee.

'The question is, what was Mr Topley doing at that time of the night in Headington?' She looked around the room.

Monty spoke first.

'This wasn't a random attack. They had arranged to meet, I think. It's possible Jacob orchestrated it, as he wanted to find out where his daughter was.'

Nish said, 'Or, he wanted to grab Ben for himself. Maybe he sent more men with Charles, but it all went wrong?'

Kristy waved her hand. 'Nope. He wouldn't send his campaign manager to grab him unless he was setting a trap.'

Nish looked at her like she had two horns on her head. 'That's exactly what I was suggesting?'

'Children, please.' Nikki laughed. 'Which hospital is Mr Topley at?'

'John Radcliffe.'

'Fine. Take a statement from him ASAP, please. Find out if he knows what Jacob knew; did he know Topley was going to meet Ben? Which makes me wonder if Jacob has been in touch with Benjamin all this time, but didn't tell us anything.'

Monty caught the thread of her thoughts. 'Which means Jacob knew that Ben, who was the last to see his daughter alive at the party, was hiding in Headington. Or maybe Mr Topley did. Either way, these two men could have been in touch with Ben, which is concerning.'

Nish said, "The fingerprints on the necklace you found matches with Charlotte. There's another set of prints on it, but it's unknown. No matches on IDENT-1. We're waiting on any DNA samples, but so far, Justin's not found any skin fragments."

"At least we know she was by the lake," Nikki murmured. "Perhaps she met Benjamin there." She locked eyes with her team. "We need to find him quickly."

# THIRTY-FOUR

Benjamin woke up to the sound of seagulls. He was confused at first, and had no idea where he was. He had that peculiar, lost feeling, stranded between two worlds in a vacuum. Then his memory returned. He was on a single bed, in a small room with damp on the walls. It was a cheap bed and breakfast, and he had paid in cash in the early hours of the morning. He sat up in bed, rubbing his eyes. He could see the street from his second-floor window. A couple of beggars sat in the bus stand. People stood waiting for the bus. In the distance he could see the outline of the ferry. One was in dock, and there was one every hour from 10 till 4 p.m. It had started to drizzle, the grey skies reflecting the shabby grey terraces and the black road. Dover wasn't the prettiest of towns.

Ben had taken out the battery of his burner phone. He wouldn't be using it again. Which meant Jacob could never contact him again. He went to the common bathroom in the hallway, which was less than pleasant. He put his holdall in the locker downstairs and went out. It didn't take long to walk to the high street. Dover's main road was depressingly shoddy. But it did have a second-hand phone shop, just what Ben needed. He bought himself another three unlocked phones with new SIMs.

Then he hailed a cab and took it to the ferry station. He wasn't concerned about missing the ferry leaving in a few minutes. There would be another fifteen in the day, according to the timetable. While in the cab, he put on a pair of glasses and a baseball cap. He got off at the ferry stop. It was a hive of activity. Regular passengers were lining up with cars, ready to roll into the upper decks. The lorries went into the lower decks. The giant ferry ships were like floating citadels. A loudspeaker was issuing reminders of the times to board cars onto the ferry.

Ben walked up to one of the checkpoints. He could see the man at his terminal through the glass windows. There was a line of cars in front of him, and the man was busy. Ben stepped closer, and he was about to rap on the windows when one of the screens on the man's terminal caught his eyes. He stopped breathing for a few seconds. His own face was staring back at him from the screen. It was an old photo on his driving licence, but there was no doubt it was him.

He couldn't believe it. Gasping silently, he stumbled backwards. The man in the terminal turned at the sound and saw him. The man frowned and came forward. He stared at Ben, who averted his face. Did he recognise him? How many more photos did they have? Ben slunk away, turning his back.

'Hey, you,' the man opened his window and shouted.

*Shit. I need to get out of here.*

Ben began to walk out of the ferry station concourse as fast as he could. A police car was parked in front, and the door opened and a burly officer stepped out, wearing his bulletproof chest rig. He had a black shirt on, and the sleeves bore the logo of Border Security Force. His radio was chattering, and he turned it up as he walked towards Ben. To his horror, the policeman called out to him.

'Excuse me, sir.'

*Damn, damn it all.*

It was possible the officer just wanted to have a word, but Ben dismissed that idea before it arrived. He wasn't calling out to anyone else, was he? He moved faster. He barged into a man's suitcase and almost fell over.

'Stop!' the officer shouted behind him.

Ben broke into a run. There was a queue of cars, lining up to get inside the ferry's cavernous breast. He jumped over the bonnet of a car, sliding across. He could hear running feet behind him. Ben swerved between people and their luggage, hoping no one stopped him. To the right, on the far side of the concourse exit, there was a tram line and a taxi rank. If he could get that far... With a screech of tyres another police car pulled up just a few yards from him. A man and woman dressed in the same black uniform jumped out, shouting at him.

Ben threw all caution to the wind. He couldn't get caught, not now. He ran full tilt, people scattering in front of him. He played football and rowed, and he wasn't short of speed or strength. He made it to the end of the concourse, then grabbed hold of the railings that separated the area from the tram station. He vaulted over just as the police caught up with him. Two of them started to scale the railings, while the other ran for gates that opened out of the concourse into the tram station.

Luckily, there was a tram just waiting to leave. Ben was able to make it in time. But so did the two cops who had scaled the railing. Ben watched in fear as they clambered up to the platform and made for the tram. With a hiss, the doors began to close. Ben ran to the next carriage just as the cops got to the door. The doors slammed shut, and the tram took off. Frustrated, one of the cops beat his fist on the door but the tram accelerated, and it left the station.

Ben sat down quickly, aware people were staring at him. He had no idea where he was going. A couple of stations flashed past, and then he got off at one called Ashmore. He came out of the station quickly. Before he left the building he looked around to make sure there wasn't a police car. To his relief, apart from the taxis and people dropping off there were no other cars. He took a taxi back to his seedy bed and breakfast. He was now glad he had parked the car miles away, in an industrial warehouse, and walked a few miles into Dover. The cops would definitely be looking for the car. He wondered who raised the alarm. As he did so, he shivered when a thought struck him. Did Topley die? Is that why... or had Jacob agreed to call the cops now that he was out of control? Well, both of them could stuff themselves.

Ben watched the entrance of the B&B for a while. He didn't see any policemen. He went in and retrieved his holdall from the lockers. He paid his dues, then went outside and flagged down another taxi.

'Folkestone,' he told the driver. 'And make it quick.'

Folkestone was close to Dover, and on the ferry lines. But he wasn't going to take the ferry. He had a better idea.

# THIRTY-FIVE

Nikki and Monty stood to one side of the gurney in the morgue. Dr Sheila Raman's assistant, Oleyemi, or Ole, for short, pushed the trolley of instruments away. Charlotte's skin was pasty white. Her eyes were open, staring blankly at the ceiling.

'Let's start at the head. A couple of small bumps and cuts, nothing major. The back of the head was pushed into grass, and I found some strands of it. And some soil as well, attached to her hair.' She called to Ole, who returned with a vial that bore what looked like a few filaments of straw.

'Looks simple but it's important. Sometimes grass, or any vegetation, can hold radioactive minerals that are unique to the region. I will look for any and if there's a match with any soil matter around here I will let you know. That way, we have a location of death.'

Nikki said, 'Maybe it was the hilltop. Or if not, you might find something.'

'Worth a try.' Sheila smiled. 'There's dirt on her shoes as well, but that will be from a variety of soil. Unusual for soil to end up on the head.'

She moved to the face. She pulled down an eyelid and asked Nikki to look at the conjunctiva.

'What do you see?'

Nikki could feel Monty leaning next to her. She said, 'Jagged black lines near the bottom of the eyes?'

'Very good. What are they?'

Nikki shrugged. 'I'm not a pathologist. Leave that to you.'

Sheila grinned. 'Sorry, I'm getting a little technical on you now. Those marks are haemorrhages. Old blood from capillaries that have burst. They burst due to an increase in pressure in the eyeballs.'

Monty murmured softly, 'And that happens when the throat is squeezed, increasing pressure in the head and neck.'

'Perfect.' Sheila beamed at him. 'We often see this in strangling. In fact, that sign is what we call pathognomonic or diagnostic of a strangling. Sometimes killers can be clever.' Sheila dropped her voice dramatically, and her dark eyes twinkled in a sort of devilish delight. 'They can brush the marks away, and using gloves often masks the pressure marks. I once had a case where the killer had used paint to cover the marks of his hands. It was the sub-conjunctival haemorrhages that gave the cause of death away.'

She leaned back like she had just delivered a performance and smiled. 'Sorry. I get a bit carried away sometimes.'

Nikki waved a hand. 'Don't be silly. It's good to know. Any other pearls of wisdom?' She was glad the ice had broken. Initially she had thought Sheila to be a little aloof. But under the hard exterior lay a soft, congenial person. Her husband had died, and she had no children. Nikki suspected she was lonely, and Sheila's work was her life.

'Moving to the nose,' Sheila continued. 'Grains of white powder seen. It's cocaine, street level, and cut with sodium bicarbonate. And from her blood test, toxicology sent me back a report that shows high levels of alcohol, cocaine and powdered MDMA, or the active ingredient in ecstasy.'

Monty whistled. 'She was having a good party.'

'She was,' Nikki said, 'until it all turned to misery. It must have been easy to overpower her, given she was so intoxicated.'

'Not only that,' Sheila said. 'The person who strangled her was most likely sober. Strangling someone when one is on a cocktail of drugs is virtually impossible. It's likely to be a man, as strangling needs a good deal of physical strength. I'm not saying it can't be a woman, but she would have to be very strong indeed.'

'I'm just thinking aloud,' Nikki said. 'All the students at the party would be in a similar state. The killer was probably an outsider.'

'Not necessarily,' Monty said. 'He might've kept himself sober just to commit the act. It gave him the perfect opportunity. She was so drug-addled she offered no resistance.'

'Still,' Nikki said. 'He would have to lure her out of the party, kill her, then deposit her body on the hilltop. It was all planned in advance.'

'The party went on till the early hours of the morning,' Monty said. 'He could have followed her outside, or hidden somewhere by the lake, out of sight. He waited until dark, then transferred the body in his car.'

He looked at Sheila, who was listening to them. 'What was the time of death?'

'Between 9 and 10 p.m., I think. It's not an exact science, as you know. I would say it's closer to nine than ten though. It was light when she died.'

Nikki frowned. 'Why do you say that?'

'She was outside. The grass in her hair meant she was lying down. There's bits of grass and vegetation stuck to her dress as well.'

'Sorry to hold you up,' Nikki said. 'Please carry on.'

'Okay. Not much to see in the mouth. Neck is the major site of trauma, as you know. No fingerprints I'm afraid. He was wearing gloves.'

She moved on to the chest. 'Neck chain still missing, I presume?'

Nikki nodded. 'The pendant wasn't recovered. Presumably the killer took it.'

'No trauma to the chest save some bruising. Also similar bruising on the abdomen.' She pointed to the blackening marks on the body. 'Interestingly, I found semen in the vaginal vault. She had sex recently. Sperm doesn't stay alive for any more than seventy-two hours, and most die within a day. I would say she had unprotected sex the day of her death. There was a lot of motile sperm in the vagina.'

Nikki nodded. 'No point in jumping to conclusions, but she was with her boyfriend at the party. By the way, the boyfriend has since assaulted her father's employee and escaped in his car.'

Sheila's mouth fell open. 'Really? I would agree he is looking like the prime suspect. If you can get a DNA swab from him...'

'To match the DNA from the semen,' Nikki finished for her. 'We need to catch him first.'

'Any idea of where he might be?' Sheila asked, zipping up the body. To Nikki, it was more than a body. A living, breathing young woman who had a bright future ahead of her and was now gone. Nikki knew she had to get closure for Charlotte's family. She hated cold cases, but they did exist. Practical realities meant a detective's resources were finite. After a few months, the trail would go cold. She shook her head. She needed to resolve this in the next few days.

'He's in the car, heading south on the M40. Probably towards London. That's all we have from CCTV now.'

'If he's heading south,' Sheila said casually, as they walked back to the dressing room, 'he could be heading for the coast. Plenty of ferries to the continent.'

Nikki stopped abruptly. 'You're right. But he might not take a ferry at all. We have his passport details.' She turned to Monty, her eyes wide. 'Oh my god.'

'What?' Monty asked.

'I think I know what Ben's planning.'

# THIRTY-SIX

'Can you please provide the names of the students who run the Piers Gaveston Society?' Kristy asked again. She was in the university administration building, a huge neoclassical, dome-shaped block on the outskirts of the main college areas. It wasn't far from Oxford train station, framed in the window in the room. Kristy was facing the window, and in between sat the assistant university registrar, a bearded man past middle age. He had a cheap blue suit and tie on, and his round belly strained the fabric of his shirt. He adjusted his glasses and cleared his throat.

'Such societies are not formal organisations recognised by the university, Miss...?'

Kristy and Nish had shown the man their warrant cards already, but he had clearly forgotten their names.

'Detective Constable Young.'

'Right, Miss Young. As these organisations are informally arranged, so I'm afraid I don't have a list of their names.'

'The students I have spoken to say that you do. They might not be officially recognised, but they do use the college

180

premises, and the university organises security for their social events. Is that not true?'

The man looked uncomfortable. 'That may be so, but I do not have their names to hand.'

Nish cleared his throat. 'The information is required in connection with a murder investigation. A student of Merton College has died. She attended a Piers Gaveston summer ball last Thursday.'

The man paled visibly. He shrank back in his chair, and then slowly took his glasses off. He licked his lips before speaking. 'Is that true? I mean, that's unheard of.'

'Not really,' Kristy said. 'Twenty years ago, another student died of a drug overdose after a similar event. There was an extensive police investigation at the time, and the university gave all assistance demanded.' She finished with an emphasis, and stared at the man. His Adam's apple bobbed up and down, and he pulled at his collar as if it was suddenly tighter.

Kristy knew why he wasn't happy. Oxford's drinking societies were shrouded in secrecy. The clubs' membership was limited to the very wealthy, and sometimes college tutors were also members. They were known to ignore the strict college rules, and get away with it, for a good reason – the tutors were often involved in organising their events.

'We can speak to our superiors,' Nish said, his tone hardening. His jet-black hair was gelled back, and his dark eyes glittered. Kristy thought he looked rather dashing.

'And we can issue a formal search warrant for the names, if that's what you would prefer.'

The registrar gaped at Nish for a while, then passed a hand through his beard nervously. 'There won't be any need for that. Let me see what I can do. Would you mind waiting outside? I need to make a few phone calls.'

Nish looked at Kristy, who nodded. They went to their car,

which they had parked in the car park of the Saïd Business School, named after the donor, Wafic Saïd.

Nish lit a cigarette, and Kristy watched him take a drag and release the smoke. 'Cancer sticks,' she said.

'Yes, right little buggers,' Nish said. 'I'm trying to cut down. Down to five a day now.'

'I gave up last year,' Kristy said, arching her eyebrows. 'Nothing but willpower. But put on weight thereafter, so not good.'

Nish shrugged. 'You're in good shape.'

'Thanks. Is that a compliment?'

Nish rolled his eyes. 'No, I'm taking the piss. Only saying what I see.'

Kristy stared at him, then grinned and looked away. It was a self-conscious grin. She felt something for Nish, but she wasn't sure if the feelings were reciprocated. They worked well together, and she wasn't sure if she wanted to jeopardise that. Also, her previous scumbag boyfriend had left her with a deep mistrust of men. He had cheated on her, then revealed he was actually married. What a fool she'd been. For a whole year, she had sworn off men. But she was warming to Nish. He was also single.

Her phone rang, breaking into her thoughts. It was the registrar. 'I got two names. They were in the register of events for a drinking event at Merton College earlier this year. The same names appear over the last two years, at various events, and all of them were for Piers Gaveston.' He paused. 'I must tell you, Miss Young, giving out these names is against university policy. For example, they are considered exceptions to the Freedom of Information Act. But I understand this is a police matter.'

'What are the names?' Kristy asked, signalling to Nish. He walked over, pulling out his notebook and pen.

'Brian Robinson and Jonathan Speller. Brian is at

Somerville, and Jonathan at Oriel. I can give you their addresses if you wish.'

'Does Brian Robinson live on Rosemary Lane, near Lady Margaret Hall?'

There was a longer pause, accompanied by the clicking on a keyboard. 'Yes.'

'Please send me Jonathan Speller's address.'

'He lives in college.'

Kristy hung up, and they decided to walk to Oriel, which was nearby, on the high street, and opposite the Bodleian Library. It was at the heart of Oxford's college complex. They took the narrow, winding lanes through the covered market and arrived at Oriel.

'It's right next to Merton,' Nish remarked. 'Charlotte Winspear was a student there, right?'

'Yes.'

They walked past the smaller Oriel College entrance, and stopped outside Merton. There was no doubt Merton was much larger, and grander, than Oriel. Of course, no Oxford college, Kristy knew, was as palatial as Christ Church, just around the corner. They could see the massive Tom Tower from here, craning its neck above all other colleges, and Oxford's High Street.

'The guv came here to take a statement from Charlotte's tutor, didn't she? That Greg Keating bloke.'

'And James Baden Powell, the politics teacher. She didn't like him much, neither did DI Sen. They wanted DNA swabs from them.'

In the hurried morning meeting they had, Nikki had told them about her suspicions regarding James.

'We could go and do it now,' Kristy suggested.

Nish demurred. 'Let's make sure this guy's not left the college. All the students are headed back home now.'

'Good point.'

They walked into Oriel College and showed their warrant cards at the porter's lodge. One of the porters took them around the edges of the ubiquitous quadrangle, and they entered the more modern-looking stone building through an arched opening. Oriel didn't look as ancient as some of the colleges, Kristy thought.

'This is the fellows' quarters mainly, but some students live here as well, in their final year.'

'Only a couple of years between a final-year undergrad and a fellow,' Nish remarked. 'After a one-year master's degree, they can become a junior fellow.'

The porter shrugged, and Kristy glanced at him over her shoulder as they went up the narrow stone staircase. Nish was bringing up the rear.

'How do you know about that?'

'I wanted to do a master's in Criminology after I finished uni. Decided to join the force instead, and save it for later. Planning to apply later this year. Might get a bursary from the force.'

Kristy didn't say anything, but she was impressed. They reached a landing and walked down a passage with doors on either side.

'Where were you planning to apply?' she asked.

'Believe it or not, Royal Holloway has one of the best Criminology departments in the country. It's close to the Holloway prison as well.'

'Why didn't you do it straight after uni?'

Nish shrugged. 'There's a number of reasons. Firstly, a job teaches you much more than a degree ever will. Learning on the job is the best lesson. Secondly, I needed the money.'

'Why do the master's at all then?'

Nish smiled. 'It's not to learn how to conduct an investigation. We're doing that now. The degree is really to understand the statistics of crime, and understand where crime comes from. I mean what sort of people commit crime, their lives, even their biology. But on a population basis, not individual.'

Kristy shrugged. The porter was walking ahead of them, swinging his keys, oblivious of their conversation.

'Sounds like you really want to do it.'

'Definitely. Crime fascinates me, like you. I mean,' he stopped, embarrassed. Kristy arched an eyebrow at him and grinned.

'Sorry?'

'I mean to say, I'm fascinated by crime as much as you are. God, that came out wrong.'

The porter stopped in front of a door and knocked. Kristy could hear the faint sound of music from inside. The door opened and a dishevelled-looking young man stuck his head out. His unruly mop of blond hair fell over his forehead. He brushed it back, standing straighter when he cast his eyes over Kristy and Nish. They didn't wear uniforms, but they looked official in their suits.

'Jonathan Speller?' Kristy asked.

'Yes?' Jonathan looked anxious. He was average height and skinny. His cheeks and forehead had a few acne spots, and he looked pale, with red-rimmed eyes. The white shirt he wore was stained and crumpled, like he'd slept in it after a night out.

Nish and Kristy showed their warrant cards. 'Can we come in, please?' Nish asked. 'We need to ask you some questions regarding Charlotte Winspear.'

Jonathan frowned, then he looked shocked, like he'd just remembered something. 'Ben's girlfriend? I mean, Benjamin Henshaw.'

'Yes.'

The room was surprisingly big for a student, and as they walked in, it became obvious it was more of a suite than a room. There was a sitting area with a TV and sofa. The bedroom door was to one side and it was shut. Pizza boxes, beer cans and bottles of wine lay on the floor, as did a woman's handbag and high heels. A few glasses rested on the table, a couple still half filled with wine. A faint smell of cigarette smoke hung in the air. Jonathan seemed to sense it as well, as he hurriedly opened the window, letting in sunlight and fresh air.

'Please have a seat.' Jonathan pointed to the sofa. 'Apologies for the state of my room. May I ask what it is about?'

Kristy studied him. His accent was polished, and it hinted at an upper-class upbringing. He had lost his initial panic and seemed more settled. His intelligent grey eyes were observing her closely, his mind trying to figure out the purpose behind their visit. From his twisting hands, and his erect spine, she could tell he was expecting bad news.

'Charlotte has died, I'm afraid to inform you. Her body was discovered on Friday.'

Jonathan's jaw sagged, and his cheeks turned pale. He sat down heavily on a chair next to the sofas. If he was acting, it was an Oscar-worthy performance.

'How could this happen?'

'Did you know her?'

'Yes, I mean, I saw her around obviously. She was Ben's girl, so I kind of knew her.'

'How well did you know her?'

'Not that well. She wasn't at my college. I only saw her with Ben and at parties.'

'Did you ever visit her house? Where she lived with her friends?'

'Once, I think they had a house party.'

'Do you know her housemates – Francine, Tabatha and Victoria?'

'Vaguely, yes. Francine came to the PG parties, and she also went out with a friend of mine. I think they broke up this year however.'

'When did you last see Charlotte?'

Jonathan thought for a while. 'At the summer ball.' His eyes widened. 'Hang on, that was last Thursday. Are you saying...?'

'Yes, we are,' Nish said. 'Her body was found on Friday, but it seems likely she died on Thursday night. We cannot confirm if it happened at the party, but it's certainly a possibility.'

Jonathan's breathing rate increased. He looked like he'd swallowed something unpleasant and needed to vomit.

'You need to think carefully about what happened to Charlotte at the party, Jonathan,' Nish said. 'You were one of the organisers, right?'

'Ah, yes. I am. I was, I mean.' He rubbed his hands together like he was trying to warm them up. 'I saw Charlotte there when she arrived, as she was with Ben, I remember that. After that, I don't recall seeing her to be honest.'

'Who was she with, apart from Ben?'

'Her friends were around, like Francine. And others whom I've seen but don't know their names, sorry.'

'Did she seem upset, or angry?'

'Not that I recall. I was busy as well, with the party.'

'Okay, this is important, Jonathan,' Nish said. 'Do you remember seeing Charlotte with another man at the party?'

Jonathan frowned, then shook his head. 'Not that I recall. She was with Ben when I saw her.'

The bedroom door opened and all eyes turned towards it. A young woman stepped out in a bathrobe. Her long dark hair fell past her shoulders. She was strikingly pretty, with an hourglass figure. Her dark eyes flashed at Jonathan.

'Darling, what's going on?'

He went up to her, and she held his hands. 'Something terrible has happened. Do you remember Charlotte? Ben's girlfriend?'

'I met her once. But I don't know her. Why?'

'She's dead,' Jonathan explained to the clearly shocked woman.

Kristy asked, 'Are you a student?'

The woman shook her head. 'I work in Oxford as a paralegal.'

'I met Natalie at a bar in the town. She doesn't know much about Oxford, and she wasn't a student here.'

'And you didn't know Charlotte?'

Natalie shook her head.

Kristy fixed Jonathan with a gaze. 'You, Brian and Ben were the organisers of the Piers Gaveston Society. Is that correct?'

Jonathan gulped. 'Yes.'

'How many members are there in total?'

Jonathan looked around the room like a trapped animal. 'Sixteen.'

'Could I please have their names?'

'Uh... not sure I can do that without their permission.'

'They were at a crime scene and could potentially have seen something important.'

Jonathan frowned. 'There were two hundred and fifty people there. What about the rest?'

'We need the names of all the guests, and we will contact all of them, starting with the people who knew Charlotte. Did any of the members of PG know her?'

'Apart from the three of us? No.' Jonathan shook his head. 'I don't think so.' He licked his dry lips, and sat down on the sofa, Natalie still holding his hands.

'Look, I don't know how this happened. It's appalling. But I really don't know any more than what I've told you.'

Nish and Kristy exchanged a glance. 'Okay, that's fine,' Nish said. 'But we still need the names of all the PG members, and everyone at the party. You must have a guest list?'

Jonathan nodded, his shoulders slumped in defeat.

* * *

Jonathan waited till the detectives left. He gave them ten minutes, then fished out his packet of cigarettes and ran out of the apartment. He went down to the quad, lit a cigarette and called the number.

'Hello,' a male voice answered.

'The police were here. Charlotte's dead.'

'I know. They came here as well. Calm down.'

'James, I told them I didn't see her with you at the party. They asked me specifically.'

'About me?' James Baden Powell's voice was sharp.

'No, not you. They asked if I saw Lottie with anyone apart from Ben. I lied. I lied for you, James.'

'Calm down. Just breathe.'

Jonathan did just that, while pulling on the cigarette. 'They also asked for names of the PG members.'

'You can't do that,' James said. 'It's against the rules.'

'I know. But what do you want me to do? I can't get hold of Ben or Brian.'

'Brian's been charged with possession of cannabis. The idiot tried to run from the cops after they discovered the hydroponics in his room.'

'What?' Jonathan stopped pacing. He felt his chest was hollowing out. 'Where's Ben?'

James paused for a while. 'I don't know. But it's not looking good. He's not answering his phone.' He continued. 'Whatever happens, don't give the police my name. I've spoken to them already. It's okay, I'll manage it. But if they know I'm a member of PG, they will suspect me.'

'But...'

'Do you want to graduate with a First?' James's tone was dead cold.

Jonathan was silent.

'Good. Then do as I tell you. And get a new phone. Never call me from this number again.'

# THIRTY-SEVEN

Seventeen years ago

Danny was now eighteen years old. The man who was his biological father had put him into a boarding school. He called his father Paul, although that wasn't his real name. They had decided that when Danny referred to his father in public, he would call him Paul Alison.

There was a knock on the door, and one of his boarding school friends poked his head in. 'The results are out,' the boy said breathlessly. 'Everyone's meeting in the main hall. Come on!'

The boy disappeared, and the door shut. Then he sat there, listening to running feet echoing down the hallway. It was August, and the A-level results were out. Unlike the other boys, Danny never felt any excitement. He didn't really understand why people laughed or cried. He felt his own pain, but that was all. At boarding school, he barely had any friends. Andy, the boy who just informed him, was one of two boys whom he knew vaguely. He was a loner and had always been so.

He heard the excited chatter of voices again as the boys

returned to their rooms. When the sounds had ceased, he rose and went down to the main hall. On the main noticeboard, behind the glass sheet, white pages had appeared, with the boys' names and their A-level results next to them. Thus the weight worked here, in this posh boarding school. It was made public, no one got individual envelopes.

A few of the boys were still standing round, some looking sad, others elated.

Danny found his name and saw he had received two grade As in Mathematics and Physics, and a B for English. He shrugged and walked past the boys, who paid him no attention. He didn't speak to anyone. His phone rang, and he saw it was his father.

'Did you get your results?'

'Yes, I did: two As and a B. That means I'm going to the college I wanted to.'

'Yes, I guess you are. Clever boy. Well done.'

Danny detected the note of pride in the man's voice. He still thought of him as *the man*. The man who had stood by while his mother's life slowly disintegrated. The man who did nothing as him and Molly were taken into care, and Molly died. The man he had to blackmail in order for him to act as his father. The man he would never trust.

Time had proven him right, because Paul had used him time and again. He suspected this time would be no different.

'What do you want?' Danny asked.

Paul chuckled. 'You know me too well. I want you to check out someone. He says he's going on business trips, but I think he's having an affair. He's a competitor of mine, and if I can expose his affair, his wife will leave him. He gets his money from his wife's family. If she divorces him, he gets nothing.'

Danny thought for a while. Although his relationship with his father was a transactional one, there were moments when he enjoyed working for him.

'What if he's eliminated altogether?'

There was silence for a while. 'What do you mean?' Paul asked.

'What if no one saw him again?'

Paul sounded cautious. 'You have to be careful. I can't have this getting back to me. What do you plan to do?'

'I don't know. I need to see where he lives and establish a routine for him.'

Danny had done this before. He had spied on a couple of men Paul had asked him to. Danny had broken into their offices and stolen hard drives, posing as an employee. Perhaps it was time now to take it further.

'Send me the details,' Danny said. 'I'll see what I can do.'

* * *

It was a dark, cold night. A drizzle had started, and it whispered against the brick wall that Danny leaned against. He wore a black hoodie that covered his face, black jeans and trainers. He was hidden, the streetlamps not reaching into the nook of darkness between the buildings. He watched the man stand outside the apartment block, smoking. His name was Mr Barrington, and he owned a media company that was publishing things about Paul that were less than pleasant. Danny had followed Mr Barrington over the last three weeks, from his mansion in Buckinghamshire, to this apartment in Soho, London. This was where his lover, an attractive brunette called Giselle, lived.

Danny slipped out of the shadows and walked towards Mr Barrington. The man was in his sixties, and he wore glasses. The street was heavy with traffic, and a truck was lurching in their direction. Mr Barrington was standing at the edge of the pavement, and he didn't see Danny sneak up beside him. As the truck bore down upon them, changing gears as it picked up speed, Danny shoved Mr Barrington into the road. The older man fell, and the last thing he saw was the glaring headlights of the truck running over him. He screamed and there was a sickening thud of his flesh getting mangled under the tyres. The truck driver couldn't stop; he had run over the unfortunate Mr Barrington by the time the wheels stopped turning.

Danny didn't stand by to watch. He ran as soon as he shoved the man under the truck. He had plotted his route out in advance. He made for the Soho canal, and jumped over the railings into the canal path. No one would see him here. He kept running, heading for the train station.

It was past midnight by the time he got back home. He called Paul to let him know.

'Well done, my son,' Paul breathed down the phone, excited. 'Are you sure no one saw you?'

'The street was quiet. I was the only one there. The rain helped. I don't think you need to worry about this guy again.'

'Excellent. I will check tomorrow. But I—'

'Hang on,' Danny interrupted. 'I want something in return. I've got good grades now, and I want to get into a top university. Use your contacts to get me in. I also want money, not just to pay for university, but to buy a house.'

'What?' Paul sounded incredulous. 'A house?'

'I took a lot of risk for you today,' Danny said calmly. 'And don't forget what I know about you.'

'Listen, you little shit,' Paul raged. 'If I wanted to, I could get rid of you by making one call.'

'But you won't. Because I'm your son. You are my dad, after all.'

There was silence filled by the sound of their heavy breathing. They had reached the impasse of their peculiar relationship again: that point where neither knew what to say.

'All right,' Paul said finally, 'you will need a new name and identity. I'll be in touch.'

# THIRTY-EIGHT

Benjamin walked the last two miles into Folkestone. The huge port area was clearly visible from the hilltop he had crested. A long line of lorries, occupying two lanes, snaked along the motorway, ending in the port. The twenty-one miles of the English Channel unfurled to the horizon, brilliant shafts of sunlight cutting in through the clouds to illuminate the choppy waters. Calais and the coast of Normandy were obscured behind rolling sheets of mist and fog. The hulk of a ferry was visible to the left, at the other end of the port. Ben wasn't interested in that.

His eyes fell on the long line of trucks. English goods travelling to mainland France and beyond. Since Brexit the lines had grown longer. More form filling and box ticking since Britain left the European Union. There were days when the queues could stretch five miles down the road, blocking the motorway. But more trucks meant more opportunity for certain people.

Ben was tired from climbing with the holdall on his back. He chugged from a bottle of water, then got up. A stiff breeze from the Channel cooled his sweaty brow. He came down slowly till he saw what he wanted. It was a tent, hidden between two jutting rocks on the hill. He crept closer and stopped when a man stepped out from behind a rock, blocking his path. The man was slim, his faded blue army coat tattered and a couple of sizes too big for him. His face was pale, cheeks and eyes sunken like he'd not eaten for days. His dark eyes stared at Ben curiously and without malice.

'Who are you?' the man asked, his English heavily accented.

'I need your help.'

'For what?'

Ben pointed at the long line of trucks. 'To get on one of those.'

A face poked out of the tent, and it was a woman. A child's face magically appeared beneath her chest. The child was no more than ten years old, and he observed Ben with fascinated eyes. His mother pushed him back inside the tent, but she stayed there, watching Ben carefully.

'What do you want?' the man said, stepping forward and blocking Ben's view of the tent. His tone was sharper.

'I told you.'

'What makes you think I can help?'

Ben put the holdall down. 'I'm going to reach inside my pockets, okay? Don't worry.'

He took out a wad of twenty pound notes and held it out. 'There's two hundred pounds in there. I've got another two hundred if you get me on a truck to France.'

The man's eyes glittered when he saw the money. Behind him, the woman asked him something. He waved a hand without looking back, shouting at her.

'I'm not undercover police. In fact, I'm a lot like you.' He smiled at the cruelty of fate that had landed both this unfortunate man and him in the same place, on a hilltop in Folkestone. 'I've got no home left any more, and I'm running away for a better life.'

'Better life?' the man smiled. 'Is that what you think you'll get?'

'Better than what I've got now.' Ben didn't smile back.

The man's face darkened. His lips turned upward in a snarl. 'I don't trust you. Why are you here?'

'I just told you. I'm alone. I have nowhere to go. I need to escape. Trust me. The sooner I get on that truck, the better.'

'We wait until nightfall. One of the men will come up from the port. There are more tents here, all holding people like me. Many with families. I speak to man who comes up the hill. You pay him. He takes you to the truck driver.'

'Okay.' Ben lit a cigarette and offered the man one. After some hesitation, he took it. Ben took a deep drag. His father always said smoking would kill him, but Ben thought he had to die of something. He tried not to think of his parents. A cloud of anguish suddenly covered him, dampening the adrenaline. His younger sister, perhaps he would never see her again. And he didn't dare call them, even on a burner phone, until he crossed into France. In fact, only when he was in Spain, his ultimate destination. His father had a villa on the island of Mallorca. Hopefully, the old man would let him stay there for a while.

'Where are the other tents?' Ben asked.

'You can't see them. They're all hidden behind rocks.'

'What's your name?'

The man looked at Ben in a strange way. Ben could understand why. Someone with his accent had probably never asked him his name. The man thought for a while, then shrugged.

'Saleem.'

'Where are you from?'

'Why do you want to know?'

Ben raised his hands. 'Look, I have nothing to gain by giving you away. I'm not with Immigration. If you don't want to tell me, that's fine.'

A funny expression flickered across Saleem's face, like he'd just heard a joke. 'Where are you from? And what's your name?'

Ben decided to lie about his name. 'John Dennison. I'm from London.'

'And you're running from your country to France... why?'

'I answered your questions. Where are you from?'

Saleem hesitated for a while. 'Syria. We landed from Calais on the back of a truck. Now waiting for a truck to take us into England. We applied for asylum seeker status in Dover immigration centre.' He raised both hands. 'We are asylum seekers because we're fleeing the civil war in Syria. But they won't give us that status. Hence, we have to do this.'

'Where will you go?' Ben asked. He couldn't help but be fascinated by the desperate, tragic life these people had.

'There's a network of illegal immigrants. I can work in restaurants as a chef or waiter. I used to be a chef in Damascus. I've cooked in the royal palace for our president.' He smiled sadly. 'But here, I have to take what I get. There's also building sites where they pay in cash and don't ask questions.'

'Where will your family live?'

'There are landlords who also take cash and don't ask questions.'

Ben could see the whole picture now. 'It's a racket. It's run by the smugglers who bring you over from Calais in the first place.' He sat down, resting his butt on a rock. The view was gorgeous, with the sun having broken through the bank of clouds. The sea was bathed in sunlight, and more of the French coastline was visible. Saleem sat down as well and lit one of his own cigarettes. The tent opened, and the woman's face appeared again. So did the child's. This time, the boy got out of the tent and walked over. His mother watched as Saleem reached out a hand and pulled the boy towards him. He wriggled on his father's lap and stared at Ben. He spoke to his father.

'My son is asking what your name is.'

'John. Nice to meet you. What's your name?'

Saleem whispered to his son. The boy said something Ben didn't catch. 'Afzal,' Saleem said. 'He's six years old.'

'Very sweet boy,' Ben said.

'Thank you.'

This was no time to be philosophical, but Ben couldn't help thinking if he had met Saleem under different circumstances, they could even be friends. Life could be strange like that sometimes.

'Keep yourself hidden,' Saleem said. 'Immigration or police don't normally come up here, that's why we're here. But they sometimes have helicopters flying overhead, or even drones these days.'

He pointed to the rock outcroppings that provided effective shelter from prying eyes. 'Get some sleep if you can. It could be a long night.'

* * *

Ben had fallen asleep in his sleeping bag, and he woke up with a start. It was dark outside, and there was a chill in the air. He could barely make out Saleem's face, who was sitting on his haunches close by.

'It's time,' Saleem said. 'The man is on his way up.'

Ben rubbed his eyes; he marvelled at how quickly he had passed out. His bones ached from lying on the hard ground beneath the sleeping bag, but at least he'd had some rest. He smoked a cigarette and packed all his stuff. When he came out of his shelter he saw Saleem had packed his tent. His wife and son sat close to him, with their bags. He heard footsteps behind and turned to see a man coming up the hill.

The man crouched in front of Saleem, and they had a hushed conversation. Saleem pointed at Ben. The man walked over and sat in front of Ben. He shone a torch in his face, and Ben lifted his hands at the sudden light.

'Who are you?' the man asked in an English accent. He lowered the torch, but kept the light on Ben. 'Don't lie to me. I'll cut you up and throw you in the sea.' He took something out of his pocket, and Ben saw the light flash on the curved blade of a knife.

'I'm running away. I can't say any more.'

'You got money?'

Ben nodded.

'One thousand in cash. I need it now, not later. Take it or leave it.'

Ben had no choice. He took the money out and handed it over. The man counted the cash, then stuffed it in his pocket. He signalled to Saleem, who walked over with his family.

The smuggler pointed down the hill. The line of trucks had grown longer in both directions. Headlights glowed in the dark like a string of garlands decorating the land before the dark sea.

They descended. Beams of light lit up the hill, and Ben could see families joining them. Babies cried and their mothers hushed them. Ben felt like he was having an out-of-body experience. Was he really here, with these sad, unfortunate people, paying a human trafficker money to get him over the Channel? He shook his head. He didn't have the luxury of such thoughts.

At the bottom of the hill, another man was waiting for them. More than half of the group diverged, going in the opposite direction to Ben. Saleem came up to him.

'Goodbye, John. Hope you find what you're looking for.' He held out his hand.

They shook hands. 'You too, Saleem. Best of luck to you and your family.'

Saleem went to say something more, but then just nodded, and he walked away. Ben called after him, and the man turned.

Ben said, 'Take out your phone.'

Saleem frowned, then did as he was told. 'Take down this number,' Ben said. 'Don't call it now, but in about a week. Say who you are, and that you met me. Use the initials BH to identify me. John is not my real name. Do you understand?'

Saleem stared at Ben for a while. Then his face crumpled, and the phone shook in his hands. In the faint glow from the trucks' headlights in the distance, Ben could see tears glistening in Saleem's eyes. Ben grabbed his shoulders. 'Don't cry. We don't have time. Take down this number.'

Ben gave him the number of his burner phone. Saleem saved the number, then grabbed Ben's hands.

'I hope we meet again.'

'I don't know where,' Ben said sadly. 'But I hope we do. And even if we can't, maybe I can help you.'

'Come on,' the people smuggler called out. 'We need to move.'

Ben joined the small group walking down to the trucks. He didn't know how he could ever help Saleem, but maybe he could try.

They came to the edge of the hill, which gently sloped down to the bank where, after a set of barricades, the motorway started. The trucks were waiting in line.

'Stay here, behind the bush. Lie low and don't make a bloody sound. Got that?' the man said. His accent was cockney. There was a murmur of assent. The man's eyes fell on Ben. 'You on your own, right? Okay, come with me.'

Ben followed the man. They bent low at the waist and scurried down the bank to the motorway. Ben remained on the ground, while the man went and spoke to a driver who was standing outside his cabin, leaning against the door. Ben kept his eyes on them. The smuggler turned and waved towards Ben. He rose and ran across.

'You'll sit in the cabin with the driver. He'll say you're his driving partner. Here's a fake passport. Show it to them. Your name's Jack Evans. Don't worry, they don't check it normally, if you're English.'

'Isn't it safer to get in the back? I can hide better there.'

'It's not that simple,' the driver said, sucking a tooth. 'Immigration checks the hold of every truck now. They also have sniffer dogs. These days, special compartments have to be made to hide immigrants.'

The man glared at Ben. 'Like I said, get in the cabin. And let him do the talking when you get to the ferry gates.'

Ben nodded, and he pulled himself up into the cabin. The driver cast his gleaming eyes over him. Ben glanced at him and sat up straighter. He wouldn't hesitate to smash his face in if he tried any funny business. It was a long drive. He couldn't fall asleep.

The truck ahead changed its lights. Ben's driver started his engine and the massive vehicle lurched forward. Ben's heart was hammering in his mouth as the black-shirted immigrant officer raised a hand at the security gates, and the truck shuddered to a stop. The driver hopped off. He presented both passports to the officer. They spoke briefly, then the officer rapped on the passenger side of the cabin. He waved at Ben.

'Come down, please.'

Ben cursed, but he had no choice. He could try and run again, but this place was busy, and it was crawling with police and the Border Security Force. Not to mention the cameras everywhere. He doubted he would be so lucky as last time.

Reluctantly, he alighted from the cabin. The officer looked at the passport, then stared at him. Ben had a sinking feeling in his heart. He should never have agreed to this. That passport probably had a photo that bore no resemblance to him. The officer ordered both of them to follow him inside the office.

Ben saw his photo plastered on the wall as soon as he walked into the office. He closed his eyes. The gates had shut behind with a soft click. Three more officers appeared out of nowhere, and they stood behind Ben and the driver.

'Mr Henshaw,' the first officer said, smiling at Ben, 'we have been expecting you.'

# THIRTY-NINE

Nikki and the others were in her office. Kristy had taken a phone call and she lowered the receiver with an excited look on her face.

'That was Kent Police. Ben Henshaw's just been handed to them by Border Security. He was caught trying to escape from Folkestone in a freight truck.'

Nikki clapped her hands in delight. 'Excellent. Where is he now?'

'In Folkestone nick. They will transfer him first light tomorrow.'

'He should be here by 9 a.m. then,' Nikki said, standing. She paced the room, suddenly restless. 'We need a DNA swab, sent to Dr Raman, to see if there's a match with the semen sample.'

Nish was sipping his coffee. 'Guv, we need DNA samples from the tutors as well. Shall we do that today?'

'Did you get DNA samples from the student you saw – Jonathan Speller?'

'Yes, and also Charlotte's housemates,' Nish said. 'Dr

Raman has the samples. She's also got the victim's parents' and brother's samples – none had a match on any of the victim's body fluids.'

Kristy said, 'No DNA match with Brian Robinson either, Ben Henshaw's housemate.' And she looked at her laptop screen. 'No fingerprint matches on IDENT1 for any of the suspects.'

Monty was leaning back on his chair, arms folded behind his head. His jacket was off, and his shirt sleeves were rolled back to his elbows, revealing muscular, hairy arms. Nikki could feel his eyes on her, and she was trying to ignore them. The more she ignored it, the harder it got.

'Seems like we have got our number one suspect,' Monty said.

'Let's go through our list of suspects, and what their motive or opportunity might be,' Nikki suggested. 'Would you like to do the honours?' she asked Monty, handing him the marker pen. He obliged, going up to the whiteboard.

Nikki said, 'Number one is obviously Ben. Then we have her father. I know that sounds odd, but consider what he had to lose. There's something not right about that man.' Monty wrote Ben's name as number one, and Jacob Winspear's as number two. 'He had a motive, but did he have the opportunity? If Charlotte was killed during or after the party, how could he have been there?'

'Unless he met her somewhere afterwards... okay that's a reach,' Nish said. He frowned at Kristy, who was shaking her head. 'What? I'm just guessing.'

'Not a good guess,' she said, pursing her lips and looking serious. Then she grinned, and Nish rolled his eyes.

'Number three would be her friends,' Nikki said. 'I'm not sure how close Francine and Taby were to Charlotte. She was definitely closer to Vicky, at least recently.'

'And Francine and Taby were at the party. But they didn't see much of Charlotte.'

'That's the funny thing,' Nikki said. 'No one saw much of her after she got there. It makes me wonder if they're speaking the truth. Jonathan Speller didn't know much, did he?'

'Nope. I asked him if he saw her there with someone else, but he denied it.'

'I asked Brian Robinson as well. He gave pretty much the same response.'

Monty said, 'Maybe she spent time with someone else. This person took her outside. Maybe that's why no one saw much of her.'

Nikki raised a hand. 'Okay, let's get back to the suspects. Did her housemates have the opportunity to kill her? Yes, they did, as they were at the party. But motive?'

She drew blank stares from all three faces. Monty said, 'We need to know more of their lives. But anyway, the way she was killed points to a man.'

Nikki pursed her lips together and frowned. 'Yes, true. But there's something about the girls I don't like. Vicky clearly didn't want to speak to us in front of Francine and Taby. And when she did, it was important. We need to find the other men Charlotte was seeing. One was someone she had known for a long time.'

'Do we need to speak to the girls again?' Kristy asked.

'Yes. I think we should bring them in, one by one. They knew her, and they were at the party. I want a statement from each one of them.'

'Guv, it sounds like you think Benjamin Henshaw didn't kill her,' Nish said.

'He had the best opportunity, but what was his motive? He has something to hide obviously, or he wouldn't run. He was driving near the crime scene just before the murder. But was it him? Why? Because he was at the party and one of the organisers. Surely he couldn't just leave like that.'

Monty said, 'Are you suggesting someone else was driving his car?'

Nikki looked at him. 'Exactly. Neither Jonathan Speller, nor Brian Robinson said he left the party, did they? His absence would've been noticed.' She raised a hand. 'Ben is still our prime suspect. But that doesn't mean we close our minds to others.'

'Right. On to number four. Her tutors?'

'Yes, I guess so. With Greg Keating, she had Vicky as her tutorial mate, so we have a witness. But with James Baden Powell, she was often alone, wasn't she?'

Monty nodded. 'And he seemed uncomfortable with the questions. We need to get him down to the station.'

'Yes. But can we first do some background checks on him, please? Do either of the tutors have any PCNs?'

'None,' Kristy said. 'Nothing on HOLMES either.' Home Office Large Major Enquiry System is the UK's largest supercomputer database for crimes.

'Okay. Build up a timeline of their movements prior to last Thursday. And delve into their employment history more. Where did they work before Oxford? Where did they live?'

'Okay, guv,' Kristy said, noting it in her diary.

'Are we going to see Charles Topley?' Monty asked. He had called John Radcliffe Hospital already, and Charles was now stable enough to take visitors.

Nikki nodded. 'Yes, and after that I want to see Mr Winspear again. Please let them know we're coming.'

The phone rang and Nish answered. He looked at Nikki. 'Call for you from Switchboard, guv. External call. He will only identify himself to you.'

Intrigued, Nikki took the phone. She assumed this was work-related, otherwise the person would've called her work phone. Her ex-husband contacted her sometimes if there was news to be shared about Rita. But this was different.

'Hello, is that DI Nikki Gill?' The smoothly modulated voice was familiar, but Nikki couldn't place it at first. Then she remembered.

'Mr Keating? Is that you?'

'Greg Keating, yes. Thank you for speaking to me.'

'No problem.' Nikki looked at her team, and she shrugged. 'How can I help?'

'It's something that I need to show you. Charlotte left a book behind after one of her tutorials. It was about late nine-teenth-century British politics. It reminded me of a place I'd seen Charlotte as well, which I had forgotten. But I think you would want to know. It would be helpful if I could see you in person. Would you mind coming to my office?'

'Yes, sure. On my way.' Nikki hung up and stood. Monty shrugged into his coat and held the door open for her.

\* \* \*

Within fifteen minutes, they were at Merton College. A different porter in the same blue uniform directed Nikki to the Fellows' Quarters where Mr Keating had his office. Monty stayed in the car; Nikki had felt, from Greg's tone, he wanted to speak to her personally.

'Please, do come in,' he said, holding the door open when Nikki knocked. 'Can I get you a drink?'

'No, thank you,' Nikki said. Greg was wearing a suit today, a nice blue cut with a dark shirt. It hugged his athletic frame. He picked up a book from his table and handed it to Nikki. It was a politics textbook, a light paperback that looked new.

'Open it,' Greg instructed.

Nikki did so, and her hand stopped at the first page after the cover. There was an inscription, written in black ink.

*To my dear Potty Lottie, Love, James xx.*

Nikki looked up at Greg, confused.

He said, 'The book was in her satchel. Her Economics books must've been at the bottom, as she emptied out her satchel and placed this book on the table. Vicky was there as well, and this happened at our last tutorial. You can ask her.'

'Who's James?'

'She came here just after her Politics tutorial.'

Light dawned in Nikki's eyes, and she felt a sudden jolt in her spine. 'James Baden Powell?'

'Yes.' Greg leaned his buttocks on the edge of his table. He looked uncomfortable. 'Look, I don't know what to make of it, but I feel I should be frank with you. I remember now that a while ago, maybe sometime last year, I saw Charlotte coming out of a house in Summertown. I was on my morning run, and it was a Sunday. I go that way into Port Meadow and then circle back.'

'Did Charlotte see you?'

'I was in my jogging clothes, and no, I don't think she saw me. I was on the other side of the road. It was winter, and there was a light drizzle, I think.'

'I see. And whose house was it?'

'It belongs to James. His family is well off, and that's how he can afford a house there, because Summertown isn't exactly cheap. He had invited the college fellows for some drinks at a garden party once, that's how I knew the house.'

Nikki crossed her arms on her chest and looked at him askance. 'Why didn't you tell me this before?'

'To be honest, you hit me with such shocking news I didn't know what to say, or do. My mind was a mess, I'm sorry.' He indicated the stack of papers on his desk. 'Plus, there's been all this to deal with: end of term exams. It's only when I found the book that my memory suddenly clicked.' He frowned and looked to the floor, then back to Nikki.

'I'm not sure what to make of it.'

'Leave it with me, please. I must say, from the language James has used, they had a personal relationship that wasn't just a standard student teacher one.'

'Yes, I have to agree.' Greg rubbed his cheek and adjusted his glasses.

'It does leave me uncomfortable though,' Greg finished.

'Like I said, leave it with us. If James ever contacts you then please let us know ASAP.' She raised her eyebrows. 'He hasn't tried to, has he?'

'No. If he does I will certainly let you know.' He paused, then clicked his fingers. 'There's an SCR dinner – sorry, Senior Common Room dinner tonight. I am invited, and I'm sure James will be as well.'

'Do you know if he's in his office now?'

Greg shook his head slowly. 'Sorry, no. You have to ask at the porter's lodge, and even they might not know. But you can try his office. I can take you there.'

Nikki wasn't sure if she would remember the narrow convoluted entrance into the building, and she didn't want to get lost. She also wanted to get Monty, but it was a bit late.

'Sure.'

She waited in the narrow, cold hallway while Greg locked his door. She followed him out to the back of the building, through a maze of narrow walkways that led to a beautiful secluded garden. Large trees shed their lily-white flowers on the green grass and there was a small pond to one side, its still waters reflecting the blue sky.

'The Fellows' Garden,' Greg explained.

'Lucky for the fellows,' Nikki said.

Greg smiled. 'The wealthier colleges, like Merton, have

209

very nice arrangements for the academics, I must say. One of the draws of coming to Oxford.'

Wealth that was centuries old, Nikki knew. Money channels now lost in the mists of time, but still producing a healthy return in the stock market. That's what kept Oxford ticking over. She kept her thoughts to herself and just offered a bland smile.

Greg walked in through a back entrance, where he presented his ID card to a digital pad. The pad beeped, and he pulled on the door handle. They went up another narrow flight of stairs, this time circular, and still cold as hell. They came out on a wider passage and Nikki recognised it now. James Baden Powell's door was in the middle of the corridor. Greg knocked on it and waited.

Nikki moved past him and tried the door handle. It was locked. She wrestled with it a few times, then gave up.

'The porter's lodge will have a key,' Greg suggested.

'Thank you. We will handle it from here, Mr Keating.'

'Greg, please.'

'Okay, Greg.' Nikki smiled at him as they walked down to the main quadrangle, where she bade him goodbye.

'I hope this helps your investigation, and I haven't caused any undue trouble.'

'Believe me, you've helped us a great deal.' Nikki waved at him and ran across the quad. She stopped by at the porter's lodge. The man in the blue shirt came out, surprised.

'James Baden Powell, the Politics lecturer. We need to find him ASAP. Do you have any idea of his schedule?'

'No, ma'am, I don't.'

Monty got out of the car when he saw Nikki running towards him. Breathlessly, she explained what happened.

'Did you get the address from Greg?'

'Yes, I wrote it down.' Nikki fished out her little black notebook from the inside pocket of her light black jacket.

'No harm in heading there now. If he's not here, then he might be at home, unless he's fled already.'

'Good idea.'

As Monty drove out, Nikki called Kristy to alert her about James.

# FORTY

James Baden Powell was glad he had the afternoon off for research. It gave him time to think about his predicament. He hoped that idiot, Jonathan Speller, hadn't panicked and told the police about him. He didn't like that Inspector Nikki Gill. She wanted to sniff around everywhere like a bloodhound. She made him uneasy. And that silent, staring great big oaf – Inspector Monty Sen. Why the hell was he even there, anyway? A fine pair they made – not!

He could feel an itching in his skin. The cops suspected something, he knew. Could they know about him and Charlotte, already? He wouldn't put it past them. Now, he regretted bitterly that he hadn't been more discreet. Lottie had been to his house, and although they'd been careful, it'd been a mistake. He couldn't turn the clock back now. Soon, the cops would realise he was a member of the Piers Gaveston Society as well, along with two other lecturers from other colleges. But neither of those two knew Lottie.

He shouldn't have been at the summer ball either. Thoughts of that evening were now like a knife twisting in his guts. Why the hell did he have to go there? Although phones were banned at the party, and no CCTV was allowed either, the students would've seen him. He turned up late on purpose, so they'd all be off their heads on the cocktails of drugs there. And Lottie... she was higher than a cloud, but once the music got pumping she got her moves going. It was electrifying dancing with her, but James also got jealous when other men tried their luck with Lottie. He saw her talking to other men as well: her friends. Truth be told, she could have any man she wanted. And she liked showing that off. It gave her a kind of power.

In any case, what's done was done. Now, it was only a matter of time. Time that was running out quickly. The cops visited Jonathan yesterday. That meant the clock was ticking. James picked up his phone and made the call.

'Thirteen fifty is confirmed?' he asked.

'Yes, sir. Will you require transport?' a female voice asked.

'No, thank you.'

James hung up and went into his bedroom. He had started packing last night, and all he had to do now was add the finishing touches. He checked the time: almost midday already. It wouldn't take long to get where he wanted. And then, he could fade away for the summer in the south of France, where his family was waiting. Hopefully, by the time he came back, Lottie's death would have blown over. The police would have some new crime to solve.

He heard a police siren in the distance and ignored it. It came again, this time closer. He left his suitcase on the bed and strode to the living room. He parted the curtains, his body taut with tension. A Thames Valley Police van raced down the road, lights flashing and sirens loud, evidently on its way to a crisis somewhere. James relaxed, sagging against the wall. He straightened quickly and rushed to the bedroom. He finished the packing and arranged his bags by the door. His phone beeped.

James frowned. He didn't recognise the number. It had

called twice before already. As he held the phone, it rang again. He ignored it. He took his passport and driving licence. His sixth sense was tingling. It was time to leave. He went to the door but the calling bell stopped him in his tracks. He put his eye to the peephole and his heart shrank. It was DI Nikki Gill and her tall sidekick.

# FORTY-ONE

Nikki pressed on the buzzer for the second time. There was no answer. They were outside a house just off the main Summertown road on Woodstock Road. A BMW M4 was parked on the front drive, and Monty took his time casting his eyes over it.

The ground-floor front bay windows had curtains drawn across them. There were no signs of life.

'Sure this is the right address?' Monty whispered.

'It's what I got from Greg, and there's no reason for him to lie.'

Monty pointed to a wooden gate to their left, between the house and the boundary fence of the next property. 'That's another way in. We don't know if he's at home though, right?'

'He's not at the college, and Kristy didn't find him booked for any lectures at the university. He should be at home...'

Her words trailed off, and when Monty looked at her, she knew what he was thinking. When a man was hard to find, and didn't answer calls, there was only one explanation. He was trying to get away.

The house was on a quiet corner, and they could hear birds

chirping in the trees. There was a deep thudding sound from inside.

'What was that?' Nikki asked. Monty was moving already. He stood in front of the wooden side door, which presumably led to the side access of the house.

'I'll give you a lift up,' he said, cupping his hands in front of the door. Nikki looked at the top. An absence of spikes, and given the door was no taller than Monty's head, she could jump over to the other side. She didn't hear a dog barking, and she would've heard that as soon as she pressed the bell.

'You coming?' Monty asked. 'Or shall I go over myself?'

Without a word, Nikki grabbed Monty's shoulders; she put a foot in his cupped palms. He lifted her up, and she was able to grab hold of the top of the door. She scrambled for purchase, and finally lifted herself over, then jumped down. Monty came shortly afterwards. Nikki was already running down the passage, and she came out into a long, narrow garden. At the far end, she could see a man running into the assorted plants.

'There he is!' she shouted and ran. Monty had longer legs, and he overtook her. By the time they got to the end, the man had slipped through a fence gate and locked it from outside. Monty pulled at the gate, to no avail. It was a sturdy gate, built into the fence. He took a few steps back, then kicked at it with all his might. It took three good kicks for the hinges on the side to break, before the gate crashed open. They heard the sound before they saw anything. That was due to the smoke that blew in their faces from the exhaust of a car as it zoomed out of the rear garage. Nikki coughed and covered her face; her eyes stung and the inhaled dust clogged her throat. She could make out Monty; his eyes were running and he coughed, then spoke into a radio.

'Control, this is MS1. Suspect escaping in dark green Range Rover, on Woodstock Road, heading north. No, I haven't got the registration.'

They went into the garage. It was a makeshift space, the roof made of cement and corrugated sheets of iron, with a floor of gravel. A stench of gasoline and rubber assaulted their nostrils. They came out into a side street. The tyres had left black marks on the road.

'Come on,' Monty said, running for the front, where their car was parked. Within minutes, he had put the siren on and reversed the car out into full traffic.

Nikki was holding on for dear life, the radio squawking from her breast pocket. 'Good job you keep up with the OCT.' The Obstacle Course Training was the annual simulated driving exam that all police force members had to do.

Monty didn't answer, but made a sound in his throat. His face was a mask of concern. The green Range Rover was visible far ahead, speeding away on an open stretch, having jumped several red lights.

'He's heading for the A40,' Nikki said on the radio. 'Attention all units.'

'Copy that, guv,' one of the traffic guys said, his subsequent words drowned in the wail of his own siren.

'Where do you think he's going?' Nikki asked.

'I don't know,' Monty said. His jaw was set tight, and a bead of sweat trickled down his cheek. 'He's got to take an exit soon at the roundabout.'

Nikki watched the Range Rover move in and out between cars, then take a left at the roundabout, heading for Kidlington. She frowned.

'He's not taking the A40 to join the motorway?'

Monty's knuckles were white as he manoeuvred the CID-issue Ford between cars that had come to a halt to let them pass.

'Maybe he wants to escape into the Cotswolds.'

'Good luck on those narrow lanes. Oh shit!' she shouted as a van almost ploughed into them from the side, missing narrowly. Monty continued to accelerate till he got to the roundabout, then took the first exit on the left at speed, the tyres screaming in protest, and the rear of the car thrusting out to regain balance. She fell against Monty, then straightened herself.

'You okay?' he asked.

'As good as you are,' she replied with a laugh. Truth be told, this was a throwback to chasing Albanian gangs on the inner-city streets of Dagenham and Peckham. She had assumed a quieter life in Oxford, but it seemed Oxford had other ideas.

Traffic thinned out as they left Woodstock Road, one of the main arteries into Oxford. A sign for Kidlington passed by and, shortly after, another for Oxford Airport. Nikki glanced at Monty. 'Airport?'

'Yes,' he said grimly. 'I can't see him though.'

At that moment, the green Range Rover emerged ahead of a van, whose wide back was covering their view. The Range Rover dangerously overtook a lorry in front of it, careening into the opposite lane, almost crashing into a car that pulled over to the side and went off the road. The car went down the grassy curve and smashed into fencing, narrowly avoiding a tree trunk.

'He's going to kill someone and himself,' Nikki said. She spoke into her radio. 'Control, this is NR1. Request heli support, over.'

'Transferring, hold on.'

Nikki knew the two helicopters for this area of TVP were based at RAF Base Benson, about fifteen miles south from Oxford. She prayed a 'bird' was available. Within seconds, she was speaking to the air marshal, who assured her one bird was available, and he could have it airborne in the next fifteen minutes.

'He's taking the exit for the airport,' Monty said.

Nikki relayed the information on the radio, asking Kristy to contact all the Cotswolds airports to ground all flights till they arrived on scene.

Monty took the exit for the airport, and Nikki was flung

against him again, and it seemed for a while Monty would lose control of the car. The Ford swerved and fishtailed, and Monty swung the wheel in the direction of the spin. Nikki braced herself. She knew going in the direction of the spin was the right thing to do, but it was scary. Like an old-time skier going off-piste, but staying on track, Monty managed to straighten the car. Ahead, the airport and its control tower loomed. This airport was a small, civilian affair, mainly managing flights for celebrities and rich people. James had money, obviously, if he could fly out of here, Nikki thought.

A couple of cars were waiting at the checkpoint, their way into the airport blocked by a bar. The Range Rover stopped, and a man jumped out. He ran across the checkpoint, past the surprised guards who, for some reason, did nothing to stop him. With a sinking heart, Nikki saw him vanish through the gates into the airport.

'Leave the car here,' she said.

Monty nodded and pulled the Ford over. They had arrived at the checkpoint, and Monty showed the guard his warrant card and quickly explained the situation. Then they ran as fast as they could into the airport building.

There was a crowd, with a few queues waiting for check-in. An information board above displayed the arrivals and departures. Escalators rose up to a first floor from the lobby area. Nikki heard the low boom of an aeroplane taking off from the runway. There was a commotion to their left, and a woman shouted. A man was running up on the escalator, pushing people out of the way. It was the driver of the green Range Rover. Monty was moving already, pushing past people. Nikki spotted a woman in a blue uniform and peaked black hat, who had an Airport Security logo on the sleeve of her right arm. The woman realised what was happening and ran past Nikki towards the escalator. Nikki pulled on her arm and flashed her warrant card in her face.

'Get an alert out for that man.'

'We heard already. All flights are grounded, don't worry. We didn't make any announcements.'

'Good.'

Nikki and the security woman ran after Monty. The man was now on the first floor, and he was running for the flight gates. From the opposite end Nikki saw another security man approaching. People stood to one side as she shouted her job title. She was panting as she skidded to the left, following Monty. The man had run into the queues of flight security, and suddenly she couldn't see him any more.

Monty had come to a standstill as well, chest heaving, hands on his waist. 'I can't see him,' he gasped. 'He's wearing a brown coat and jeans.'

'He's taken them off. He wasn't wearing a cap earlier. Spread out. Look for a man with a cap on.'

Two more security men joined, and they filtered down the lines, looking at all the faces. Nikki saw a man bending down to tie his shoelaces. He wore a white shirt, and the back was sticky with sweat. He also wore a black baseball cap on his head, and he looked familiar. His chest was moving as he breathed heavily, like he'd just run a mile. He'd been clever, getting rid of the coat and putting the cap on. But there was no place for him to escape, and he knew it.

He didn't look up as Nikki approached. She stopped in front of him and bent her face down to his. Sweat covered his face, and he wouldn't look at her. It was James; she recognised him easily.

'You're under arrest, Mr Baden Powell, for driving recklessly, and also as a suspect in the murder of Charlotte Winspear.'

# FORTY-TWO

With the culprit in the meat van, Nikki and Monty drove back in the Ford. The adrenaline rush was fading, and Nikki was suddenly feeling tired. Her personal phone rang, and it was Rita. She answered.

'Hi, Mummy.'

'Everything okay, darling?'

'Yes. Am I coming this weekend?'

'Of course you are.' Wires had been crossed, clearly, but she'd never say no to her daughter. 'I'll pick you up from the station on Friday, usual time. And you're staying for the whole week, yes?'

Rita didn't reply for a few seconds, which meant she'd made plans with her friends. It wasn't fair on the teenager, who was on the cusp of having her own life. Now she had to divide that life between London and Oxford. It deepened Nikki's guilt. Unhappy as her own childhood had been, she hadn't had to go between two homes. When Rita was born, Nikki had promised she would give her a good life. And now...

'Why don't we talk about it when you're here?' Nikki said

softly. 'We've got stuff to do. Going up to Stratford–upon-Avon, right?'

'Oh yeah, cool,' Rita replied brightly.

'See you on Friday, but if you want to come sooner, just call me, okay?'

'Okay. Bye.'

'Love you, darling.' Nikki wanted to make kissing sounds, but she didn't want to in front of Monty. She hung up and sighed. Rita was happy when they were together. She just hoped she was happy back in London, where her friends and school were, and logically, her life as well. They had to make the best of a difficult situation. Nikki'd had to leave the Met after that case that went horribly wrong. She was injured and off sick for almost two months, and she had to deal with the guilt of the dead family. London's gridlock of streets had become a prison for her.

'Coffee?' Monty asked.

'Oh yes,' she agreed; it was just what she needed. They stopped at a café and recharged with coffee, and Monty had a quick cigarette. Nikki had stopped smoking, but she eyed him with envy. A drag of nicotine was just what she needed now. Instead, she sipped her coffee. That was good enough. Her time off in London had taught her she needed to take care of herself. She was overworked, dealing with a dead marriage, and she had a child to raise. Life was making too many demands on her, and she was running on empty. She had to prioritise. That meant looking after herself, for Rita's sake. She loved that girl more than anything else.

'Both suspects are in custody now,' Monty remarked, bringing her back to the present. He crushed the ciggie butt in a bin.

'We should speak to Charles Topley before we get back to the nick,' she said. 'The John Radcliffe is on the way.'

'Good idea.'

* * *

They drove to Headington. Visiting was still ongoing, and the nurse showed them to Charles's bed. He wasn't there, and they found him in the sitting room, reading a murder mystery. He had a white bandage wrapped around his head. The charge nurse introduced them, and Charles looked carefully at their warrant cards, before nodding his approval. The nurse took them to a private interview room and closed the door.

'Do I need a lawyer?' Charles asked first.

'That depends,' Nikki said. 'You're not under suspicion, but we need to understand why you saw Benjamin Henshaw that night.' She didn't add any more details about Ben just yet.

Charles took his time to answer. He was in his sixties, but he was obviously strong and able, still. Despite his injury, he seemed calm; he gazed at Nikki with clear eyes.

'When you have lived for as long as I have, Inspector, you want to leave the world without regrets.'

The comment surprised Nikki, but she sensed it was a portent of something important.

'What do you mean?'

'I have known Jacob most of my life. He's a close friend, and now a business associate. Well, I spearheaded his campaign.' He picked up the newspaper from the chair next to him and showed Nikki the first page. It was the *Oxford Gazette*, a local newspaper. There was a headline on the right column of the first page:

Tory Councillor Jacob Winspear becomes Member of Parliament for Oxford West and Abingdon.

'It seems your campaign was successful,' Nikki said, glancing at it.

'But for every success there's a price.' Charles paused and

bowed his head. 'Jacob was worried what Charlotte's political interests would do to his campaign. He's a well-prepared man. He met Benjamin when Lottie invited him to the house one day for dinner. Jacob took his number and stayed in touch with him. Eventually, he asked Ben to report on Lottie's activities.'

Charles paused. Nikki rose and filled a plastic cup with water from the dispenser in the room. She gave it to Charles.

'Thank you,' the older man said. He drained the cup. 'After Brian was caught, Ben got scared. He knew he had to escape.'

Nikki raised a hand. 'Hold on. When we went to search their house, Brian obviously ran and we had to chase him down. But Ben had already gone. We didn't find him, and he never came back to the house. So, what you're saying doesn't make sense. Ben knew something was wrong *before* we came to their house. Is that correct?'

Charles paused for a while, his eyebrows lowered as he thought. 'I'm not sure. You see, I wasn't in touch with Ben. Jacob was. He can tell you more. I'm not sure why Ben wasn't there. But I do know he was hiding in Headington, and Jacob asked me to see him.'

Monty looked at Nikki. This was an important revelation, and they both knew it.

'What did Jacob say?'

'He wanted me to collect Ben's Range Rover, which he knew the police were looking for. I guess Ben told him. I was meant to drive it to a garage in Botley, where Jacob knew the mechanic. He would get rid of the car. Please don't ask me how.'

'Why did you agree to do this?' Monty asked. 'Surely you knew the risks involved?'

Charles was quiet and downcast. 'Over the years, Jacob has helped me in my career. Introduced me to influential people in the media. And he was paying me well for this job. I owed him.

He sold it to me nicely. It was about getting Lottie back, he said. Ben could help us, but we needed to get him out of trouble.'

'At that time, Jacob didn't know that Lottie was dead?' Monty asked.

Charles spread his hands. 'I don't know. I realised there was a lot Jacob wasn't telling me. I was foolish to agree; like you said, I should've known the risks. I did it for a friend, but he's not my friend. He uses people to fulfil his aims, and he's used me.'

'What do you think Jacob knew about Lottie's recent movements? Did Ben tell him she was at the party?'

'He was always worried about Lottie. Her radical left-wing views, her drug-taking and social life were a concern. He thought it would affect his campaign. Horrible as it sounds, I can't deny that her being out of the way helped him.'

Nikki repeated her question, and Charles shook his head. 'Sorry. Short answer is – I don't know what he knew. Lottie didn't come home after the party on Thursday. It wasn't until Monday that Jacob felt something was wrong, and that's when you came to visit him. It all exploded after that.'

Charles looked at them in turn. 'Was Jacob behind Lottie's death? No, I don't think so. She was a difficult child but, deep down, he loved her like any father loves his daughter. Her death was a surprise to him.'

'Do you think Ben did it?' Monty asked.

The question hit a nerve. Charles's face lost colour, and his nostrils quivered. 'It was him who tied me up and...'

Nikki nodded; no further words were necessary. 'Unless he had an accomplice, which we doubt. We have CCTV footage of him driving your car.'

'If he can do that, what else is he capable of?' Charles whispered.

'Did you meet Jacob in the days before Charlotte went to the party?'

'Yes. We were stressed and busy with the campaign, obviously. He kept getting phone calls, and sometimes I heard him say Ben's name. I think he was getting updates about Lottie's whereabouts from him. He said so, in fact. She was a leading member of the group determined to take the statue down. It caused him a lot of strife. I was struggling to keep the media at bay.'

'The Basil Bones statue? The one that's creating a national furore.'

'Indeed, and it troubled Jacob greatly. Anyway, he was in regular contact with Ben in the days leading up to that party last Thursday.'

Monty asked, 'Did you see much of Charlotte?'

'I've met her, obviously. But I didn't know her well.'

'What did you think of her?'

'Honestly? I thought she was glamorous even though she had this hippy vibe. Pretty girl.'

'Do you know if she had other boyfriends, apart from Ben?'

Charles shook his head. 'I don't know, I'm afraid.'

'Do you know who killed her?'

Charles's face fell at the abrupt question, and he stared at Monty. Nikki knew what Monty was trying to do. It was a time-honoured interrogation tactic. Drop in the main question when they're least expecting it.

'I don't know,' Charles whispered.

# FORTY-THREE

Danny stood outside James Baden Powell's house as the two cops went in. He even saw the tall man give the female inspector a leg up to get over the side gate. Minutes later, he saw James escaping in the green Range Rover. He smiled to himself. It was all coming to the logical conclusion. It had been his life's work, his obsession. He saw the police car chase James, and he knew it wouldn't be long. He sat down at a roadside café in Summertown, enjoying the sunshine. He got busy on his laptop. Almost an hour later, he saw the police van and two squad cars returning. He knew they had captured James. He rubbed his hands together. That idiot had it coming. And where was Ben? Danny didn't know, but chances were he was close to getting caught. If he wasn't in prison already. None of them had planned for this like Danny had. Now he just needed to lay down the finishing touches. Like an artist signing his name on the picture.

That reminded him. There was still unfinished business. That Inspector Nikki Gill had a bee in her bonnet about Lottie's death. She had a shark's nose, and they could smell molecules of blood from miles away in the sea. She would keep coming after him, he knew that. In a way, he had enjoyed sparring with her. He needed to keep a closer eye on her. He had followed her back from the Kidlington South police station one day. He knew where she lived.

So far, it looked like she lived alone.

If Nikki Gill became too much of a problem, he would have to eliminate her. But there was a much easier prey. A prey who might end up giving him away. He needed to get to her before that dumb bitch thought of a clue that might expose him.

Danny packed up his stuff. He needed to get a move on, before it got too late. He drove to Cowley and parked outside the house. He had no choice but to wait. He did have the girl's phone number, but calling her was weird, and it might make her suspicious. It was a long wait, and he whiled away his time by marvelling at how good his plan had been. Danny liked congratulating himself. He had deflected all attention, and now he could be scot-free. Well, just a few loose ends to tidy up.

It was almost evening when he saw the door open, and Vicky stepped out. She was dressed in jeans and a top, and she carried a bag on her shoulders. She started walking towards Magdalen Bridge, and Danny followed. Vicky stopped on Cowley's High Street and went into a food shop. It was an Indian place, one of many in Cowley that sold spices and oriental food. This was his opportunity. He parked on a side road and rushed into the shop. He spied Vicky browsing a shelf near the rear. He placed himself right behind her, so she would see him when she turned. Which she did, and he feigned surprise.

'Vicky, how nice to see you.'

She smiled at him but her face was drawn and tired.

He frowned. 'Are you okay?'

She didn't answer.

He reached out and touched her shoulder. 'It's all right. You can talk to me.'

She stared past him. There was no one else in the shop. She lowered her voice. 'Have you heard about Charlotte?'

His face twisted in what he knew was an expression of pain. He could be a great actor when the occasion demanded it.

'Yes, unfortunately. I sent you a text when I heard but you didn't reply, so I left it. I'm so sorry. I knew you were close to her.'

Tears brimmed in Vicky's eyes. 'I still feel so bad about it.'

'Me too. Look, shall we go somewhere and have a cup of coffee to talk?'

Vicky thought for a minute, then she nodded. She paid for her stuff, and so did Danny, although he picked up things he didn't need. Better that than arouse her suspicions.

'I know this place in Iffley, not far to drive. I can drop you off when we're done.'

Vicky nodded. They got in his car and drove. He took the turning for Iffley, because he had a place in mind. He knew the Iffley ran along the River Thames. The river was wide in places, and Iffley was well known for its sixteenth-century lock from where the Oxford regatta used to start. There were many secluded paths along the river, and it was easy to get lost in the woods.

Danny went down a dirt track and the car bounced along. Vicky looked at him, the first hints of fear on her face.

'I'm sorry,' he said, smiling. 'The pub is by the river, and we could walk there, but this is a short cut. Walking would take much longer.'

He could see her hand had snaked inside her bag. She had her phone there, and what if she called someone? But his words seemed to have the desired effect, and she relaxed.

They could see the river up ahead. Its waters caught the sunlight and glittered between the trees. The path had come to an end. Danny switched the engine off.

'We have to walk from here.'

Vicky was frowning, her eyes scanning his face. 'Why did you bring me here?'

He shrugged; his mannerisms relaxed. The hard work was done. The fly was caught in the spider's web.

'To talk. I know you've been worried about what happened.'

She was still giving him a strange look. Then she nodded and cleared her throat. 'Okay. Let's go.'

He smiled. They got out of the car. As soon as she was out, Vicky turned and ran. She left her bag behind; and she was faster than he had thought. Danny set off in pursuit, but she'd surprised him and had a head start. For a short, dumpy girl, Vicky was quick. He struggled to catch up with her. The road was visible now, and he needed to stop her before she got there. He increased his pace, his chest heaving with the effort.

Vicky got to the road before he did. She ran out into the middle, trying to flag down a car. The car couldn't stop in time, though. It hit Vicky with a sickening thud. She flipped over the bonnet, rolled over the roof and collapsed in a heap behind the car.

# FORTY-FOUR

Nikki stared at Benjamin till he averted his gaze. His solicitor was a harassed-looking middle-aged man in a cheap suit. Nikki hadn't seen him before. She was wary of all lawyers. The posh ones in pinstripe suits were the worst.

Kristy was with Nikki, and she did the honours for the recording machine. Ben looked calm enough, and he probably had accepted his fate. He was dressed in the blue vest that the custody sergeant had handed to him yesterday, and wore matching trousers, and crocs on his feet.

Nikki started the questions. 'Where were you last Thursday night?'

Ben looked at his lawyer, who leaned forward and whispered in his ear.

'At the Piers Gaveston summer ball.'

'Indeed? And yet, your car was seen on CCTV that evening around seven thirty p.m., near Waterperry. Were you driving the car?'

Ben glanced at his lawyer, who nodded.

'Yes, I was.'

'Were you driving under the influence of alcohol?'

Ben nodded.

Nikki said, 'Can you speak up, please?'

'Yes, I was.'

She scribbled on her notebook. 'Why were you there, in your car?'

'My girlfriend, Charlotte Winspear, sent me a text. She wanted to see me, and she was there.'

'Can you confirm she was at the party with you?'

'She was, but so were a lot of other people. I lost her in the crowd. I didn't know where she was, in fact, till I saw the text.'

'You didn't text her back to ask what was happening?'

'I did, but she wanted to see me there. I also asked her how she got there, but she didn't reply. I was worried, actually. Hence, I took the risk of going back home, then driving to see her.'

His lawyer looked pleased, and he smiled at Ben, who sat back with a smug appearance. Nikki didn't like it. For all he had done, Ben was looking far too relaxed. His statement made it sound like he was the caring boyfriend.

'And what did you see when you got there?'

Ben's face changed. His jaws relaxed and he broke off eye contact. 'I walked up the hill, to where we had met before. Then I saw her lying on the grass. I tried to wake her up but then I realised she was dead.'

'How did you try to wake her up?'

'I shook her shoulders, patted her on the cheek. She was warm, but had no pulse.'

'And why didn't you call the police?'

Ben looked at Nikki. He had clearly waited for this moment. 'I knew what it looked like. You guys would think I did it. So, I went back home, packed my things and left. Looking back, I know I made a mistake. I should've reported it. I'm sorry.'

He shifted in his seat and looked at his solicitor, who was still looking pleased. He smiled at his client.

'You didn't call Jacob Winspear, her father?' Nikki asked casually.

Ben's face fell. His eyes darted around the room, and his lawyer leaned in and whispered in his ear. Ben licked his dry lips, now nervous.

'No, I didn't. I wasn't thinking straight. To be honest, I thought of the worst, that the police would accuse me of the crime. Hence, I tried to run away. That was an error.'

Nikki changed direction. 'Is it true that Jacob Winspear stayed in close contact with you?'

The lawyer cleared his throat. 'Miss Gill, does this have anything to do with the current case? Who my client chooses to be in contact with is surely his own business.'

'It is relevant in this case, as the person in question is the victim's father.'

The lawyer had a hushed chat with his client, and Ben nodded. 'No comment.'

Nikki looked at the lawyer again. For the first time, she realised he might've been hired by Mr Winspear. Ben had asked for him specifically; he wasn't a duty solicitor roped in for the case. She looked at her notes.

'Mr Carter,' she addressed the lawyer. 'We have evidence to prove that Mr Winspear actively stayed in touch with the defendant right up to the moment of his escape from Headington. In the light of the above, I think your client's comments are critical.'

Mr Carter's face went rigid, and his eyes cold, flat. He looked at Ben and shook his head slightly.

'No comment,' Ben said with a stony face.

'Okay,' Nikki sighed. 'So you assaulted Mr Topley, Mr Winspear's right-hand man, and you took off in his car. Essentially, you left him for dead. Care to explain that?'

'I didn't know who he was. I was afraid he had come to attack me. He tried to get into my room and I acted in self-defence.'

'So you didn't know who he was? We know that Mr Winspear let you know that he was coming.'

Mr Carter whispered in his ear, but Ben looked uncomfortable this time. Nikki now knew for certain Mr Carter had an angle to protect Jacob.

'You were expecting Mr Topley, but, by this time, you had lost trust in Mr Winspear. You didn't know what Mr Topley would do to you. You were scared for your life. Only desperate people do what you did, Ben. So, you beat him up, and then tried to vanish.'

Ben breathed heavily, his cheeks mottling red. Mr Carter spoke to him again, but it didn't appear to have any effect.

Nikki's voice became cold as steel. 'You had to escape because you killed Lottie.' The accusation made Ben's head jerk straight. His wild eyes stared at Nikki.

'You took her in the garden of Bloomfield House during the party. You strangled her to death, which was easy because she didn't struggle as she was on drugs. You couldn't leave the body there so you put her in the car and drove it down to Waterperry. That's the real reason you had to escape. Correct?'

'No,' Ben whispered, a sheen of sweat forming on his forehead.

'How much money did Mr Winspear offer you? A lot, presumably. But he didn't ask you to kill his daughter, did he? You messed up, Ben. Maybe you heard about Lottie's other affairs. You were jealous. You were drunk and high. You had an argument and things got out of control. Did she accuse you of working for her father? You wanted to shut her up but she wouldn't listen. You got angry and slapped her. She fell to the ground and you got on top of her and put your hands on her throat—'

'No!' Ben shouted, rising from his chair. His face was trembling, beads of sweat sprouting under his hairline. His face was crimson, nostrils flaring.

'I didn't kill her. I swear I didn't.'

'Really? Then why did you run?'

'I told you, I made a mistake. I shouldn't have. I panicked and thought...' He looked around him like a trapped animal in a cage.

Mr Carter was up and speaking to him. He turned to Nikki. 'Inspector Gill, these are baseless accusations. Total hearsay. The CPS will have a laugh, and you know it.'

'I think your client should answer the question.' She looked at Ben, who was leaning against the wall and rocking, his face ashen.

'What happened, Ben? Did you think Mr Winspear was coming after you? That Mr Topley had arrived with goons to take you away?'

'Yes,' Ben whispered. His head lowered. Mr Carter's shoulders slumped.

'I thought Jacob was going to make me look like the killer. I was there, with Lottie's dead body. What if someone hid in the bushes and took photos of me? I would get framed. If that didn't work, he would get rid of me. I went with Lottie to all these communist party meetings. I pretended to be interested, but I was reporting back to her dad.'

'Carry on.'

'Jacob's powerful. He knows people in the police. I could vanish without a trace. That's why I ran.' His chest heaved with emotion, but his eyes held Nikki's. 'I'm telling you the truth.'

Nikki rose and stepped towards him. She didn't get close; she leaned against the table and folded her arms across her chest. 'If you didn't kill her, then who did?'

Ben was miserable. 'I don't know.'

# FORTY-FIVE

While Nikki was interrogating Benjamin, Monty and Nish were with James Baden Powell. The interview rooms were all the same in the Kidlington South HQ. Lime-green walls and lino floors, with the table and chairs screwed to the floor. A one-way viewing glass on the wall to the right of the table, and a camera on the wall from either end; one facing the officers, the other on the suspect. The clock ticked loudly on the wall. James was nervous, Monty noticed, which was reassuring, in a way. Seasoned criminals were calm and knew how to use the law to get away.

'Please state your name, date of birth and address for the recorder,' Nish said to James. He had already mentioned their names and job titles.

The lawyer was a duty solicitor, and he looked like he needed sleep. He was young, with eyes deep in the sockets and a week's stubble on his cheeks. His name was Mr Solomon.

James did as asked, and Monty got the ball rolling. 'Why did you evade being questioned today?'

'No comment.' An answer prepared in the briefing with the lawyer, no doubt. Monty wasn't surprised. James had little in the way of defence. As far as Monty knew, he couldn't plead insanity. He needed a very good reason for a judge to not send him down for dangerous driving, at the very least. And that was the tip of the iceberg. No wonder James looked nervous.

'You had a private chartered flight booked for Nice, France. Why were you travelling?'

'Vacation.'

'Is that why you raced off, risking several lives in the process?'

'No comment.'

Monty tried a new approach. 'Did you know Charlotte Winspear?'

James blinked, and his hands stopped moving. He glanced at his lawyer, who nodded. 'Yes, she was a student.'

Nish took out the textbook which James had presented to Charlotte. He placed it on the table and spoke for the recorder.

'Suspect being shown evidence item number one.'

'You gifted this book to Miss Winspear,' Monty said. 'You refer to her as *Potty Lottie*. I take it that's a term of endearment.' It was a statement, not a question. James was breathing a little faster. 'Are you on such terms with all your students?'

'No.'

'So there was something special about Miss Winspear?'

James licked his dry lips and had a hushed chat with Mr Solomon. Monty leaned forward.

'James, if I may call you that, please make this easy on yourself. We have evidence and witnesses to prove that you and Miss Winspear were having an affair. Is that correct?'

'No comment.'

Monty ignored him. 'And you are a member of the Piers Gaveston Society, and you were present at the summer ball last Thursday. It is likely you saw Miss Winspear there. Can you confirm that?'

James swallowed hard, then opened his mouth to breathe.

'No comment.'

'Having met her there, you proceeded to have sex with her. I assume there will be a DNA match between yourself and the semen sample. After sex, you decided to kill her because you didn't want knowledge of your affair to become public.'

James's cheeks were turning beetroot red. Mr Solomon whispered in his ear.

'No. I didn't do that.'

'What did she do, James?' Monty asked. 'Did she threaten to expose you? You've been doing this for a while, right?' He looked at Nish, who opened an envelope and removed some papers.

'These are PCNs, James, filed by two women who were postgraduate research fellows at Merton College. You made sexual advances towards them in the Senior Common Room, and then followed them around. One woman states you tried to grope her in your office. The cases didn't go to court as you reached an out-of-court settlement with them.'

Monty laid out the papers in front of James, one by one. Nish and Kristy had done their research on James and discovered his past. Mr Solomon looked bored.

'This is all past history, Inspector Sen. My client has acknowledged it. Can we please get to the point?'

Monty smiled. 'Of course. James, so you couldn't get your way with these women. But Charlotte was younger, and she was vulnerable. Over three years, you groomed her. Did you threaten her with bad grades if she didn't submit to your attentions?'

A deep frown was creasing James's face. 'No,' he growled.

'You saw her often at the drinking society meet-ups. Not to mention the one-on-one tutorials. Finally, you had what you wanted. A woman you could control. Only, that wasn't the case. Charlotte had a mind of her own. Why were you angry with her? Did you find out she was with another man? Is that why you strangled her?'

'No,' James seethed. He covered his face in his hands. 'Please stop.'

'Inspector Sen. What are you charging my client with?' Mr Solomon was frowning. 'We know he faces three counts of dangerous and reckless driving. Is that all?'

Monty was silent for a while. James was staring at him.

'James Baden Powell, you are charged with the murder of Charlotte Winspear. You don't have to say—'

'No! No!' James was white as a sheet, gripping the edges of the table. 'I didn't kill her. I swear to you, I didn't.'

'Then why don't you tell us what happened at the party?'

James lowered his head. 'I saw her there. We danced. I got there late, and the party was in full swing. She was distracted, and drunk, obviously. I wanted to talk to her more, but she didn't want to. After a while, I didn't see her.'

'What did you do then?'

'I was there for a while, then I got a cab back.'

'Can anyone vouch for you?'

James frowned. 'Yes, I think so. I can provide you with some names of students, including the ones I said goodbye to.'

'So, you got back home and stayed there?'

'Yes. I didn't leave until the next morning when I went to work. In fact, if you give me my phone, I can even tell you the cab company that gave me a lift. The driver will confirm that he took me straight home.'

'What do you think happened to Charlotte at the party?'

'I don't know.' James looked skywards. 'Look, as it happens things were coming to an end between us. She was moving out of Oxford to pastures new. I wouldn't see her as much. We had already grown distant.'

'Did you have sex with her at the party? Or recently?'

'No. You won't find my DNA in that semen sample.'

Monty made a note of this, and he looked at his notebook. 'Did you know that Charlotte was seeing another man, apart from her boyfriend, Ben?'

James shook his head. 'You mean, she was three-timing us? No, I didn't know.'

\* \* \*

They reconvened in the office upstairs. Nikki listened to what Monty and Nish had to say.

'James isn't off the hook yet. If his DNA shows a match with the semen found in Charlotte, then he's back as main suspect. I'm leaning more towards him now, than Ben.'

'What did you think of Ben's statement?' Monty asked.

Nikki thought for a while. 'It seems Jacob Winspear was manipulating him behind the scenes. Ben ran for his life. I could be wrong, but I don't think he's a murderer. But James, I'm not sure of. Given his past history, he could've done it.'

'I agree,' Monty said, and the others nodded. 'These women lodged a PCN, but there could be others who never came forward.'

'Did you charge him, guv?' Kristy asked.

Monty shook his head. 'Not yet. Although he has these previous cases against him, murder isn't one of them. He's a dangerous idiot, and he needs a conviction for his previous crimes, I think. But I'm not sure he murdered Charlotte.'

'Unless there's a DNA match,' Nish said. 'We'll know tomorrow.'

'Yes,' Nikki agreed. 'We need to see Jacob now. He's got a lot to answer for.'

There was a sharp rap on the door, and Justina, one of the uniformed sergeants, walked in.

'One of the girls who lived with your victim was in an RTA. Her name's Victoria Davies. She's in the Radcliffe, in a critical condition.'

# FORTY-SIX

Jacob Winspear stared at his phone in confusion and disbelief. His hands shook. The screen showed photos of Charlotte lying on the hill. They were taken from different angles, and clearly the sender was alone with her. Jacob checked the number quickly. It was unknown. How did they get hold of his number?

His fingers shook as he thought of responding. Before he could, a text arrived.

Did you enjoy them?

Anger and revulsion sparked in Jacob's heart. He threw the phone down on the sofa. It started to ring. He stared at it for a while, then picked it up. It was the same number.

'Who are you?' he ground out. In the chambers of his heart, he felt he knew the answer. And it made him sick to the core.

'Ben's in prison. Charley's in hospital. And you know what happened to Lottie. Not looking good for you, is it, Jacob?'

'Danny. Is this you?' Jacob ground out.

'Oh, hello, Dad.' Danny laughed. 'You recognised me, after all.'

Jacob slumped on the sofa; he held his forehead in a palm. He was unable to speak for several seconds.

'Cat got your tongue, *Dad*?'

Jacob moaned softly. 'Oh god. Danny, what have you done?'

'What have I done? I'm only following on from what you did. I haven't heard from you in years. Forgotten all about me?'

A slow rage was kindling in Jacob's guts. 'You son of a bitch. Did you really do this? You killed Lottie?'

'And what if I did? To be honest, I did you a favour, correct? She was a thorn in your side. All her left-wing politics was getting embarrassing for you.'

'Shut up!' Jacob shouted. 'What have you done, you fool?'

'Only what you taught me to do. You never gave me a home, or love. But you told me to be ruthless. You made me what I am today.'

Jacob's hands shook, and his whole body trembled. 'You're finished now, Danny. You're done, you hear me? I'm coming after you.'

'You want me to go to the cops? I can tell them about Janet, my mother. Also about Mr Barrington, whom I killed for you. Would you like me to do that, Dad dearest?'

Jacob closed his eyes.

Danny chuckled. 'No, I didn't think so either. You will pay, Father. You will pay for what you did to my mother and sister. Molly died because of you. She should have lived in that house where you are now. You should've given her a home. Instead, you let her die. It's time for you to pay.'

'I looked after you, didn't I?'

'Only after I forced you to. It was always a transaction. If I hadn't blackmailed you, would you have looked after me? I can't think of a father who does that to his own son.'

Jacob gripped his forehead. This was going from bad to worse. He should've got rid of Danny years ago.

'What do you want?'

Danny took his time to answer. 'I want you to name me as your sole heir. Get rid of Rupert, and your wife. Lottie's gone already. I want to come into the business now, and I want to stay there until you die, then take sole ownership.'

Jacob's mouth fell open. 'You're mad.'

Danny laughed, a chilling sound. 'That's what they all say, don't they? But only you and I know the truth, Father. No one else will, unless I tell them.' He paused meaningfully. 'Do you want me to tell them? Shall I ring the newspapers?'

Jacob was silent, his teeth grinding together as his jaws clenched.

'I didn't think so. Get the papers ready. I want my name on your business, right now. Only mine, apart from you.'

'That's never going to happen.'

Danny took his time to answer, which made Jacob nervous.

'Then get ready for what's coming next,' Danny whispered menacingly.

# FORTY-SEVEN

Nikki and Monty were standing to one side of Vicky's bed in the intensive care unit. She was intubated, and the tube coming out of her mouth was pumping oxygen into her lungs and removing the carbon dioxide. An assortment of intravenous lines were attached to her elbows. Her eyes were closed, and her chest rose and fell in cadence to the soft beeping of the artificial ventilation machine on her right. The consultant was a short, thin Asian man called Dr Verma, and he stood next to Nikki.

'Pelvic crush fracture, with major damage to all the organs within. She had massive haemorrhage and went into multiorgan failure. Which basically means she can't survive without being hooked up to these machines.'

Nikki felt sick looking at the innocent face, and sad. Could she have done more to protect Vicky? Maybe. She knew more than the other two girls, Francine and Taby. Nikki had already dispatched a squad car to the girls' address, and they were under police protection now. They could only leave the house if they were accompanied by a uniformed officer.

'What are her chances?' she asked.

'Slim to non-existent, I'm afraid. The car which hit her was travelling at high speed. It was a deserted stretch of road, and I can't blame the driver. She suddenly popped up in the middle of the road, and even after the driver braked, the car moved for twenty yards before stopping. She was almost dead a few hours after hitting the ground. We're keeping her alive, as she's young and the parents want it.'

Monty said, 'But sooner or later you have to make a decision?'

Dr Verma's large eyes dominated his face, and they were dulled with sadness. 'Unfortunately, yes. It's rare to see a young woman in this state, but it does happen.'

'Is there any chance she will talk?'

'I doubt it. We will keep trying. She has twenty-four hour one-to-one nursing support. If she utters even one word, we will know.' Dr Verma looked at Nikki, then at Monty.

Nikki left her card with Dr Verma and stepped outside. In the intensive care lobby, the pale-faced driver was flanked on both sides by uniformed officers. Inspector Tony Rodrigues, who had brought the driver there, introduced him.

'Steven Moore. He's given a full statement and will cooperate as necessary.'

Mr Moore looked like he might faint any moment. He was a slim man, dressed in a black T-shirt and jeans. 'I'm so sorry,' he whispered.

Nikki indicated the seat, and then sat down next to him. 'Tell me what happened.'

'I was driving to pick up my son from cricket practice, and I was late. I was rushing. The speed limit is fifty there, and I was doing a little more. There're no cameras there, but I wasn't doing seventy or anything stupid.'

'Even if you hit her at fifty miles an hour, I doubt the situation would be any different,' Nikki assured him. 'Please, carry on.'

'She was a blur. She came from my right. I was adjusting the heating on my dashboard. I looked up and for that fraction of a second...' Mr Moore's head lowered in his hands. 'I'll never be able to forget that moment. It's like a nightmare.'

Nikki put a hand on the man's shoulder. He was clearly traumatised.

'What happened after that?'

'I stopped. I got out of the car and ran to her. She wasn't moving. All this blood was appearing around her head. And I also saw this man.'

He paused. 'He was standing to the right, by this dirt track in the woods, where the girl had come from. He watched me for a few seconds, then ran back. I didn't really think much about it at the time. But now I wonder if he was with the girl.'

'Can you describe him, please? Height, how heavy? What was he wearing?'

'A white man, younger than me. In his thirties, I'd say. He was wearing a full-sleeve dark shirt and dark trousers. He had trainers on, blue, I think.'

'Did he wear glasses? Or a hat?'

Mr Moore thought for a while, then shook his head. 'No glasses. His hair was dark. Longish and heavy. That's all I remember. I didn't see him for that long. He ran back into the woods, and I thought it was odd. He must've been chasing the girl. Correct?'

'I think so,' Nikki said. 'Did you see how far he went?'

'That dirt track curves around and it's hidden by the trees. He ran fast and I couldn't see him. Sorry.'

'Then you checked on Vicky, and you called the police?'

'Yes. And I waited. I rang my wife and told her. She picked up my son.' Mr Moore's hands trembled as he passed them over his face. 'This will haunt me forever.'

'I'm sorry.' Nikki gave him a few minutes to compose

himself. 'While you waited for the police to arrive, did you see that man again? Maybe in a car, coming out of the woods?'

Mr Moore thought for a while. Then his brows crinkled. 'No, I didn't see him again. But now that you mention it, I did see a van coming out of the woods. It was a black Toyota van. It emerged from behind where I was and went in the opposite direction. This happened after I had made the police call, and I was waiting. My mind was a mess, so I didn't really think of it till now.'

Nikki put her elbows on her thighs and leaned closer to Mr Moore.

'Think carefully. How many people were in the van?'

'I couldn't tell. The driver, definitely. I'm not sure about anyone else, sorry. I also can't remember the registration number, but the car wasn't old.' He concentrated hard, shutting his eyes. '2020 reg, or 21. Yes 21. It was a 21 reg van.'

Monty asked, 'And are you sure it was a Toyota?'

'Yes. I know because I used to own one just like it.'

Monty and Nikki looked at each other, and she saw his eyes gleam with excitement.

Tony Rodrigues stepped forward. 'I'll get Traffic on it now. There's no CCTV in that stretch. But he could've headed into Iffley High Street, and we'll get him there.'

Tony went off to speak on his phone. Nikki thanked Mr Moore and went outside with Monty.

'This man was someone Vicky knew, right?' Monty asked. 'Or why would she meet up with him?'

Nikki nodded. Both of them knew that most victims were murdered by people they knew.

'If it was a date, they wouldn't be in those woods. Unless it was a man she was seeing already, and they wanted some private time.'

'Let's take a look at the crime scene,' Nikki said. 'I know it was an RTA, but I think Vicky was running from this man.'

\* \* \*

Monty drove them down to the stretch of road on the outskirts of Iffley, a road that snaked around the Thames as it broadened, cutting a wide gash through the land on its way down to London.

The road was closed to traffic. Blue and white crime scene tape fluttered across the road, and a squad car was parked on the side. A uniformed officer came out of the car and took down their names and ranks. Nikki and Monty walked down the dirt path. The woods were dense here. Shafts of sunlight broke through the dense canopy of foliage above their heads, but the dimness, even in daylight, was palpable. Through the gaps in the trees, Nikki could see flashes of sunlight sparkling on water.

'I would run away from here too,' she said out loud. The path curved, like Mr Moore had said. Tyre tracks were visible on the dark-brown earth. Monty bent down to examine them.

'Fresh tracks. Made today obviously. Good job it hasn't rained.' He took photos to send them to scene of crime. They had a database of tyre tracks, and hopefully they could get a match, if the car was stolen.

'Footprints,' Monty said, from where he was sitting on his haunches. Nikki leaned over his wide shoulders to see where he pointed.

She could make out a small print, made by a child or woman's shoes. This was an unusual place for a child to be alone. Monty rose and walked forward, while she squinted at the prints.

'More here,' Monty said. 'And bigger; a man's print.'

Nikki rushed over, excited. Some of the prints were disturbed, but she could make out a man's boot print. She had little experience of forensic gait analysis, but Hetty would have a field day here, uploading the photos to the national database. Gait analysis and boot prints were invaluable tools to catch a criminal. Monty was busy snapping away. Nikki walked around, and then peered closely at the grass verge of the track. She walked along it, observing the ground closely. She had moved back along the way she came when she found something.

It was a shiny object, like a can of soup, but smaller. She put on her gloves and bent closer to have a look. It was a can of turmeric spice, the brand logo glittering on top. She turned it around. It was brand new, never been opened. What was it doing here? Did it fall out of a bag? What were the chances that bag belonged to Vicky?

She joined Monty, who was staring down the other end of the track, to where it curved out of sight.

'He went that way.' He pointed at the tyre tracks. 'The track must come out on that side. Oh, turmeric spice. I use that in my cooking.' He grinned when he saw what Nikki was holding up to his face.

'This place isn't exactly a picnic spot though, is it?'

'Nope. Did you see anything else?'

'No. I was thinking that if Vicky was running down here, maybe something fell out of her bag? She must've had a bag when she left the house. Maybe the man followed her when she was shopping. He's picked up everything else, but missed this.'

'We can ask the brand which shops they supply to. Check CCTV. Worth a try.'

Nikki spoke to Nish on her phone as she followed Monty. They followed the tyre tracks until they reached the end, where the dirt path opened out into the main road. Behind them, the squad car was parked at the scene of the accident.

'These tracks must belong to the Toyota van Mr Moore saw. I can't see any other marks.'

'Yes. Let's head back to the nick. We have work to do.'

* * *

Nish and Kristy were waiting at the office. 'We're going through Vicky's phone. Managed to get a call list. Looking to see if there's any matches with the numbers we have.' Kristy waved an A4 printout sheet that bore the call log.

'Francine and Taby were out when this happened. They didn't know where Vicky went, or who she saw.'

Nish added, 'But they do think Vicky had a man in her life. He never came to the house, but she said she was going out on a date with Michael.'

'Michael?'

'Yes, guv, that's all we have so far. Sorry.'

'Okay, keep searching for this Michael. Do the girls know if Michael drove a black Toyota van? Please ask them.'

Kristy made the call while Monty went out to his desk. 'What else did we get from the crime scene?'

'Nothing apart from her phone and clothes. She didn't have a bag.'

Nikki took out the jar of ground turmeric and put it on the table. 'We need to ring the company and ask them which shops in Oxford they supply to. Then we can ask the shop owner if they have CCTV.'

Nikki interlocked her fingers and leaned back on her chair. Thinking things through. One thing was certain now. She had got this all wrong. Neither Benjamin nor James could have been involved in Vicky's accident: Benjamin was in custody, and she and Monty were chasing James at the time. So someone else was involved, and she needed to find out who. She closed her eyes and thought back to what Mr Moore said about the man who had appeared to be chasing Vicky. *In his thirties... His hair was dark. Longish and heavy.* She sat forward. There was one man they'd spoken to recently who matched his description.

Greg Keating.

Nikki remembered how Mr Vardy had reacted when she asked him about the presence of lecturers and academics at the

PG Summer Ball. He wasn't just uncomfortable, he was hiding something.

She grabbed her phone and thumbed down to his number, then called Greg Keating.

'Mr Keating, this is DI Nikki Gill. We spoke to you recently in connection with our investigation into the death of a student of yours, Charlotte Winspear. Can I ask where are you right now?'

His tone was calm; he sounded a bit surprised. 'At my office. Is anything the matter, Inspector?'

'I need to ask you about a recent development. I will be there in fifteen minutes. Can you stay in your office till I get there?'

'I'm a bit busy—'

'This won't take long. Please stay where you are, and I will see you shortly.'

# FORTY-EIGHT

Mr Keating opened the door at the first knock. He stared at Nikki and Monty for a few seconds, then stood to one side. He wore a suit, shirt open at the collar. His room had the same organised mess it had before.

'Has anything happened?' Greg asked.

'Yes. Victoria Davies was run over by a car in Iffley today. She will not survive her injuries. She is in intensive care.'

Greg's eyebrows shot up. His mouth relaxed till it formed an O. 'What... when... did this happen?'

If he was acting, Nikki thought, then he was a professional. Liars find it hard to control the muscles of the neck, a behavioural psychologist had once taught her. They learn to keep the facial muscles relaxed, but the neck compensates. Greg's neck showed no sign of contraction.

'Today. Around three hours ago. Can I ask where you were at the time?'

Greg's face changed. He blinked several times, then frowned. 'Why are you asking me?'

'Please answer the question.'

'I was here, as it happens. I've been here since this morning.

253

You can ask them at the porter's lodge.' He indicated his desk. 'I have a lot of paperwork to finish up before we break up for the summer.'

'What time did you arrive?'

'Around nine a.m. I had lunch in the Senior Common Room. In fact, you can ask some of my colleagues who were at lunch with me. That was, in fact, almost three hours ago. It's now almost four p.m.' He looked at his watch to confirm.

'Which colleagues saw you?'

Greg thought for a few seconds. 'Marcus Botham, who's a professor of Classics. And also Jenny Quint, a lecturer in Maths. There were various others, and you can ask the waiters who were there as well.'

Nikki knew there would be CCTV at the porter's lodge. If Greg was lying, he would be caught easily. She began to relax.

'What type of car do you drive?'

'I drive a Lexus electric car. It's at home. I walk or bike to work.'

Nikki wrote down the registration number of his car, and she texted it to Kristy. It would be easy enough to check. She also took down the contact details of the two academics he had lunch with.

'Please don't leave Oxford over the next few days. We might need to speak to you again. Did you see Vicky recently, by the way?'

Greg shook his head. An expression of sorrow overlaid his features. 'I should have made more of an effort, I think. She did the tutorials with Lottie and me. She was affected by her death deeply, I think. I never spoke to her, that's just my assumption. Are you sure she didn't commit suicide?'

Nikki frowned. 'Why would she do that? She didn't seem depressed when I questioned her.'

'I'm sure you've checked everything out,' Greg said. 'I was just wondering what happened today.'

Nikki was silent for a while. She was wrong about Greg. Clearly, he wasn't the man she was looking for. She had to ask the witnesses, but she doubted he was lying.

'Thank you for helping us with James Baden Powell.' She filled him in about how he tried to escape and was caught.

'Goodness me.' Greg was shocked. 'Even if he was having an affair with her, surely his actions were excessive.'

'You'd be surprised what people can do when they're desperate.' She rose. 'Thank you for your help so far. Please remain in Oxford; as I said, we might need to speak to you again.'

'I'm at your service.' Greg smiled, also rising. 'No plans to go anywhere, too busy here.'

\* \* \*

Nikki and Monty went outside, and she rang the two academics. Both of them answered, and both confirmed they'd seen Greg that day in the Senior Common Room. Nikki asked at the porter's lodge, and the porter, who had been on duty the whole day, said Greg came in just before nine, and hadn't left the building till now.

'Problem is, our man is getting desperate now. He knows the two suspects in custody will speak the truth and might even get exonerated. He's going to strike again.' Monty said anxiously.

'That's exactly what I was thinking,' Nikki said, her mood darkening. She knew she was close to figuring out who this cold-blooded killer was. She could see his cunning, meticulous plan. Ben and James had been simple-minded in comparison. They sought to escape, but Nikki now knew the real culprit was hiding in plain sight.

She also knew the killer might strike again. He would try to hide his tracks, and Nikki didn't want to have another young girl's death on her hands. They were walking past a bench, and she sat down. Monty joined her without question, and they sat together in silence. Monty was the first to speak, his voice low and sonorous.

'Taking it from the beginning, what do we know? Something happened in Bloomsdale House, where the PG society had the party. Charlotte was there, and she ended up dead on a hill in Waterperry.'

'And we still don't know how she got there.'

Nikki's heart raced. They were getting somewhere. Instead of Monty's face, she saw a sudden bright, thunder light whiteness, like a lightning flash that illuminated her mind.

'Bloomsdale House,' she whispered, almost to herself. 'Who else was there that night, apart from the party people, the groundsmen, and the security staff?'

Monty raised his eyebrows. 'No visitors allowed, that's for sure. But people attended to set up the stalls—'

'And food,' Nikki interrupted. 'Catering staff. There had to be.' She gripped Monty's arm.

She phoned the housekeeper, getting straight into her questions. She put him on the loudspeaker so Monty could hear as well.

'Who else was here that night? What about serving staff, or caterers?'

Mr Vardy spoke slowly, as if he was recalling details. 'Yes, the drinks are served by staff recruited from outside. There is some food as well, and although it's a self-serve buffet, the caterers are on hand.'

'Do you have the name of the catering company?' Nikki asked, glancing at Monty.

'Yes, I do,' said Mr Vardy. 'Do you want their details?'

'And also of the security company, if you don't mind.'

'Sure, no problems. Actually you asked me about something unusual, and I remember now. We normally have the same catering company, and I help them to set up shop inside. There's about three of these summer balls here every year, and over the years, I've got to know the catering staff. There was a new guy this year. He always wore these dark glasses and a cap. Almost like he didn't want to show his face. I found him a bit weird. But it's not just that. I saw him coming up from the grounds that night and going back into the main building. I didn't understand what he was doing outside.

'I don't think he saw me. He was walking fast; he went back inside the house. I wanted to speak to him, but there wasn't enough time.'

'Can you describe him?'

'Slim build, white man. Just your average joe, really.'

'What colour hair? You said he wore dark glasses. Anything else?'

'Brown hair, quite dark and thick. He had his hat off when he was outside. Clean-shaven. Nothing else comes to mind.'

Nikki and Monty shared a glance. The description wasn't ideal, but it matched the man who had chased Vicky out to the road.

'It stuck in my mind as the waiters don't really go outside. They lay the food out, then help people to load their plates. Then they pack everything up and move out. They can stay quite late, as sometimes the guests want to snack and there's no other food shop around here. I saw them leave. This man with the dark glasses drove his own vehicle, like some of the staff do.'

'What sort was it?' Monty asked. His face was animated and Nikki knew he was sensing the same excitement as her.

'It was a black Toyota van. But what I remember is that this guy had a rolled-up carpet he put in the van. Then he drove off. I've never seen the catering staff do that.'

'Is there any CCTV at Bloomfield House?'

'There is, but unfortunately the night of the party the

257

cameras are switched off. It's one of the requirements the organisers make.'

'Mr Vardy, please think carefully. Are you sure this man was driving a black Toyota van? Can you remember the registration number?'

'No, sorry. But it looked new, if you know what I mean.'

'Can you guess why he would have a rolled-up carpet?'

Mr Vardy said, 'Not sure. I thought at the time the caterers had brought it with them. That could still be the case. But I've never seen them bring carpets before. I might be wrong though.'

'We need their details, ASAP please,' Nikki said, adrenaline spiking in her blood.

# FORTY-NINE

Royal Caterers was still open when Monty pulled up outside their office in Witney High Street. Witney was a pretty town northwest from Oxford on the A40. It was a respectable, solidly middle-class place, and the cobblestone high street epitomised the tourist-brochure look of Cotswold villages. The workers of Royal Catering weren't prepared for Monty bursting in through their doors, Nikki close behind.

'Where's your manager?' Monty asked the scared-looking young receptionist. She gaped at him, then pointed a manicured red fingernail to the rear of the open-plan office. Royal Caterers was a big operation, Nikki could see that. She could count roughly thirty employees, some of them on the phone to customers, others staring at her.

She followed Monty to the office at the rear. The white door bore a sign that said, *Manager, Steven Leadenhall.* A sharp knock on the door got them inside. Mr Leadenhall was an average-sized man wearing a half-sleeve shirt, with glasses on the bridge of his nose. He was black, with curly hair that was going white. He frowned at them.

'Who are you?'

Monty showed him his warrant card, and so did Nikki. She said, 'We need to ask you about the PG summer ball at Bloomfield House last Thursday.'

Monty had shut the door behind them. Mr Leadenhall removed the glasses. 'Sorry, I don't follow.'

'This is a murder inquiry. A woman was killed at the party, and we believe that one of your members of staff might be a key suspect.'

Mr Leadenhall's jaw dropped. 'That's not possible. My staff are all vetted. They had CRB disclosure checks, and I never hire anyone with a criminal record. I've actually had complaints about that, but I don't care. People trust our brand. I would never jeopardise it by hiring dodgy people.'

'That's fine. But the kind of person we're looking for might not have a criminal record, or even have come into contact with the police. Have you hired any new staff recently?'

'We've expanded, so yes, some new hirings took place. Why?'

'We need their records. The man we're looking for is average height, Caucasian, slim build, no glasses. Thick brown or dark hair. Young to middle-aged, no more than forty. He drives a black Toyota van. Does that ring any bells?'

Mr Leadenhall frowned. Then his eyes widened. 'Yes, it does.' He opened the top two drawers of his desk, then slammed them shut. He clicked on the keyboard and looked at the monitor on his desk. Then he turned the monitor so Nikki could see. She saw an application form, made out in the name of – Salvatore Garibaldi. There was an address in a town called Wheatley, which wasn't far from Oxford, if memory served.

Mr Leadenhall said, "There are Data Protection and confidentiality issues at stake here. Strictly speaking, I'm not allowed to show you these documents. But as this is a murder inquiry, I assume disclosure of a suspect's documents is allowed?"

"Your assumption is spot on," Monty said.

'Salvatore Garibaldi looks like the man you described,' Mr Leadenhall said. 'And I'm pretty sure I saw him get into a black Toyota in the car park at the back.'

'Don't you have a photo?'

Mr Leadenhall searched his file on the computer. He showed them his CRB and police checks, which were all clear.

'I'm sorry. I don't seem to have a photo. We normally ask for a driving licence or passport, and this is all he gave us.'

Monty had memorised the address, and he was already on the phone, asking a squad car to head over to Mr Garibaldi's house.

'Did he attend for an interview?'

'It was an online video interview as it was lockdown at the time. I can look and see if I can get a copy of it.'

'Yes, please. After last Thursday at the summer ball, has he done any other work for you?'

'No. But summer is a busy time for us, and now with the country opening up we have a lot of bookings. We might need him again, or not, as the case may be.' A look of concern rippled across his face. 'My god, you really think he murdered someone at this party?'

'We don't know for sure. How many times has he worked for you?'

'This was the first time. And obviously, the last as well.'

'Did anyone else in your office come into contact with him?'

'Well, the other waiters did. None of them are here today. But I can give you their details and you can contact them.'

'Yes, please.'

\* \* \*

When they left Royal Caterers, Monty pointed the car towards Wheatley. The town was less affluent than most in the region, with a depressed-looking high street. Boarded-up shops, barber shops and kebab joints that had groups of youths hanging around outside – young people who should be in school, or working. They took a turning off the main road, and after a few roads, came to the address. The squad car was already there, and a uniformed sergeant was at the door.

'No answer, guv,' the burly sergeant said. His name badge identified him as Derek.

Nikki went up to the terraced house that was similar to all the others down the road. They had seen better days. The red bricks were faded to orange, and the paintwork had chipped on the rotting timber of the window frames.

She turned to Derek. 'Ask the neighbours. I want a door to door of all the houses. Find out when he was last seen, with who, and what car he drives. Get another unit down here.'

'Yes, guv.' Derek went to the car to speak to his colleague.

Monty was knocking on the door with little success. He raised the letterbox flap and shouted. Again, no response.

'Break it down,' Nikki said.

Monty took three steps back, then hurled himself at the door, kicking it with all his might. It took two solid hits from his boots for the hinge to crack, and the door smashed open. Monty went in first.

'Police! Anyone here?'

The carpet was a faded brown, and it was threadbare, with dips in places where the floorboards had sagged. A flight of stairs led upwards. The living room had two sofas and a TV, with photos on the shelves, along with books. The windows were shut and curtains drawn. Monty had his gloves on, and he pulled the curtains apart carefully, having inspected around the edges of the bay window. He touched the layer of dust on the window ledge.

'No one's been here for a while.'

Nikki also had gloves on and she took down one of the photos from the shelf. It showed a youngish-looking man with dark-brown hair. He wore a brown shirt, and dark trousers. He was standing next to another man, and their physical proximity suggested more than friendship. She assumed one of them was Salvatore Garibaldi; the description from the car driver and Mr Vardy matched the man on the left. Monty came over and looked over her shoulder.

'That's him on the left, correct?'

'Yes, I think so.' The man on the right wore shorts, a white top and sunglasses. He was shorter, and blond.

Nikki felt a churn of adrenaline and danger in her guts. She was getting closer. She stared at the man's photo for a while, memorising it. She put the photos in their frame in her bag.

'He's still not answering his phone,' Monty said, stuffing his mobile back in his pocket. They had tried several times on the drive down here as well. There was no response. She had looked at social media. She got several hits with his name, but they were either Italian or American, or the wrong age.

Monty went out the door and came back with a stack of envelopes. 'All addressed to him. He's not been reading his mail.'

The dining room/lounge was the next room, and it led to the small garden. Monty opened the door and they stepped outside. It had been mown a few weeks ago, the grass starting to grow again. The dining table was empty; and another sofa set and larger TV lay closer to the garden. Nikki went back in to check the kitchen. The fridge had some food in it, and the milk was out of date by a few days. There were no plates in the sink, and there were dirty plates and cutlery in the dishwasher.

'He's not been gone long. Probably realised the game was up and left quickly.'

'I wonder where he's been hiding?' Monty remarked. 'He surfaced to get to Vicky. He must think Vicky knows about him. Maybe Vicky saw him with Charlotte?'

'Well, she told us Charlotte was seeing another man. That's

probably him.' She narrowed her eyes as she concentrated. 'But I see what you mean. Why Vicky? Why not Francine or Taby? It's possible Charlotte told him that she confided in Vicky. Or Vicky saw something. Or maybe he was just after her. Creeps like him follow women around. It wouldn't surprise me.'

'I checked on the team outside the girls' house. They're okay, but shaken obviously.'

'We need to find this guy soon,' Nikki fumed.

They went upstairs, Nikki taking her time to stop at the ledge of the window at the landing. There was another framed photo, this time of Salvatore on his own. He was bare-chested, wearing swimming trunks, sitting on a beach by the sea. His arms were spread wide, and he was smiling. It wasn't a great photo for Nikki's purpose as the sunlight obscured the face, but she put the photo in an evidence bag anyway.

She sniffed the air. Nothing but an old musty smell, the kind that came from the windows not being opened for a while. A dead body's stench would've been obvious at the door. Monty had gone ahead, and he was standing under the trapdoor that she presumed led to the loft. He opened the bathroom door in front and went in. He emerged with two evidence bags, which he held up for Nikki to see.

'Toothbrush and razor. Enough to give us DNA samples.'

Nikki nodded, and she followed Monty into the first bedroom. The curtains were drawn here as well, and he turned on the light, then opened the curtains. The double bed was made up, and Nikki took off the cover sheet and duvet. The bedsheets indicated it was slept in, and the depression on both sides meant two people had used the bed. Salvatore and his nameless lover, Nikki thought.

The wardrobe was almost empty. All the clothes removed, save a couple of old shoes at the bottom. Monty bent down and looked underneath the bed. He pulled out an old suitcase and went through the contents. Then he slid underneath the bed. Nikki walked over to him as he emerged, holding a blue manila folder in his hand.

'It was taped to the underside of the bed,' Monty said, his eyes glinting. He put the folder on the floor and opened it. Inside they found four photos of Charlotte. All were taken at university, and two of them showed her wearing sub fusc, the formal attire required for exams, outside the examination hall. The other two photos were intimate one of Charlotte naked on the bed, one leg crossed over the other, and the other with her posing on top of the bedsheets.

Monty held up a typed A4 page that was clearly a timetable; it had Charlotte's name written on the top right. Parts of the timetable were underlined. The other documents were some more photos of Charlotte posing, this time with clothes on.

'We found him,' Monty whispered. He glanced at Nikki, then stood, grimacing as his knees clicked.

'But he's with this blond man, right?' Nikki said as Monty put the evidence in a bag. 'I'm sure that's his boyfriend.'

'Maybe he likes a bit of both. Either way, he's our man.'

'Yes.'

Nikki checked the other, smaller bedroom. The single bed was not slept in, and the room contained old boxes, and a wardrobe with clothes that were clearly not used. She left Monty to look through the boxes to see if he found anything interesting. The small study was the final room upstairs. It had a desk and a printer. There was no desktop computer, and the router wires were disconnected. She searched for a laptop to no avail. Monty came back and shook his head.

'Old junk. Paperback books and old CDs, DVDs.'

Questions were swirling in Nikki's mind like a tornado. 'Let's get back to the nick. We have work to do.'

# FIFTY

Monty held the steering wheel with one hand as he drove. 'I'm interested to see what traffic found on CCTV. If there's nothing, we should check CCTV in Witney, outside Royal Caterers, and on the high street. We might be able to pick up a black Toyota van.' Back at the nick, Nish and Kristy were going through the films with traffic. Nikki stared at the countryside rushing past the window. She couldn't stop thinking about the train of events that had led her to Salvatore. If she hadn't visited Bloomfield House and questioned Mr Vardy, she would be in the dark. *What else was she missing?*

She had focused on Benjamin Henshaw and James Baden Powell for too long. They were both dangerous and unpredictable, James much more so. She needed to question him more, and he was definitely going to be convicted for his crimes of dangerous driving at the least. Ben had acted more in self-defence. And neither of them had killed Charlotte. Nikki shook her head in disgust and gripped her temples with one hand. How could she have been so stupid?

'Don't kick yourself,' Monty said calmly. 'We're dealing with someone who's an expert at flying under the radar. He didn't even submit his passport for the job with Royal Caterer. I think his only weakness was actually Vicky. She must have seen him. He had to get rid of her. That's why he risked everything to come back.'

Nikki nodded. 'You're right.'

'Charlotte was a complex person. She loved attention from men, and probably enjoyed stringing them along. I'm no psychologist, but maybe it was her way of taking revenge on her father. Clearly, she didn't get along with him.'

'We need to bring him in, I think. He's guilty of manipulating Ben, anyway. And we have evidence from Charles Topley. He's going down. But not for the murder of his daughter. He's got an alibi anyway. From his wife, who said he was at home with her on Thursday night.'

'Who the hell is Salvatore, anyway?' Monty murmured. 'I wonder if he's lived here all his life, or he's fresh from Italy.'

'Could be Latino. Don't make assumptions,' Nikki corrected him. 'By the time we get back, Kristy should have all his details.'

They stopped to pick up coffee and pizza for the team. Nish met them downstairs at the car park to help them carry it upstairs. In the office, Nikki bit into her first slice of pepperoni and realised how hungry she'd been. Well, so much for no carbs today.

Kristy read from her laptop screen. 'Salvatore Garibaldi was born in Italy; he came to this country when he was five, with his parents. Used to live in Grantham, in Lincolnshire, and then went to university in Manchester. He came down here to Oxford to work for a newspaper, then lost his job when the paper folded. For the last six years he's been doing a variety of odd jobs.'

'Has he always lived in Wheatley?'

Kristy scrolled to the bottom. 'No, he's moved around. Was in Cowley for a while, then in Botley.'

'Anything on HOLMES?'

'Nope. No PCNs, and I've done a search from his date of birth.'

Nish said, 'I spoke to Francine and Taby on the phone. They don't know who he is. Interestingly though, they agreed with Vicky's story that Charlotte had another man on the go.'

Nikki puffed out her cheeks then exhaled. 'Put another team on their surveillance. I want those girls to be checked night and day.'

'Did Charlotte have other friends who might have seen her with Salvatore?'

'Maybe. But we need to focus on finding him now. What about CCTV?'

'Thanks for the reminder,' Nish said. He finished eating his slice of pizza, then wiped his hands. His fingers flew across the keyboard, then he brought the images up on the screen. Nikki and the others crowded around him, and Nikki couldn't help noticing that Kristy had her hand on Nish's shoulder as she leaned forward. As if conscious of her action, Kristy swiftly removed her hand. Nikki suppressed a grin.

Nish pressed play and the four boxes on the screen showed traffic moving on Witney's High Street. The top two showed the high street from both directions. The bottom two showed the roads the high street joined.

'There it is, guv.' Nish pointed to the top-left screen. A black Toyota van came down the road and indicated left to the Royal Caterers offices. The car park was at the rear of the building, where several businesses had their offices. The black van parked, and a man came out. Nish stopped the film and zoomed into the man's face. He was wearing sunglasses and a baseball cap. It was sunny, and he wore a T-shirt and jeans. He didn't have any tattoos on his arms.

'He looks like the man in the photos,' Monty said, and Nikki agreed. 'And the description fits the man Mr Moore saw after the accident.'

Nish speeded the tape up, and they saw the van emerge and join the traffic. Nish followed through several frames, fast forwarding till it joined the M40 motorway.

'The van was last seen going up towards Birmingham, at junction fifteen. That's the exit for Walsall.' Nish showed them the clip, with the van circled as it took the exit. It was visible again at a couple of junctions, before vanishing down a deserted country road.

'CCTV dark spot.' Nish raised both hands and shrugged.

Nikki noted the date. 'This was Monday, two weeks ago, which was just over a week before the PG summer ball. He comes back into Oxford before the ball last Thursday, we know that. Then he drives to Bloomfield House.'

'There's no CCTV around Bloomfield, guv,' Nish said. 'Traffic have scoured the cameras, using ANPR now that we know the van's reg number. They found nothing.'

'It's possible he changed the number plates,' Monty said. Everyone nodded. It was a common tactic used by criminals to avoid their cars getting detected by ANPR.

Nish continued. 'On DVLA, the van is registered to the address in Wheatley. No name. And yet, there is no sign that the van was parked there since last Thursday. But it was there before.'

Nish opened up a new tab, and he uploaded some more video files. 'Traffic looked at films from four weeks ago.' He stopped scrolling the images. 'Is that him?'

Nikki and Monty got closer. Nish clicked on Play. A man, dressed in a dark full-sleeve shirt, came out from the same house as Nikki had just visited in Wheatley. He got into a black Toyota van. Nish froze the image and magnified the man's face until it was in danger of becoming blurred and pixelated.

'Yes, that's him,' Nikki said. 'Any more views of him? Notice how he wears dark glasses. Mind you, it's sunny now.'

Nish looked at a few more CCTV files. He found another two that showed Salvatore parking the van and walking up to his house in the evening, or leaving in the morning. He was also seen going for a walk. He was always alone.

'Funny,' Nikki said. 'He did have a partner. The blond man. Where's he?'

'Blondie didn't have any mail addressed to him,' Monty said. 'Well, all the mail and bills came in Salvatore's name.'

Before dropping off the evidence with Forensics, Nikki had taken photos. She zoomed in on one of the photos of the blond man. She looked at him closely, noting his face, neck and chest for any visible moles, necklaces, tattoos or marks. She found nothing. For some reason, the face looked vaguely familiar. She'd had a similar feeling when she first saw his photo in Salvatore's house, but now it was stronger. She asked the others. Everyone shook their head, including Monty.

'Is that the only photo of him we found?'

Nikki nodded. After Monty and herself had left, the Uniforms had searched all over the house. They found nothing of importance. The door to door was still ongoing. Nikki hoped the neighbours might be able to shed some light.

'Send Salvatore's photos to Mr Moore, the driver who hit Vicky. Let's see if he can do a positive ID. Did you send the photos to Francine and Taby?'

'Yes,' Kristy said. 'Nothing so far.' She called Mr Moore and spoke to him briefly, then sent him the photos.

Nikki called Hetty Barfield, the head of Forensics, who also did gait analysis work. Hetty poked her head inside the door a few minutes later. She was business and bustling as usual, a twinkle in her eyes, cheeks cherubic.

'I hear you want to test my gait analysis software. Only

special people get their hands on it.' She sniffed and lifted her nose in the air.

'Has to be me then.' Nikki laughed. 'What have you got for me?'

Hetty pulled a face and put a hand on her voluminous hip. 'Precious little, I'm afraid. The shoe marks from that dirt track didn't show any matches. It's a man obviously, and there's a woman's tracks. That was more useful, as we have casts from Vicky's shoes. It's definitely hers.'

'At least we got that,' Nikki said, disappointed. 'Any prints from that can of turmeric spice?'

'Yes, but again, no matches on IDENT1.'

'Speaking of which, guv,' Nish said. 'I spoke to the manufacturer, who gave me the number of the supplier for this area. I've got a list of shops in Oxford where that brand is stored. There's six of them, spread all over Oxford. The cans also have a serial number that corresponds to which area in Oxford they are stocked at. I'm going through them to see if there's any of interest.'

'Let's assume that can came from Vicky's bag. Or even from her attacker's, who had to be Salvatore. In which case, if we can find the right shop, we can get hold of CCTV in that area. Worth a try.'

'What time would Vicky have been shopping though? Or Salvatore?'

Nikki shrugged. 'Got me there. But let's hope she did her shopping before she came out. She, or Salvatore, wouldn't just be walking around with a can of turmeric spice in their bag, would they?'

Monty cleared his throat. 'Hang on. That brand, it's stocked in how many shops in Oxford?'

'Six.'

'How many of those six are in Cowley? I'm asking as Cowley has a big population of Asian and black people. This spice is always used in their diet.' He grinned. 'I know because my mum used to put it in her cooking. So why don't we look at the shops in your list that happen to be in Cowley?'

'Great idea,' Nikki said. 'Vicky lived in Cowley as well, right? So she could've just walked there for some shopping. The serial number on the can should tell you if that can was stocked in Cowley.'

'I'm on the case, guv.'

Nikki closed her eyes and sighed. She felt tired, and she wanted a drink. But they were close, so she pressed on.

She said to the room, 'We should get another statement from Jacob Winspear before it gets too late.'

Monty nodded, and she picked up her jacket from the back of her chair.

# FIFTY-ONE

Jacob Winspear parked his vintage Corvette and looked around him. He was at a newly derelict warehouse outside Donnington to meet Ryan Siddle, the Labour MP. The man never spoke to Jacob on the phone; they always met in person, without any phones.

Ryan was waiting inside. He was pacing the empty hulk of the disused warehouse, scratching his beard. He stopped when he saw Jacob.

'Are you alone?'

'Yes, of course I'm alone.' Jacob frowned. Ryan looked agitated. His eyes swivelled behind Jacob, and his face worked overtime.

'Give me your phone.' Ryan put his hand out.

'I keep it in the car, with the battery off. You know that. Where's your phone?'

'I do the same. But you're not keeping your end of the bargain.'

'What do you mean?' Jacob relaxed as he understood what was troubling Ryan. 'The stadium permits? Don't worry. I've won the election now, thanks for your help. I don't forget my friends. We'll keep pushing for the land and permits on behalf of the contractor, but he won't succeed. You have my word on that. All you have to do is keep resisting and look like a hero.'

'Not that, you fool.' Ryan's eyes blazed as he stepped closer and lowered his voice. 'Someone called my office and wanted to speak to me. He knows about you and me. Some guy called Danny. He wouldn't give me his full name.'

Jacob felt a cold sinking numbness claim his limbs. For a while, he couldn't speak. His lungs squeezed air out, and his chest felt empty.

Ryan crinkled his eyebrows. 'Who is he? What's he got on you?'

Jacob closed his eyes. He ran a hand down his face, trying to control himself.

'How the hell does he know about us?' Ryan hissed.

'Okay.' Jacob raised a hand. 'What did he tell you?'

'Not much. Asked me how you are, and when we're meeting. He didn't go into any details. But the threat was clear. He hung up as I asked him questions.'

'Oh my god.' Jacob looked skyward. He hadn't smoked in years, but he could do with a cancer stick now. And a triple whisky.

He heard a sound behind him and whirled around. A man was loitering at the gate of the warehouse.

'Don't worry,' Ryan said. 'That's my security man. He checked out this place before we arrived. It's clean, and no one's seen us.'

Jacob gaped at him. 'You don't trust me?'

'How could I after that phone call? You gave me your word, and now someone knows about us? Do you know what this could do? It'll be the end of both our careers.'

Jacob shook his head as if this was a bad dream and he needed to wake up. He needed to placate Ryan. 'Don't worry. I'll take care of it. I'm sorry this happened.'

'How? How does this guy know?'

'I don't know, okay?' Jacob shouted, losing his cool. 'I don't even know who he is, for heaven's sake.' He cursed loudly. 'He calls me up and threatens me, just like he did with you.'

They were silent for a while, each grappling with their own emotions. Jacob couldn't believe it. He had to sort this problem out, once and for all. He'd lost Charles now. He turned out to be a traitor. Ben was in police custody. And now this Danny…

'I helped you.' Ryan raised a finger and shook it in Jacob's face. 'You wanted me to cut our resistance, and we did. I even kept an eye on your daughter. I'm sorry about what happened to her, by the way.' A funny look came over his face like a thought just occurred to him.

'Are you in some kind of trouble, Jacob? First your daughter dies, and now this random guy seems to know about us.'

Jacob couldn't say anything. His hands were on his waist as he stared at his shoes. 'Listen,' he said eventually, 'I won't let this get out of hand. I promise you that. No one will know anything about us. When this guy rang, did you trace the call?'

'No. It came to the main office who put it through to me. I hope to hell no one was listening. This could really damage us.'

'I know.' Jacob's jaws clamped tight. 'I'm going to sort this out now.'

He said goodbye to Ryan and went back to his car.

\* \* \*

He stopped at the first service station on the motorway. Danny answered on the first ring.

'I need to meet you,' Jacob growled.

'Oh really? Why the sudden interest, Father?' Danny laughed. It was a curious, whiny, high-pitched sound.

'Don't call me that,' Jacob shouted. 'I'm not your father.'

'No? Don't you remember Janet, my mother? And the

DNA evidence I sent you? If you don't believe me, maybe I should go to the media. The public might believe me.'

'I'm going to finish you.'

'No.' Danny's voice hardened. 'I will finish *you*, unless you do as I demand. Sign over the entire estate to me. I am now your sole heir.'

'To discuss that, we need to meet.'

Danny laughed again, and Jacob shivered at how unpleasant it sounded. Like listening to a sick horse neighing.

'You think I'm stupid? I meet you and you ambush me with some hired goons. What's the urgency anyway?' He was suddenly quiet. 'Ah, I know. You've met your friend Ryan Siddle, haven't you? Did he tell you about our little chat?'

'You bastard,' Jacob snarled. 'You know nothing.'

'Well actually, I do. You see, I used to follow you around. I planted a tracking device on your car. I saw you went to this deserted industrial estate and I wondered why. So one day I followed you. I heard everything. I taped it as well. I tape all our conversations.' His voice hardened. 'That's why you want to meet, so you can ambush me. I'm not Ben, or Charles that you can order around.'

'What do you want?'

'To start with, I want fifty million pounds. Then, ten million pounds every year, for as long as I want. That should drain your wealth till there's nothing left, and you even have to sell your house.'

'You're mad.'

Danny laughed again in that funny way. 'No, Father, I'm not mad. I'm just getting even.'

# FIFTY-TWO

Monty and Nikki were standing at the imposing front door of Jacob's mansion. The guards let them through the gates when Nikki brandished her warrant card. At the end of the long, curving gravel drive, the impeccable white house stood blazing in the sunshine. A big, burly man scurried down the steps as Monty pulled up. His shoulders and biceps almost burst out of his tight suit.

'Hello, I'm Mr Kirk, Mr Winspear's PA.' The man's unsmiling face drew level with Monty, who was the same height as him, but a skinnier version.

'We don't want to see you,' Monty said. 'Where's Mr Winspear?'

'Do you have a search warrant, Inspector Sen?' Kirk said, glancing at Monty's warrant card. 'If you don't, I suggest you leave the premises.'

Nikki broke in between them. 'We don't need a warrant, or permit to speak to Mr Winspear. We have new evidence about his daughter's murder. Where is he?'

The two men remained staring at each other for a few

seconds. Kirk was the first to back off with a sardonic smile. He glared at Nikki.

'I don't know. He's gone somewhere.'

'Not a very good, PA, are you?' Monty said. 'Or is your main role acting as a steroid-pumped bodyguard?'

Kirk gnashed his teeth and stepped in front of Monty again. 'Listen, you. I'll give you five minutes—'

'Or what?' Monty said calmly. 'You'll assault me? That would look nice, for a man who's a suspect in a murder case.'

Kirk's face blanched as his eyes narrowed. Nikki found the situation interesting. Jacob must be losing control if he was employing men like Kirk to guard him. He wasn't his PA. More like private security thug to protect him. What had changed?

'Excuse me,' a woman's voice from the top of the stairs interrupted them. Beatrice appeared. She was dressed casually, in a blouse and slacks. She came down the stairs, and Kirk stood to one side deferentially.

'I'm Beatrice, Jacob's wife. You're the police, aren't you?'

'Yes, ma'am, we met last time,' Nikki said. 'Sorry to disturb, but we need to speak to your husband.'

Beatrice's eyes were lined with grief. She looked tired, and the lines on her forehead and temples seemed deeper. She searched Nikki's face.

'He's not here right now. Can I help?'

'When will he be back?' Nikki asked, eyeing the house.

'I don't know.' Beatrice turned to Kirk. 'Leave us alone.' Kirk glared at them one last time, then nodded and left.

'Sorry about that,' Beatrice said. 'He's new, and attached to Jacob like a shadow. Not sure why he's even been hired.'

Nikki said, 'Did you hear about Benjamin and James being arrested?'

'Yes, I did. Someone called Kristy from your team rang. I'm shocked, of course. Not sure what Ben was doing, but James

Baden Powell's behaviour is appalling. We had no idea about any of this.'

'Did you know James?'

'Not at all. This is all a very unpleasant surprise.' Beatrice squared her shoulders. 'So, tell me. Who do you think did it?'

Nikki sighed. 'Can we please go inside?'

They walked into the same drawing room where Nikki had been before. Beatrice faced them on the sofa opposite, looking anxious.

Nikki told her about Vicky's accident, and the events leading to the identification of Salvatore.

'Did you ever see, or hear of a man like him, in relation to Charlotte?'

Beatrice's mouth was open as she digested the information. Then she blinked and swallowed. 'No, I didn't. Lottie kept a lot of her life private.'

Nikki showed her a photo of Salvatore on her phone. Beatrice shrugged and denied ever seeing him.

'Thank you. Please tell your husband about this as well, and ask him to attend the Kidlington South police station as soon as he is back.'

They said goodbye and left. As they got in the car, Kirk appeared on the steps, staring at them. They drove off, ignoring him.

Nikki was tired. It had been a long, eventful day. The sky was darkening, and it was almost 7 p.m. They drove back to the station, where Kristy had some news.

'Dr Raman called. No DNA matches between Benjamin or James and the semen sample.'

'Now we have to wait for Salvatore's DNA,' Monty said. 'I've dropped off his toothbrush and shaving kit. Did Dr Raman get those?'

'Yes, and so has Hetty. We should get a result tomorrow.'

Nish opened the office door and came in. 'I heard back from

the door to door on Salvatore's house. The neighbours said he keeps himself to himself. They don't see him much. He's lived on that street for the last couple of years. It's a council house; he was on benefits. For the last couple of weeks, he's not been seen.'

'What about his partner? The blond guy?'

Nish shook his head. 'No one's seen him either.'

'Any more CCTV footage?'

Nish turned down his lips. 'None of the black Toyota, sorry. I've told traffic about the shops on Cowley High Street, where they sell that turmeric spice can. They're sending me the images soon, but it will be tomorrow now.' Nish stifled a yawn.

'Go home,' Nikki ordered. 'I need you fresh for tomorrow. Thanks for your help.'

Kristy's phone rang and she picked it up. She listened then hung up slowly. Nikki knew it was bad news.

'That was Dr Verma. Vicky Davies just passed away.'

Nikki felt a mixture of sadness and anger in the pit of her stomach. Another innocent young life lost. She was getting closer, but that wasn't enough. She had to find Salvatore.

'I put out an all-points bulletin,' Monty said, breaking the silence that had suddenly dropped on them like a lead balloon. 'Any port Salvatore checks into, he will be stopped.'

'Let's hope it's not before he takes another life,' Nikki said grimly.

# FIFTY-THREE

Nikki couldn't get to sleep. Monty had dropped her off. She had her ready meal from the fridge, washed it down with two glasses of white wine. That helped to ease the headache, but sleep was harder to come by. She tossed and turned, wishing she could sleep, assailed by visions of Vicky's tearful face. Vicky had confided in her, and she hadn't been able to help the girl. As the long night dragged on, she became increasingly exhausted.

Just as she had finally faded into oblivion, her phone rang, waking her up. She cursed, then fumbled with the table lamp switch. The phone rang insistently. Groaning, she held it up to the light, squinting. It wasn't a number she recognised. She checked the time. It was 5 a.m. That meant she'd had some sleep, but she still felt as tired as the night before.

'Who is it?'

'DI Nikki Gill. I'm sorry to bother you at this hour. This is Greg Keating.' Greg's voice was shaky and disturbed.

'Hi, Greg. What's the matter?'

'I got a call from Francine. She's with a man called Salvatore Garibaldi, who wants to meet me. She sounds panicky.

This man says he will hurt her unless I meet him. He will only let Francine go when I arrive.'

Nikki was instantly alert.

Greg said, 'I hope you don't mind me calling you. Did I do the right thing? I hope so.'

'Yes, you did,' Nikki said, putting him on the loudspeaker. She put on her clothes quickly.

'Where did Francine say you have to meet her?'

'It's in a house in Houghton, ten miles outside Oxford. I spoke to the man as well, who gave me the address.'

'Text it to me. Stay where you are, don't go anywhere. I'm going to alert the duty teams to meet me there.'

'No, wait,' Greg said. 'Will you please come and pick me up first? This Salvatore wants me. He won't let go of Francine until I get there. He wouldn't tell me why. He also told me to come alone, and not call the cops.'

Nikki thought for a while. If she went without Greg, then there was a chance Salvatore might escape.

'Okay, I'll pick you up. Be ready in fifteen minutes.'

Nikki hung up. She brushed her tangled hair, wincing in the mirror. She got ready quickly and grabbed a grain bar from the fridge, her rush breakfast. Light was glinting yellow and white in the corners of the horizon as she drove down Kidlington's High Street.

* * *

The roads were deserted, and it didn't take long for her to reach the outskirts of Botley, where Greg lived. Her satnav took her to the address. Botley wasn't the most affluent of places, and Nikki was slightly surprised at where Greg lived. He had the ground floor of a terraced house, converted into a flat. The neighbourhood didn't quite live up to the image of the suave lecturer she had met. But then again, she knew that academics weren't paid a great deal and renting in Oxford was expensive. Buying a house was even more so, and most of her police colleagues couldn't afford to live in places like Oxford. Academics wouldn't be much different, unless they had family money.

The light was on in the porch, and Greg opened the door as soon as she rang the bell. He blinked nervously behind his glasses.

'Thanks for coming. Sorry to bother you like this. I didn't know who to call.'

Nikki went in and Greg shut the door. He led the way down the corridor to a living room, which led to a kitchen and dining area. The living room was lined with bookshelves. There was a desk, overflowing with papers. Books and magazines were strewn on the floor.

'Apologies for the mess,' Greg said. Hastily, he removed some of the junk to the floor and made some space on the sofa for Nikki. 'Have a seat, please. I'm making a cup of coffee, would you like some?'

'When did Salvatore ask you to meet him?'

Greg checked his watch. 'In half an hour. It won't take long to get there.'

Nikki wanted to get a move on, but she also didn't want to get there too early. And she didn't have coffee before she left. 'Okay,' she nodded. 'But only if it's quick.'

'It will be. Please have a seat.'

Greg bustled off into the kitchen. Nikki sat down, but soon got up, feeling restless. She walked over to the desk. Exam papers littered the desktop. A red piece of paper caught her eye. She removed some documents and realised it was actually the corner of a passport. A red British passport, the way they were before Brexit. Intrigued, Nikki picked the passport up and flicked to the photo page. She wanted to see what Greg had looked like in a photo.

She didn't recognise the photo. It was a colour photo of a

man with brown hair and dark eyes. He looked familiar to Nikki. Then she caught the name and, suddenly, she felt the ground slipping beneath her feet. A hollow sensation bloomed in her chest like a silent explosion. She couldn't speak. She couldn't even think.

The passport belonged to Salvatore Garibaldi.

She stared at it, eyes bulging, breath fluttering in her chest. From her frozen brain there suddenly came an electric surge, lighting up the dots, blazing across her synapses. In a flash of light, the macabre picture exploded in her mind.

Greg had pointed her towards Benjamin. And then towards James Baden Powell. He had regular tutorials with Vicky and Charlotte, and Vicky might have suspected him. He wanted her dead. Greg's description matched the man Mr Moore, the driver, had seen, and also of the waiter in Bloomfield House, observed by Mr Vardy. The waiter that she thought was Salvatore.

She glanced behind her. Greg was still in the kitchen, but she couldn't hear him. She was alone in the room. With shaky hands, she moved more of the papers. Then she opened the first desk drawer. She found some photos. Some were blown up, others were taken from a distance. They were all of the same person: Jacob Winspear. A memory sparked in her mind.

The photo of that older man in Greg's office. Now she knew why it was so familiar. It was a photo of Jacob, in profile, like he wasn't even aware the camera was aimed at him.

Underneath the photos there was a lab report. It was a DNA analysis, which showed Greg's DNA was an eighty-five per cent match with Jacob's.

Confusion reigned supreme in Nikki's mind. An eighty-five per cent match was only possible with a first-degree relative. Greg was young enough to be Jacob's son. But how... She heard a sound behind and whirled around. Greg was standing there.

She hadn't heard him. He had latex gloves on, and a piece of rope was hanging from his right hand.

'I told you to sit there. If only you had listened.'

Nikki was gasping. Words only emerged from her mouth with an effort. She held up the passport, her fingers cold and numb.

'How did you get this?'

Greg smiled. 'It was a stroke of luck meeting Salvatore. We started chatting at the bar, and he told me about his job, and when he was going to Bloomfield House. It was a sign from above. The heavens were in my favour. It all clicked together.'

'What do you mean?' Nikki had to keep him talking. He was watching her intently; if she tried to reach for her phone he would lunge at her. She stood still.

'Can't you see? I became Salvatore. I nicked his passport first, then had to kill him. It was necessary to achieve my goals. Lottie and I were getting closer. That party was the ideal place to get to her, when her guard would be down. But I wasn't invited. James laughed when I wanted to go. It was for members and their guests only.'

He inclined his head to the left, a gleam in his eyes. 'But then I met Salvatore, and it all changed. I could now attend the party, and everyone would think I was a waiter.'

Nikki was rooted to the spot like she had nails driven in her shoes. She gasped. 'Mr Vardy saw you put the body in the van. In the rolled-up carpet.'

'Yes. I didn't like that man. He kept looking at me very closely. But who cares? No one questioned a waiter putting a carpet in his car. Everyone was off their heads.' Greg laughed, a strange, high-pitched sound. 'One of the security guards even asked if I wanted a hand.'

Nikki pointed a trembling finger at the photos in the drawer. 'And these... are you related to Jacob Winspear?'

'My father, as it happens.' A dark shadow came over Greg's

face; and with alarm Nikki noted the slow snarl in his lips. 'It's payback time for him; vengeance for little Molly.'

'Molly?'

'The sister I couldn't save. My sister, and me, who Jacob left behind.'

Nikki couldn't believe her ears. 'Jacob's your father?'

'Yes. Didn't you see the DNA report?'

Nikki stared at him, then down at the drawer. She needed to get out of here. But Greg was blocking her way. She had to get past him, and then hopefully the door wouldn't be locked. She looked up fearfully as Greg took a step closer. He held up the rope in his hand.

'I'm sorry you got caught in this. I was trying to divert you, but you keep getting closer.' A cold, dull glaze covered his eyes. 'Time to end this.'

Nikki moved, but Greg was faster. He closed the gap in two quick steps and his body slammed against Nikki's, pressing her against the wall. His hand closed on her neck and crashed her head backwards. Pain mushroomed in her skull in a blinding yellow haze. She kicked her leg, but Greg didn't seem to notice. Her head smashed against the wall again, and the world went black.

# FIFTY-FOUR

'Where's guv?' Nish asked, putting his phone on the desk. Kristy was already in, staring at her laptop screen.

'Not sure. She should be here any minute.'

'It's eight. She's normally here already.'

Kristy sipped on her coffee, then glanced at her watch. 'Yes, you're right. Monty might know.'

Nish went out into the open-plan office and found Monty's coat draped over the seat, but no sign of the man himself. Then he spotted him coming out of the kitchen with a cup of coffee.

'Have you heard from guv?' Nish asked.

Monty put his coffee cup on the desk, then checked his phone. 'I had a missed call this morning around half five. I called her back, but she didn't answer.'

'She's late, which is unusual for her.'

'That's true.' Monty pressed his lips together. 'Let's ask Switchboard if they have any messages from her.' He picked up the receiver and pressed zero. He spoke to them, and Nish watched his eyebrows shoot upwards.

'Salvatore Garibaldi's got Francine in a house in Houghton. Greg Keating rang Nikki this morning. She's alerted the duty uniform team, who got to the address. Nikki instructed them to wait for her, as she was arriving with Greg, whom Salvatore wants to see.' Monty put his coat on. 'But Nikki never arrived. Do you have Greg's address?'

Nish went off to get it, while Monty called Greg. There was no response. From the corner of his eye, Monty saw Tony Rodrigues, the uniform inspector, rush into the office. He spotted Monty and headed quickly towards him.

'The address in Houghton is a derelict house. No one's lived there for a long time. All the windows are boarded up. I checked with the council; it's a condemned building. Needs to be destroyed.'

Monty and Tony walked to Nikki's office. 'Did Salvatore give Greg a false address? Why?' Tony asked.

'Maybe because he wanted Nikki and Greg to get there and then he'd ambush them. He's got Francine anyway, right?'

Kristy was on the phone, and she said a few words, then hung up. 'I just rang Francine. She's at home, and she says didn't meet anyone called Salvatore last night.'

Monty stared at her, his mouth opening slightly.

Nish said, 'Oh my god.'

All of them rushed to where Nish was staring at CCTV footage on his laptop. 'Yesterday I asked for the films from Cowley High Street, for the shops which stored that brand of turmeric spice. There were two shops, and we found Vicky in one of them.' Nish pointed at the screen, where Vicky's face was circled.

'Look at the man next to her,' Nish whispered. He clicked on the image and zoomed in. The man next to Vicky was wearing glasses and a baseball cap. But there was no doubt. It was Greg Keating.

Nish scrolled the image, and they followed the couple walking down the high street. They turned into a side road, and the cameras changed. The couple were seen again, getting into a black Toyota van.

'It's Greg Keating. He took Vicky on her last journey.'

'Roll it forwards. See where the van goes,' Monty said.

The black Toyota was circled in red, and as Nish ran the images, the van moved from Cowley further south towards Iffley and the river. Soon, they lost it as the car took a turning into a road without cameras.

'That's the road where Vicky was hit,' Monty breathed. He put a hand to his forehead and swore. 'Get traffic to focus where Greg lives. I'm heading down there now.'

'I'm coming,' Nish said.

'Me too,' Kristy rose from her seat. Monty shook his head. 'No. One of you has to stay here in base. Fill in Patmore when he arrives. Go through the CCTV from Greg's house with traffic and let us know what you find. Nish comes with me.'

Kristy said, 'Okay. I'll track guv based on her last call.' She clicked on her screen and brought up a map. 'It was from Greg's address in Botley.'

'Let's hope they're still there,' Monty said. Tony Rodrigues was already out the door, barking orders into his radio. Monty and Nish ran behind him.

# FIFTY-FIVE

Nikki couldn't breathe. There was a dull ache in her head, and it felt heavy. Slowly, her senses started to come back. Her body was moving. Was she on a boat? Her eyes blinked open, and all she could see was blackness. It pressed down on her, making it almost impossible to see anything. Nausea lurched in her throat, and she turned to one side and retched. Pain flared in the back of her skull. Her memory returned. Greg had hit her... then she didn't remember anything.

Her hands were tied behind her back. Lying on her side eased the pain on her wrists. Her body lurched again, and she steadied herself with her leg, which hit something hard. A strong smell of gasoline filled her nose. She realised she was in the boot of a car. Her mouth was gagged, and she could only breathe through her nose. She forced herself to be calm. From the slivers of sunlight coming through the cracks of the door, she could tell it was still morning.

She tried to move her hands, but they were tied tightly. She shuffled with her legs and tried to move sideways. Her fingers scraped the floor, trying to find something, anything. The car lurched over the road, and her head hit the floor hard, making her cry out in pain. She lay still for a while, then moved again. Her fingers resumed their search, moving her body by feeling with her feet. She felt something soft, like a piece of cloth. Further down into the boot, she came across a bag. It was zipped up, but with some effort, she was able to pull on the zipper. Inside, she felt something hard and metallic. They were screwdrivers, she thought, of various sizes. She pulled out a small star head screwdriver. She bent her left foot. Thank god her feet weren't tied. By contorting her body, she was able to put the small screwdriver down her sock.

She gasped, sweat pouring down her head with the effort. Her face and neck were caked in it; and her left cheek vibrated from lying on the floor. She rested, feeling the car move. Soon, she passed out again.

She didn't know how long had passed, when she woke up with a start. The car wasn't moving any more. She strained her ears to hear sounds. Footsteps approached, and the car jolted, but stayed in one place. The driver's door slammed. Then she heard someone fidgeting with what she thought was the boot lid, and suddenly a flood of light blinded her. She cowered, screwing her eyes shut. But it was a relief to smell fresh air again. She breathed in with her nose and coughed. Then she gagged, her face heating up and lungs burning. Mercifully, her captor leaned forward and removed the gag.

To say that was a life saver was an understatement. Nikki opened her mouth greedily and sucked in lungful's of air. She couldn't see her captor's face yet, but felt his rough hands search her. He didn't touch her socks. Then he grabbed her waist and pulled her outside. He leaned her against what she now could see was a van. A black van. Her legs buckled, and almost gave way, but somehow, she managed to half stand and lean against the van.

Greg observed her quietly. His glasses were off, so he must be wearing contacts, she thought. He slammed the back doors shut. Nikki looked around her. Her hands were still tied, but she could run, if there was any strength left in her legs. She tried a couple of steps. She was still wobbling all over the place.

To her right lay the rusty, dilapidated carcass of an old factory. Its corrugated-iron sheet doors were broken, and they lay on their hinges. She could see nothing but darkness inside it. Around her it was only fields, dotted with occasional farmhouses. She was out in the country, but she didn't have a clue where. The van had driven up a dirt track and, far behind, she could see the black strip of a road, curling around a forest and vanishing. She couldn't see any road signs. She scanned the horizon and found an electricity pylon in the distance, but nothing else.

Greg was suddenly in front of her, and she flinched. He was too close for comfort. She could smell his stale sweat, and it was revolting. He pulled on her arm.

'Come on.'

She didn't budge. 'Free my hands first. They hurt.'

'Not yet. Come in, first.'

'If you haven't tied my legs, why my hands?'

Greg was pulling her, and he stopped. 'Because you can't run anywhere. There's nothing around for miles. You can scream and shout, but no one will hear you.'

'My team will find out where we are. They're going to come after you. Make it easy on yourself, Greg. Let me go.'

'Shut up!' he snarled. He pulled on her arms till she stumbled and almost fell against him. She had no choice but to follow. The dark space inside was large; and disused farming machinery lay littered around the corners. Greg dragged her right to the back, where light fell through a crack in the ceiling. He had put some old furniture here. A couple of old sofas and a chair. There was a rectangular storage unit which she recognised as a freezer, and it was switched on. A table had been fashioned from bits of wood and timber, and there was a kettle and mugs.

Greg gave her a push, and she fell to her knees, then crawled to one of the sofas. 'I need a drink,' she gasped.

He didn't reply. Nikki got to her feet and walked towards him. 'Did you hear what I said?'

Greg ignored her. He opened up the long freezer. Nikki saw inside, and her heart froze. Revulsion crawled on her skin, and nausea churned in her guts. There was a dead body inside. A man, clothed in jeans and shirt. She recognised the face. It was Salvatore. Greg turned towards her.

'There you go. That's who you wanted, correct? It's too hot to leave a dead body outside, and I didn't have time to dig a grave. I could chuck him in the lake, but he'd float up somewhere. Best to keep him here, don't you think?'

Nikki stumbled back, feeling weak and exhausted. She slumped on the sofa. 'Please. I need a drink.'

'Patience is a virtue,' Greg said, turning his back on her. Nikki fell to the floor and closed her eyes. She lay there for a while, aware Greg was watching her. He came forward and slapped her cheeks once. She didn't respond and he slapped harder, twice. Nikki moaned and acted like she was waking up. She fluttered her eyelids once then sagged down on the floor again.

Greg cursed and got up. He filled a cup with water from a container. Nikki watched him. The kettle was plugged to a black object, which she thought was a battery charger. How could he get electricity here? Then she remembered the electricity pylon she had seen, with the large overhead wires looping over the countryside. She knew he couldn't get an electricity supply from there; the voltage would kill him. He was an academic, not an engineer. But could there be an electric supply nearby? If there was, she might be able to do something with it.

Greg turned, and she closed her eyes and went limp. He slapped her again, hard. It stung, but she only moaned once.

'Get up,' Greg said. He grabbed her by the shoulders and pulled her back on the sofa. She slumped to one side. Greg cursed loudly again. Nikki knew he couldn't make her drink while she was on her side. She also suspected he didn't want her to die. Not right now, anyway. He could use her as a bargaining chip if the police got closer to him.

'Hey!' Greg shouted, bringing his lips close to her ear. 'Can you hear me?'

Nikki didn't flinch. She lay with her eyes closed, body relaxed. She shook her shoulders, once, then her body, to make it look like she was trembling. Greg straightened and sighed. He moved away. She didn't open her eyes till she heard his footsteps fading. He walked to the gates, then went outside to the car. He couldn't see her from that angle. Nikki looked around her without moving, then with some difficulty, she sat up.

Hulks of machinery lay all around her. Her hands were still tied, and no matter how much she rubbed her wrists together, they didn't come loose. The ties were either cloth, or rope. They didn't feel like plastic. She could also feel the screwdriver nestled against her right sock. Her hands had to be free to get it, though.

Nikki got up and went to the kettle. The black object was not a battery. The kettle was plugged into it, but there was a wire from the black object snaking across the floor. She glanced over her shoulder to make sure Greg wasn't coming back. She tiptoed across the floor, following the wire. It snaked underneath the ground at the wall, and then went outside. It must be a live wire, Nikki assumed. Greg was using a transformer to capture the electricity – that was the black object.

She foraged around the decaying machinery till she found what she was looking for: a sharp metallic object that was upright. She didn't know what it was, but it stood up from the floor of a forklift truck. It was probably a gear or crankshaft that had been chopped off for some reason, and it left a flint-like edge sticking up. It was rusty, and looked disgusting, but it was the only hope Nikki had.

She turned around and had to adopt an undignified position, squatting on the floor of the derelict machine, in order to get her wrists against the sharp object. She could see the door from here. If Greg stepped in now, he would see her. True, she was at the back, and the light here was less, but he only had to walk for less than a minute in order to see her.

She had no time. She set to work. It was her thighs that balanced her, and she could feel the burn in them. She rubbed her wrists against the sharp edge, wincing as the metal cut into her flesh. Tetanus jab later, she promised herself.

She heard a sound from the door and her heart froze. She rose from her squatting position. Greg walked across the doorway, making her pulse surge. She got ready to scurry back to the sofa. But he walked across the door, whistling, still busy doing something with the van. Nikki exhaled, thanking her lucky stars. He obviously thought she was still out cold on the sofa.

Nikki resumed rubbing her wrists against the old metallic shard. She gritted her teeth as sweat poured down her face, blinding her eyes. Her breath came in gasps. She couldn't do this for much longer, but neither would she give up.

She didn't want to end up in the freezer like Salvatore.

# FIFTY-SIX

Nikki could feel warm blood coursing down her fingers. Her wrists were burning, and the pain in her shoulders was immense. Her thighs had become blocks of rock, and she doubted she could move much after this. But she could feel a give in the ties, and her hands were a little looser. With one last burst of strength, she kept going. Then she heard the van door slam. A few seconds later, Greg appeared at the doorway, and this time, he walked right through, heading for her.

Nikki couldn't waste any more time. She jumped off the forklift truck. She bent low at the waist and ran round the edge of the little domestic area, to lie down on the sofa. Her heart was pounding so loud she thought her chest would explode. Had Greg seen her? He was walking over fast; she could hear his steps. They came closer. She kept her eyes closed and tried to control her breathing. But how could she? Her chest was heaving with the exertion, and her pulse was surging in her ears. One look at her flushed face and Greg would know she'd been up to something.

She felt him next to her, looking down. She licked her dry lips and moaned again. She blinked her eyes open.

'Water... water please,' she croaked. Greg didn't move. Then she saw him kneel and bring his face closer. She tried not to flinch. He reached out with one hand and tucked a hair strand behind her ear.

'What's the matter?' His voice was soft, almost caring. 'You're sweating.'

'I... I don't feel well,' she croaked again. 'Please. Water.'

He didn't move, observing her with fascinated eyes. His face was flat and cold, but his lips were stretched tight, and he couldn't take his eyes off her. Nikki felt sick to her bones. He was enjoying this. She closed her eyes, and her head lolled to the side. She heard him get up. He had gone to the water container and had his back to her.

He brought the cup of water back, and she sat up, hands still behind her. He helped her sit straighter by pulling on her shoulders. Nikki drained the glass held to her lips. It felt like heaven, and she asked for another. Greg gave her a long look and went to the table again. This time, he didn't turn his back. He watched Nikki as he poured another glass of water and then brought it to her.

Nikki needed to buy more time. She hoped Monty and the others would be suspicious of Greg by now and, with any luck, they would have launched a search.

'What happened to your sister Molly?'

Greg stopped and looked at her. He seemed to weigh up the question in his own mind. 'Why do you want to know?' he whispered.

'I can see Molly's death had a deep effect on you. You spoke about it, and how angry you are at Jacob for leaving your family in that state.'

'Family? You having a laugh?' Greg's posh accent had slipped, a feral tone underlying his words. 'That bastard got my mother pregnant, hooked on drugs, then did a runner.'

'Tell me what happened.'

'What do you think happened? My mother died.' Greg stopped suddenly, and his eyes stared into the distance, like he was suddenly in a world of his own, his mind lost in memory. Then he snapped back to reality, and he blinked. 'Then we got taken into care.'

Greg talked about the abuse little Molly had suffered, until one day she threw herself out of the window of a tall council apartment block. She fell fourteen floors to her death. She had been nine years old.

'I'm sorry,' Nikki said, and she meant it.

Greg carried on detailing the horrible events of his child-hood. He stopped to catch his breath, his face red.

'Then I found him. My so-called father. I made him look after me. True to form, he continued to use me. But he also paid for my education, and he helped me get into Oxford.'

While Greg talked, Nikki worked harder on her wrists, trying not to move her shoulders, which was almost impossible. Greg glanced at her, and she stopped.

His face twisted with pain. 'But I'll never get Molly back. She was let down by her own mother and the care system. Finally, I couldn't save her either.'

Nikki stared at him, all of a sudden his words hitting her in the middle of her chest like a cannonball. Is this not what happened to her half-brother – to Tommy?

Tommy was taken into care, and then he was abused until he too sought freedom in death.

'That's my real regret,' Greg whispered. His fists tightened, and his jaws clenched. His eyes bulged into hate, and he snarled suddenly. He looked at Nikki like he wanted to kill her.

'Until the day I die, I will avenge Molly. The blood of my so-called stepfamily will flow until she's at peace.'

Nikki chose her next words carefully. She was scared out of her wits, aware Greg was now in a dangerous and unstable frame of mind. But she hoped her words would cut through the red mist in his mind.

'I also lost my sibling, my brother. He was in social care, and they let him down badly. He ended his own life, too. He was called Tommy. No one stood up for him. No one listened.' Nikki bowed her head. She wasn't acting, not any more. The grief layered inside her like shifting sand. Eventually, she looked up to find Greg staring at her.

Neither of them could speak. She was also lost in her thoughts. This monster standing in front of her – was he really an evil, twisted being, or had fate bent him into that shape? What would've happened if Greg had been born into a normal family, where he had love and support as a child?

And... her own heart twisted at the thought that always plagued her – what would Tommy have turned out like, if he was still alive? God forbid, would he have turned out like Greg?

'Why was your brother in care?' Greg asked.

Nikki told him about Tommy. It felt surreal, opening up to a man who was a cold-blooded killer, and a man she had to bring to justice. She knew she had to keep going, because Greg was genuinely interested.

Greg frowned after she finished. 'You're a police officer. Did you not look into his history and find out the men who were responsible?'

Nikki's wrists hurt, and she felt warm blood between them. 'Yes, I did.' She had his attention. If only she could get free. She squirmed, and Greg narrowed his eyes.

'What's wrong with your hands?'

# FIFTY-SEVEN

Nikki realised her mistake but it was too late. She feigned nonchalance and pressed further back into her seat.

'Just a tickle, that's all.'

Her heart thumped loudly as Greg came over. 'Let me have a look,' he said; his eyes narrowed. He swept Nikki's protests aside and pushed her forward. The knot was looser than before, but she was still tied up. She desperately tried to free her arm so she could protect herself but it was no use.

Greg shoved her face down on the sofa and swore loudly. 'You bitch,' he shrieked. He tightened the knot of ropes over her hands, then sat her upright. He faced her, his face shaking with rage.

'You're all the same! All of you! I was starting to trust you, see how you let me down? I bet you're lying about your brother just to buy more time.'

'No!' Nikki cried out in anguish. 'I'm not lying about my brother. Greg, you need to stop this. I'm sorry about what happened to you, but look at how many people you hurt just to take revenge on your father. Charlotte, Vicky and Salvatore. Three innocent people dead. How many more lives will you take? Nothing will bring Molly back. If Molly was alive today, she wouldn't want you to do this.'

Greg's face was livid, eyes burning with hate and pain. 'She's not here though, is she? And she never will be.'

'Just like Tommy,' the words slipped out of Nikki's mouth. Despite the terrible danger she was in, a sadness suddenly overcame her.

'You're lying,' Greg whispered. 'You're like the rest of them. And to think, I was starting to trust you.' He looked around, his eyes checking the ceilings of the warehouse, and he did a 360 degree. He spun back to face Nikki. He grabbed her hair, and she screamed in pain, but he pulled her to standing. Then he grabbed her elbow and dragged her to the gates. Nikki fought the best she could, but it was no use. Her hands were now firmly tied, and although she kicked with her legs, Greg delivered a rocking blow to her head that almost felled her. The world swam before her eyes, turning black.

Dimly, she was aware that she was being pulled over a dirt track, then across a field. Cold wind whipped at her hair, and she winced as her head hurt. She was on a hill top, she realised. She could see other hills around her and dark clouds in the sky. The air smelled fresh – of heather and gorse. She was somewhere in the Cotswolds, but she could be anywhere.

Her feet bounced along the ground as Greg dragged her to a spot and then lay her on the ground. Nikki was lying on her back, and she rolled over. The sight took her breath away. They were at the edge of a steep drop. The land opened up in a deep green valley, hundreds of feet below. Apart from dense vegetation, she couldn't see anything else. The hills formed a ring around the horizon, and storm grey clouds threatened rain. The wind picked up, whining in the trees.

Nikki saw Greg standing at the edge, staring down. Her heart did a somersault. She shouted his name. At the second call, he turned his neck slowly, but his body remained at the edge.

'There's a way out of this,' she said, her voice raspy. 'Hand yourself in. Give me your phone, and I can make the call. I will make sure Jacob is punished for what he did. I give you my word.'

Greg walked over to her. He raised her up, his face inches from hers. He snarled in fury, then dragged her over to the edge. Nikki looked down and froze. The fall was worse than she could've imagined. She could barely see the trees far below. A few small rocks broke free from beneath Greg's boots and skittered into nothingness.

Greg's eyes bore into hers. Nikki's throat was dry, but she managed to get the words out. 'Please stop. Don't do this.'

His next words surprised her. 'Did you really have a brother called Tommy?'

'Yes.'

Greg's face softened, and the snarl subsided. 'And you told me the truth about him?'

'Yes, I did.'

Nikki heard sirens in the distance. Their long, wailing sound rose above the wind. Greg heard them too, but he was suddenly calm. Nikki heard the sirens get louder, and then the crunch of tyres on gravel. She heard car doors slam, and then running footsteps. She dared to glance sideways. She couldn't see anyone, but she knew help had arrived.

'How did Tommy die?'

The words took her breath away. She suddenly felt a pain squeeze her throat, darkening her soul. Her lips quivered.

'He jumped from a hill... Oh god.'

Greg smiled sadly. 'You know what I wanted? For Jacob to call me his son. I wanted him to call Molly his daughter. That's all I wanted.'

Tears welled in Nikki's eyes. Greg's face dissolved in a cascade of bitter memories and regrets.

A voice shouted her name. It was Monty. 'Nikki!' She heard him run forward, and then skid to halt.

'Step away from the edge!' Monty shouted. 'Do it now.'

Greg appeared not to have heard him. His attention was focused on Nikki. She sniffed, her arms paralysed, hands unable to wipe her own tears.

Greg said, 'I just wanted a home for Molly and me. A home with two parents. That's all I ever wanted. But I know that will never happen. Just like it never happened for your brother.'

Nikki choked, then found her voice. 'Greg, please...'

With savage force, Greg hurled Nikki away from him, to the ground. In the same movement, he jumped into empty space, his hands outstretched like he was skydiving, but without a parachute.

Nikki felt Monty's arms reach around her shoulders and pull her back to safety. A scream ripped out of her chest, and she fought Monty, trying to get to Greg. Monty held her down as she kept screaming, her feet kicking up dust, fighting Monty to stand up and rush to the edge.

Greg was nowhere to be seen, just the whine of a desolate wind where he once stood.

He was gone.

Monty was saying something to her, but she couldn't hear. She dissolved into tears, kicked and snarled and fought to be free, to break away from him. He was too strong, and finally she gave in, head buried in his chest as sobs shook her body.

# FIFTY-EIGHT

Flecks of light bobbed up and down, like boats in a dark lake. Whispers came and went like the sound of distant cars on the road. But the granite blackness remained, pressing on her eyes. Where was she? Nikki had no idea. The whispers became louder. She felt herself moving, shaking. The darkness began to retract from the edges of her mind. The light was brighter, but it was painful, and she winced. The movement stopped, but the voice was louder. A man's voice, and one she knew.

'Nikki. Nikki!' The voice was more insistent. She wanted to answer, but couldn't. It was Monty, that much she gathered.

'We need to move her,' Monty said. 'Can't wait for an ambulance. Grab her legs. Let's put her in the back seat. Here, open up.'

She had passed out. The shock of the moment, and the similarities between Tommy and Greg had finally overwhelmed her senses.

Nikki felt herself being lifted. The pain surged at the back of her head, and then spread through her spine, sending electric jolts down her legs. She cried out, but it came out as a moan.

The light was brighter now, and the speckles had gone,

replaced by a gentle wash of yellow. She blinked, and the light was tolerable.

The first person she saw was Nish, and two uniformed officers, sitting by her feet. Behind them, the flashing blue lights of two squad cars outside the gates. In the distance she could hear sirens.

'That'll be the ambulance,' one of the uniformed officers said.

Nikki remembered everything, and a deep remorse overcame her again. She found Monty's eyes staring at her.

'It wasn't his fault,' she whispered, regret scratching at her throat, wetting her eyes. 'He suffered too much.'

'Good to hear you speak,' Monty sounded relieved. 'Who are you talking about? Greg?'

'Yes.' She couldn't speak any more. There was no point. Words had become useless now.

Nish gave her a cup of water, and she drank it greedily. He refilled it, and she thanked him. She tried to smile at his concerned face.

She turned to look at Monty. His jaw was set in stone, but his eyes were soft.

'How did you find me?' she whispered.

'Kristy got CCTV images from the front of Greg's house. We saw him leave. It was the black Toyota van; he had changed the number plates. With the new plates, ANPR picked him up near the Chiltern Hills area.'

Nikki sat up straighter. Monty moved, but remained close in case he had to catch her. She couldn't deny the comfort she felt from leaning against him, smelling his familiar aftershave.

'That's where I am? Chiltern Hills?'

'Yes. Luckily, Greg didn't drive far from the motorway. We caught up with him on CCTV when he took the exit. It leads to a little village, and one of the farmers saw his van speeding up this country lane.'

Something flickered in his eyes. A glint of anger, but also remorse. 'But we didn't get here in time. I'm sorry.'

She shook her head. 'You did your best.' She looked at Nish and the uniformed officers. 'All of you. It was kind of my fault to pick up Greg on my own. I should've gone with backup.'

The siren had grown louder, then tamped down as it pulled up outside. Monty put an arm around her shoulder again.

'Come on, let's get you up.'

They walked to the waiting ambulance, and two paramedics came out. They took Nikki inside the ambulance and checked her over. Monty and Nish hovered outside. Nikki called them.

'I have to go somewhere.'

One of the paramedics said, 'I'm sorry, but you need to be seen in hospital. You had a concussion.'

Nikki stood. She was dizzy but she managed to get down from the ambulance. Monty frowned at her.

'What are you doing?'

'I made someone a promise, and I'm going to keep it.'

# FIFTY-NINE

'I really don't think this is a good idea.' Monty's jaws were set in a hard line. His hand gripped the steering wheel tightly as he drove. Nikki closed her eyes, and she clutched a bottle of water in her right hand. She appreciated Monty's thoughts for her wellbeing, but she didn't need them right now. Her mind was set on the current course of action.

She was driving back to the station with Monty. Nish had gone ahead, back to the station to get the paperwork ready for the next stage.

Her head was throbbing. The paramedics had tended to her bruises, but she had no lacerations or active bleeding, which helped. She didn't need any stitches. Her body was wracked with pains, but the painkillers were starting to have an effect. She took another long swig of water.

'It's better to sort this out now,' Nikki said, her eyes still closed. She could tell Monty was looking at her. The car had stopped at a set of traffic lights.

'Okay,' Monty said, his voice gentle. 'But I'm coming with you.'

'Yes, I'd like that.' Nikki opened her eyes and glanced at

him. He was focused on the road, his face like granite. A muscle ticked in his temple, and his knuckles were rock hard on the wheel.

'I am okay, you know,' Nikki said. 'What happened wasn't your fault.'

'But I should've seen it. After James Powell, Greg Keating was the only person who had close contact with Charlotte and Vicky. To be honest, I can't believe I missed it.'

She touched his forearm, and it was tense. He flinched, as if he didn't want her to touch him.

'Pull over,' Nikki said.

'We're almost there. Just a mile away.' Nikki agreed, as they could talk in the car after they'd parked.

Once they got to the nick, she made sure he parked a distance away from the other cars, where they could be alone. Monty looked at her, his eyes full of concern.

'I'm sorry. At the very least, I should've been there with you.'

'It was my decision. Nothing to do with you.' She put a hand on his shoulder and felt it relax. She leaned towards him, the best she could with a bloody gearbox in the way. Monty tried to do the same, reaching out with his hand, which she grasped. It was the first time they'd held hands. His large hand enveloped hers, the brown skin a soft glow in the sunlight. The clouds had relented, and the day was brighter.

He lifted his other hand and touched her forehead lightly, next to the bruise. His fingertips were gentle and soothing, and she relaxed under his touch.

'I just wouldn't forgive myself if something happened to you,' he whispered.

'Nothing did, so it's fine.' She shook her head slightly. 'His childhood was similar to Tommy's in so many ways. But he didn't break, like Tommy did. He got twisted instead, and became... what he was. He got in touch with Jacob and forced

308

him to look after him. Clever kid, to be honest.' She told Monty about Greg and Jacob.

'Blimey,' Monty whispered, when she finished. 'That's some life. I see what you mean about him and Tommy.'

'That's why this isn't over yet,' Nikki said. 'Let's go.'

She walked slowly, holding on to Monty's offered arm, although she didn't need to. The walking helped in fact, and she was getting back into her stride.

'Tom Armstrong is here. He arrived just before we left. He wanted to come with us, but he's still on leave, so I told him to stay,' Monty said.

'Is he?' Nikki smiled. 'Will be good to see him.'

They reached the back entrance, where two uniformed sergeants were smoking. One of them greeted Nikki.

'We heard about what happened, guv,' one of them said. 'Glad you're all right.'

'Me too.' Nikki smiled at them. She walked inside and along the green lino corridor, and felt a strange sense of relief to be back where she worked. So much of her life was spent here, and it felt like she belonged here now. Monty stopped at the canteen to pick up coffee and bagels, and she suddenly realised how hungry she was.

Tom was standing at the door of the open-plan office, and he hurried forward when he saw them. His anxious eyes scanned her face.

'I heard from Nish. So glad you're okay, guv.'

'How are you?' Nikki shook hands with Tom.

'Coming back to work soon. I decided it's time.'

'Good to hear that. We need you back on board.'

They went inside, and Nikki acknowledged the greetings and words of encouragement that came her way from the assembled detectives, and the uniformed officers.

She sank down at her table and bit into one of the bagels that Monty offered her.

'Are we ready?' She looked at Nish and Kristy, who were standing by with the paperwork.

They nodded.

'Then let's do this.'

* * *

The two cars churned gravel under their wheels as they drove down the long drive that took them to the massive main entrance of the Winspear residence. Kristy and Nish had rung ahead, and there was a figure waiting for them at the top of the stairs.

As they got closer, Nikki realised it was Beatrice, Jacob's wife. She went up the stairs, and Beatrice met her with an anxious look on her face.

'What's this about? Have you found who killed Lottie?'

'We need to see your husband, Mrs Winspear. We asked him to be present, not you.'

Nikki saw movement across the open door behind Beatrice. Jacob's short, podgy figure bustled across the large reception hall.

'What do you want?' he asked belligerently. 'I'm busy and don't have time to waste.'

*Neither do I,* Nikki thought to herself in silence. Monty and Nish stood on either side, flanking her.

Nikki cleared her throat and fixed Jacob with a stare. 'Mr Jacob Winspear, I'm arresting you for being an accessory to the murder of Charlotte Winspear. You have the right to remain silent—'

'Wait, what?' Beatrice stopped Nikki. Jacob turned a shade of green, then bone white. His shoulders were slumped.

Nikki ignored Beatrice and read out the rest of the formal statement. Jacob had recovered somewhat.

'You cannot do this. You need a warrant to come into my house.'

'As a matter of fact, we can, but we have a warrant as well,' Monty said, producing an envelope from his pocket and handing it to Jacob.

Beatrice's face was pale, but there was also a glint in her eyes Nikki hadn't seen before.

'What proof do you have for this, Inspector?'

'Mr Winspear was in close contact with Greg Keating, a lecturer at Merton College, who killed Charlotte. Mr Keating happens to be Mr Winspear's son from another relationship. We have DNA evidence to prove that, and also phone call evidence which shows they were in touch, even recently. Mr Keating's real name is Daniel Hardy.'

Jacob was speechless, his mouth open. Beatrice glared at her husband.

Nikki said, 'Mr Winspear also used Benjamin Henshaw, Charlotte's boyfriend, to monitor Charlotte's activities. His adviser, Charles Topley, also helped him in this regard.'

Monty stepped forward with handcuffs. Jacob retreated, fear spasming across his face.

'Wait, you can't do this. I didn't kill Lottie, for heaven's sake.'

'But you were an accessory to her murder. Mr Keating was your son, and Charlotte had become an obstacle to your political aspirations. You had the motive and the opportunity. Through Mr Keating, you had the means. You are under arrest, Mr Winspear.'

Beatrice focused on her husband, her cheeks slowly turning crimson. Her hands became claws, and they shook as she clenched them.

'You bastard,' she hissed, and then hurled herself at Jacob. Monty and Nish stepped in deftly. Monty held Beatrice, while Nish pulled Jacob to one side. Nish took Jacob down to the car.

'This is ridiculous,' Jacob yelled. 'I want my lawyer.'

'What you need,' Nikki said, staring down at him from the top of the stairs, 'is to understand what you did to Greg and his sister, who died at the age of nine. The daughter you never cared for, Mr Winspear.'

Jacob went white as a sheet, and he trembled, looking up at Nikki.

Nish put him inside the car and slammed the door shut.

Beatrice said, 'I'm coming with you. I want to know everything.'

# SIXTY

Nikki was sitting in the garden with Clarissa. It was a mild September evening, the portent of autumn in the air, but still not chilly. The sun refused to die, melting clouds with its winking rays. There was no breeze, and it felt warm enough to wear shorts.

Clarissa had brought a few more photos of Tommy that she had unearthed, and Nikki was glad she did as she hadn't seen them. Two of them also showed Steven, Tommy's father.

Nikki shook her head as futile regrets surfaced again. Hesitantly, she had told Clarissa of Greg Keating, or Danny, without mentioning any of the names. Though Clarissa wouldn't tell anyone, she knew.

'What if Tommy had grown up to become like him?' Nikki asked.

Clarissa took her time to answer. 'He was a gentle soul. Too soft for his own good, I think. I don't think he'd end up... like the person you described.'

And that's why he died, Nikki thought to herself bitterly. She leaned back on the chair and looked at the shades of grey between the surprisingly blue sky. She had closure about

Tommy. It was time to let go, but not to forget. She thought about Greg again, and his strange, tumultuous life. She had comforted Beatrice, who had lost her daughter. There was no sense in this life, this vortex of loss and despair, and she knew Beatrice, like herself and Clarissa, would carry the wounds of her past with her. An invisible cross to bear. And that was life for some people; they had no choice.

Jacob was charged with being an accessory to murder, but as Nikki had expected, it did not stick. After all, it was Greg who engineered the whole event. But the whole event had ended up in the newspapers, and Jacob's political career was dead in the water; and his business was also suffering. A crowd of media vans had camped outside his mansion, and his life had become a nightmare. To Nikki's mind, Jacob deserved far worse.

Benjamin Henshaw would serve a six-month sentence for assault and battery, for his attack on Charles Topley, and evading justice. But ultimately, Nikki felt his heart was in the right place, and he would make better choices later in life.

She reached out and held her mother's hand, feeling the warmth under her wrinkled skin. At least she had reconnected with Clarissa and had been able to start a new phase of her life. Rita was coming back in two weeks, and this time, she had decided to spend a weekend with Clarissa, which had delighted Clarissa no end.

One chapter in Nikki's life was drawing to an end, but she was turning over to a new page, new words appearing like the stars that were beginning to glimmer in the early evening sky.

# A LETTER FROM THE AUTHOR

Dear Reader,

I hope you enjoyed *Silent Girl*, the second in my Detective Nikki Gill series.

If you'd like to join other readers in keeping in touch, here are two options. Stay in the loop with my new releases with the link below. You'll be the first to know about all future books I write. Or sign up to my personal email newsletter on the link at the bottom of this note. You'll get bonus content and get occasional updates and insights from my writing life. I'd be delighted if you choose to sign up to either – or both!

www.stormpublishing.co/ml-rose

If you enjoyed *Silent Girl* and could spare a few moments to leave a review that would be hugely appreciated. Even a short review can make all the difference in encouraging a reader to discover my books for the first time. Thank you so much!

Join other readers in hearing about my writing (and life) experience, and other bonus content. Simply head over to www.BookHip.com/VKKKXJB

Street drugs destroy lives, and its victims are young families. I wanted to write about this, for a long time. Danny's (Greg) character came to me one day while I read about a man whose life had been spent in social care as his parents were drug addicts. He suffered with terrible anxiety, and became an alcoholic himself. The flawed and tragic character of Danny slowly took shape. There's no excuse for him becoming the twisted monster that he morphed into, but the seeds were there in his tragic childhood.

I enjoyed creating all the characters, Nikki especially. She remains defined by the terrible events of her own childhood. Yet, she pours every ounce of herself into the job. This case becomes personal for her, like a lot of her cases. She can't help feeling that way. She will always be impulsive, headstrong, damaged, but brilliant at her job. I like Nikki, I like her a lot. She resembles Arla Baker, my first female detective character.

I hope you enjoyed reading Nikki's latest case. If you did, please leave a review, they take two minutes of your time, but guide other readers forever.

Thank you for reading,

M.L. Rose

 facebook.com/arlabake

Printed in Great Britain
by Amazon

38513806R00182